DAYS ARE COMING

BY

PAT SIMMONS

Developmental Editor: Chandra Sparks Splond
Proofreader: Miriam "Cookie" Mitchell
Beta Readers: Evangelist Charlotte Townsend; Stacey Jefferson
Interior Design: Kimolisa/Fiverr.com
Cover Design: @designerqueen3/Fiverr.com

Praise for Pat Simmons

OMGreatness...5 Stars for Day Not Promised

My, my, my, my and MY!!! This book was so intense and emotional that I found myself interacting with the story as I read it. Pat Simmons' "Day Not Promise" had me praying, crying, speaking in tongues, lifting my hands, and rejoicing. You cannot read this novel without thinking about your salvation and those that The LORD has put in your pathways. –Reader Viv

Inspirational faith-filled demon slaying... 5 Stars for Day Not Promised

Whew, this was so inspiring with scriptures on fighting the enemy who comes to kill and destroy. But with praying intercessors, faith, and believing in God's will, anything can happen in His time. I loved how, one by one, the crew was saved. There was some tragedy, but God showed up with his angels on guard to prevent Satan's schemes. I want to be so in tune with God that I can see the enemy of darkness and be able to call on the name of Jesus to send in his army. Glory. Can't wait to read the next book. Omega and Mitchell are the Holy Ghost power couple. He truly was her hero. —Sheryl, Michigan

Timely and Sobering... 5 Stars for the Day She Prayed

Day She Prayed captures the sense of urgency we all need as Believers. It's twofold: first to work out our own salvation with fear and trembling and then to win lost souls to Christ. I was moved to feel sadness, hope, laughter, joy, tears, and gladness as

I read the book. Randall and Tally's story was so real, and just like the two of them, I feel complete after finishing. — Cameisha Barnes.

Awesome and Powerful Read… 5 Stars for Day She Prayed

I am such a fan of Pat Simmons. Her writings have truly blessed me over the years. This series has really ignited my prayer life. – Reader

DAYS ARE COMING

Chapter One

For, behold, the days are coming, in which they shall say,
Blessed are the barren, and the wombs that never bare,
and the paps which never gave suck. —Luke 23:29

I'm coming for the children, God whispered.

Jude Morgan stirred but didn't open his eyes as he sank deeper under the covers. Nothing was going to rob him of his sleep. He hadn't hit the bed before midnight for three days because of working overtime for Boeing, church meetings, and other commitments. Jude was determined to get a total of seven hours of sleep.

I'm coming for the children, God repeated.

Jude's eyes popped open, looking to his left, then right in his dark bedroom. Was he dreaming? Did he hear a voice? The hum of his central air was ready to lull him back to sleep. Holding his breath, Jude remained alert but didn't leave his bed. He questioned whether he heard right.

I'm coming for the children, God thundered.

The Lord's disturbing edict caused Jude to jolt up. As a youth minister at Christ For All Church, Jude believed in praying and then taking the time to listen to Jesus.

He waited to see if the Lord would reveal a vision to understand the message better. Being one of God's sheep and an intercessor, he recognized his Shepherd's voice.

That wasn't a warning or prayer request. Jude began to weep as he slid out of bed and dropped to his knees. If King David in the Bible could cry out to the Lord, then Jude had no shame. "Lord, what do you mean? Not the children." He stared into the darkness, and God's presence created a blinding light.

This world is increasingly wicked. Man has sacrificed the souls that I created and gave them to idols, inside and outside the womb, to Molech and Chemosh, the Lord said. *Demons are waiting for their mutilated bodies to torture them.*

With his face bowed in submission, Jude's heart ached as the Lord mentioned the names prominent in the Bible for fake gods. If there was one thing God hated, it was idolatry—past and present.

In Biblical times, people would burn their children, including babies, alive to their pagan gods called Molech. King Mesa of Moab had offered his eldest son, a prince, in a burnt offering to Chemosh in front of his enemies to win a war he "ultimately" lost.

Who is sacrificing children? Jude thought. It was hard to visualize the brutality carried out throughout history.

Knowing his thoughts, God answered. *The heart of man is wicked. They have become their own gods, butchering babies before they are born. Their souls are Mine!* The room shook from the Lord Jesus' anger, and Jude trembled in His presence. *When they are born, they are realigning their sex. I am God, the Creator of Heaven and earth. I make no mistakes!*

"God, have mercy on us," Jude pleaded.

Men take innocent babies and use them for sex. They do not teach them about Me. Guns are their toys. They prostitute their children for money, drugs, and evil acts. I have been watching. God called out deeds done in darkness from the world.

"God, what can I do?" Jude pleaded for guidance.

Judgment has been set, God spoke, and then an unsettling quiet filled Jude's bedroom. This was not good. He glanced at the time displayed on his phone: 2:32 a.m. After what he'd just experienced, how could Jude even think about falling back to sleep? His body told him to try.

A year shy of forty, Jude wasn't married, nor did he have children, but a church member and single mother, Sinclaire Oliver, had three, and Jude spent time with them, mentoring her oldest son, Carlton.

His friends at church, the Addamses, and Franklins, were two married couples eager to start families. What did this mean for them?

Renewed with a mission, Jude began to pray. Yep, his spirit was too active to get a restful night's sleep.

In his mind, he wondered who would repent and return to God.

Jude was exhausted when he climbed back into bed after praying for hours.

He felt drugged and weak, and his head and heart ached. Jude needed coffee for physical strength. Nope. He shook his head. This situation called for fasting and prayer.

I'm coming for the children kept reverberating in his head.

There was no way Jude was going into the office, nor would he work from home today. He called his supervisor. When Jude got Kenneth's voicemail, he left a message, then emailed him. His boss would think Jude wanted a long weekend.

The next call was to Pastor Rodney.

The church secretary informed Jude that their pastor was out for a conference and wouldn't return until Saturday night.

"Great. Thank you." Jude began his morning routine at the kitchen table with his Bible open.

No television.

No satellite radio.

No phone calls.

For the rest of the day, Jude prayed and read his Bible.

Jude's heart remained heavy as he sang praises to the Lord to end his fast day. "Lord, You are a righteous God, and let Your will be done on earth as it is in heaven, in Jesus' name. Amen."

On his way to the kitchen, Jude patted his whining flat stomach, courtesy of a consistent gym schedule. Opening the refrigerator, he found a container with leftovers from his mother's house.

Jude warmed up her chicken Alfredo. Stepping out on his deck, he ate under a nice June breeze. The day was calm, with no hints that God's judgment could happen anytime.

His thoughts went to Sinclaire Oliver. What did God's judgment mean for *her* children?

He grabbed his phone, scrolled to her name in his history, and tapped.

She answered with a "Praise the Lord" greeting.

That always made Jude smile—no, grin—as he remembered how Sinclaire fought against the church and Jesus' salvation. Her son, Carlton, was the witness she needed to draw her to Christ.

"Praise the Lord, Sinclaire. What are you and the children doing tomorrow night?"

"Taking Sissy to a birthday party."

"Hmmm." He couldn't mask his disappointment. "Well, I wanted to hear your voice and know you and the children are okay." If he had the strength, Jude would drive the half hour to see them now, but Friday evening would be better.

"We are. Jude, are you okay?" She sounded concerned.

He nodded as if she could see him while his spirit screamed no.

"Do you mind if I stop by on Saturday then?"

Sinclaire sighed. "His father has visitation rights, beginning at noon."

Jude would not be deterred. He had to see his favorite little friends, not knowing if they would be spared in God's judgment. "How about I bring breakfast and visit before Harrison comes?"

"You know how he feels about the men at Christ For All. He thinks every brother and minister is trying to steal Carlton from him, and I'm not in the mood to go head-to-head with Harrison about insecurities and attitude."

"I get that, but I just want to see them."

"O-okay. See you about ten?"

"I'll be there at 9:55." They chuckled and ended the call.

Hours later, when Jude laid his head on his pillow, a tear fell as his heart was full of sorrow for what was yet to come.

God is righteous was his last thought before he closed his eyes.

Chapter Two

On Friday morning, while Jude showered and dressed for work, he prayed for joy. The Bible said it was the source of Christians' strength. Jude needed supernatural strength today! He and a group of church members were designated intercessors.

God revealed spiritual warfare to them that others didn't see. They were the actual Ghostbusters, but the battle with demons wasn't for the faint at heart. It was a matter of life or eternal damnation of one's soul.

The Christians the Lord selected as intercessors needed to be fearless, know how to pray without ceasing, and fast for spiritual strength. That was Jude, except this time, it seemed personal.

Aren't all souls personal to the Believers? God asked, and Jude felt the rebuke.

Chastened, Jude repented, walked out the door, and then drove to his office, where he hoped to distract his mind for eight hours.

One more day, and he would get a glimpse of the Oliver family.

Jude didn't have much time to spend with Sinclaire's children before Carlton's father, Harrison Sr., arrived, so he didn't plan to be late. He bought breakfast crepes and mini cinnamon rolls topped with white icing and bits of pecans at Carlton, Sissy, and TJ's favorite place. Even their mother was okay with the sugary treats ever so often.

The aroma inside the bakery triggered Jude's stomach to grumble for the first time since Thursday morning. It was a good sign because his appetite had waned since the Lord woke him. Jude ate on autopilot for daily nourishment since his taste buds seemed numbed. He was still on spiritual alert.

Once he arrived at Sinclaire's apartment building, Jude opted to hike the stairs to the second story rather than take the elevators. He was eager to see the family that inspired him to hope that one day God would bless him with one of his own—if God would send any more children into the world.

Jude rang the doorbell and waited, hearing the children's excited voices. When Sinclaire opened the door, he was already smiling and in a better mood.

Sinclaire was refreshing. She was a pretty lady—fair skin, sandy brown hair, and a shape that turned heads, which was not her focus since surrendering to the Lord.

She had made lousy dating choices, resulting in three children from two men. Sissy and TJ favored Sinclaire. Carlton, not as much.

"Praise the Lord, Jude." Sinclaire greeted him with a contagious smile. She took the bags out of his hands and stepped back.

Carlton, who would be ten by the end of the summer, was getting taller. Jude wouldn't be surprised if the boy reached his height of six-three in high school. "Hi, Minister Jude."

"Hey, buddy." Jude wrapped him in a hug and kissed the top of his head. Jude might not be his biological father, but he believed a child could never have too much attention and affection.

Clare, who was six years old and everyone called Sissy, stretched out her arms. Tyler Jr., age four, was named after his father but called TJ. Both children had the same father. Jude heaved them up with little effort.

"Follow the food to the kitchen," Sinclaire teased as if she had been the breakfast chef instead of serving takeout. "Wash your hands before you touch anything," she instructed her children when Jude set them on their feet, and they raced off.

Sinclaire studied him, then lifted her chin and nodded. "You had me worried the other night. You didn't sound right."

"Tired." He rolled his shoulders. "I was up...praying." *Lord, please don't let her ask me why.*

She didn't. "That's what us saints do, especially you, minister," she said as she took the food out of the bags and set it on the counter.

The children returned with grins and water dripping from their fingers. Sinclaire fussed and reached for the kitchen towel. "When you wash your hands, make sure they're dry before you leave the bathroom."

Jude waved her off. "I got this." He took a paper towel and squatted and dried their small hands.

Carlton pulled out the chair for his mother. Pleased by his actions, Jude nodded. As his mentor, Jude groomed him for manhood. Carlton bowed his head and blessed the food.

His younger siblings mumbled Amens and reached for the mini rolls first. Sinclaire had set glasses of milk by their plates.

The discussion was lively, and they vied for Jude's attention. He didn't disappoint. He wanted to make promises for summer fun now that school was out: picnics, museums, and other activities to show them how much they were loved. Jude couldn't make plans, not knowing if God would take them away from Sinclaire...and him.

Twenty minutes later, the children were fed and returned to their rooms to play. Jude helped restore the kitchen. "Seems like I haven't seen you in so long."

Tilting her head, Sinclaire smiled. "I guess that means we're missed."

"Most definitely," Jude said, then let it rest. He wanted to be a friend to her first, then build from that foundation. One thing Jude didn't want was for her to think he was like the other guys who were attracted to her, only to deceive her.

Sinclaire's eyes sparkled. "The children and I miss you too." She turned her back to him to wipe off the table. "Have you heard the big fuss on social media about women who say they don't want to have children for selfish reasons like keeping their money, having uninterrupted quiet time, and not subjecting their conditioned bodies to unnecessary pain for a child? *Hmph.* I can't believe a lot of women agreed."

Not knowing where the conversation was going, Jude was cautious in his questioning. "Do you feel that way? Regrets?"

"I regret my vulnerability with two men, but then I look at my children. I know I will always have them to keep me company, make me proud, and care for me when I'm old. No regrets with the gifts God gave me."

"Amen."

She chuckled. "But I guess it's true because I heard a report last night that the number of births is down to the point where medical schools are reducing admissions in that specialty," she said with her back to him.

Jude's heart crashed as his body froze at the news. Had the judgment started? Sinclaire chatted away with little care in the world.

She turned around. "I'm not surprised. Women are smarter. What woman wants to fall for a man who isn't interested in her feelings but only in her bed? Twice, I fell for it. If I could go back, I would change many things about my life." Sinclaire bowed her head in shame.

Jude stepped closer to her. He wanted to rest his hands on her shoulders to encourage her but didn't. Jude knew his boundaries with the sisters in the church and didn't cross them, especially with this one who had his heart, but she didn't know it. Plus, some women didn't like to be touched because of whatever physical abuse they had suffered in a relationship before Christ saved them. Jude respected boundaries.

"Don't beat yourself up. We were all born in sin. Sin is in our bloodline, and Jesus' blood on the cross was the transfusion we needed. Sin is a sickness that only Jesus can heal. You repented, so your sins are forgiven, sis."

"Thank you for the pep talk, Jude."

The doorbell rang, and Sinclaire sighed. "Carlton, it's probably your dad. Are you ready?" she called.

"Yes, mom." The boy appeared.

Jude stayed in the kitchen while she opened her door. He was glad Sinclaire never invited Harrison Wakefield inside. She confided in him that Harrison had no interest in her romantically and barely had a civil relationship after she petitioned the courts for child support.

"Be good for your dad, son," Sinclaire told Carlton when he came to the door.

"He's my kid. I know how to keep him in line. C'mon." Harrison's rough tone begged for a hit to the jaw or a beat down from the Lord. Harrison could pick his poison.

Jude didn't like the man's tone, but he had no right to demand anything as he continued to watch from the kitchen.

Vengeance is Mine, God whispered. *Your job is to minister to sinners.*

"Yes, sir," Carlton answered in a respectful tone. The boy looked forward to his parental visits with Harrison.

"Where are you two going today?" Sinclaire asked in a friendly tone.

"I'm not sure. Maybe to the park or a baseball game."

"Baseball? Yay." The child hugged his mother.

"Come on, Carlton," his father demanded impatiently.

"Love you, son," Sinclaire said as she closed the door.

She twirled around and sighed. "*Whew.* Can we say extra?"

Her phone rang. She grabbed it off the counter and answered, "Hey, Omega. What's up?"

Jude watched as the blood seemed to drain from Sinclaire's face with whatever Omega Addams told her.

Not only had Tally Addams helped Sinclaire get employment at the company where Omega worked, but they were also friends and church members.

Jude came to her side as Sinclaire dropped the phone and ran to the window. He picked up the phone, watching Sinclaire, who was shaking. "Praise the Lord, Omega. This is Jude." He put the call on speakerphone. "What's wrong?"

"God showed me a vision. Harrison has a gun and plans to kill Carlton. Sinclaire said they had just left. Do you know where they went?"

"What?" Jude held his breath, balling his fist at Harrison, hoping God would spare Carlton. This had become Jude's worst nightmare.

"They're gone." Sinclaire bawled and shook her head. "I don't. This is Harrison's scheduled weekend, so they could go anywhere, but he mentioned a park or baseball game."

Omega's husband, Mitchell, added to the conversation. "Can we do an Amber Alert?"

"No. Carlton wasn't taken." Sinclaire's voice shook. "Can I file an endangered child report?"

Mitchell said, "I'll call my brother-in-law to see if there is a file on employee cars and license numbers. We can give authorities that information so they can look out for his vehicle."

Harrison worked at Randall Addams' company and had no idea that Randall's sister, Omega, had befriended his ex-girlfriend Sinclaire, the mother of one of his children.

Without warning, Jude released an agonizing cry. "Lord, not Carlton. Not Carlton." He dropped the phone and fell to his knees to pray.

Sissy and TJ came out of their rooms and patted his back.

"It's okay, Minister Jude. Jesus will fix it," Sissy said, unaware of the possibility that this could be God's will not to fix it.

Sinclaire joined him on his knees with a gut-wrenching cry. Jude had no choice but to pray God's divine will and comfort for what was coming.

Chapter Three

*For he shall give his angels charge over thee,
to keep thee in all thy ways.* —Psalm 91:11

Carlton glanced out the window from his passenger seat in his dad's truck at the passing scenery. This was not the way to the baseball game or the park near his house.

He frowned, looked at his dad, then opened his mouth to ask but didn't, judging from the stern look on his face. Where was his father taking him?

Though you walk through the shadow of death, fear no evil, I am with you, God whispered.

Smiling to himself, Carlton remembered Psalm 23 from Sunday school and began to recite it. "The Lord is my Shepherd. I shall not want…"

"Shut up that nonsense," Harrison snapped, lifting an arm to smack him.

"Yes, sir. Sorry, Dad." Carlton lowered his voice and slid down in his seat, trying to keep from shaking. He wanted to go home. Minister Jude was there with his brother, sister, and mom. He was always nice to them.

I am your Shepherd, Carlton. Never apologize for believing in Me, God whispered.

"Your mother messed things up for me," Harrison growled. His teeth appeared as long and strong as animal fangs. His eyes darkened like evil was behind them.

What Carlton saw wasn't real. It wasn't human. His father was tall but not taller than Minister Jude. Carlton shivered from fear as if an invisible poison were seeping out of the air conditioner to kill him.

"Sinclaire didn't need help raising you. You don't even love me—and I'm your father," he snapped.

Hiding his hurt from the accusation, Carlton needed to defend his family. "Mom was sad sometimes because she couldn't give us what we wanted, and Jesus told me to love everybody. I love you, Dad."

"I told you I don't want to hear any of that Jesus stuff." Harrison twisted his mouth as if he tasted something sour.

He gripped the steering wheel. Was he going to yank it free from the truck? A yellow light flashed, then it was red. He sped up and zoomed through the intersection, missing a collision. Cars honked, but his father didn't stop and shouted curse words that his mom said he was not to repeat if he heard them.

A monster flashed before Carlton's eyes. Was this what demons looked like? A growling sound reminded him of a dog that was once behind a fence and ready to attack.

"I hate you," he spit at Carlton. "I hate my life. I don't know why I fooled around with silly women like your mama." Harrison released a beast inside with those words as slime dripped from his mouth.

A hungry one.

Carlton tried to be a big boy but couldn't stop the tears from falling. He was scared. Harrison pulled out a gun from inside his jacket.

Suddenly, a police car pulled beside them, and Carlton tried to get their attention.

Duck, God thundered.

Carlton bent over at the same time he heard a pop and felt a sharp pain in his shoulder and back. *I'm afraid, Lord.*

He closed his eyes.

Chapter Four

*Continue in prayer, and watch in the same
with thanksgiving... —Colossians 4:2*

Jude did his best to comfort Sinclaire, but it was a struggle. Carlton was a part of Jude's life as if he was his son. They met by accident. Carlton was a third wheel on what was supposed to be a getting-to-know-you date. Jude had been impressed with the boy's intelligence and zeal for the Lord.

The *I'm coming for the children* warning ran track through Jude's head. Thousands—millions—of children in the world, one of those children had a face and name.

And Carlton was in danger.

The doorbell rang while the adults pleaded with God for intervention. Jude doubted any of them knew about God's judgment. He opened the door to their friends and church members.

Omega Franklin marched through the door with her husband, Mitchell. Both wore fierce expressions, hands balled into fists, ready to battle. The intercessors had arrived to wage war on the spiritual battlefield. Omega had been the protégé of the late prayer warrior, Mother Helena, who possessed many spiritual gifts of the Holy Spirit and nurtured Omega's gift of visions.

Omega's brother, Randall Addams, was Harrison's employer, and he had come too. Randall and his wife, Tally, pushed their way inside the apartment.

Both women entered praying, rebuking the powers of darkness, and praising the Lord for pulling down the strongholds.

Their presence instantly revived Jude's spirit.

Randall took charge and calmed Sinclaire down. "God's in control." He led her to the sofa, and they sat. "Can you remember anything out of the ordinary today about Harrison, whether it was something he said or how he acted that might have hinted he wasn't in his right mind?"

Sinclaire shook her head. "Harrison was his same old rude self, telling Carlton to hurry up." Her lips trembled as tears fell. "I tolerate him and ignore his snide remarks for our son's sake."

Omega and Tally walked away into the kitchen, where they released gut-wrenching petitions to God.

Jude silently prayed as he tried to distract Sissy and TJ.

Once Randall felt he had gathered enough information, he called the police. "We believe a child is in danger. Can you issue an Amber Alert or something? Carlton Oliver is with his biological father, Harrison Wakefield Sr." He searched for notes on his phone. "Harrison drives a Ford truck, Missouri license plate WTB-349." As Sinclaire dictated the information, he relayed Carlton's physical description and what he was wearing. "He's nine years old, about four and a half feet tall, weighs sixty pounds…" He paused, listened to the dispatcher, and frowned. "A reason for our suspicions?"

Putting the phone on mute, Randall walked into the kitchen for help. He tried to coax his sister out of prayer for guidance but couldn't.

To say Omega saw a vision of danger wasn't an attention grabber for people in this world.

Jude prayed, *Lord, give Randall what to say.*

"I'm Harrison's employer. He has been acting irrational lately and upset about child support payments…." Randall paced the room, layering on one reason after another until he ended the call and exhaled. "They agreed to relay an all-points bulletin, but it doesn't constitute an Amber Alert since Carlton wasn't taken without permission."

"Let's pray God's will in heaven be done on earth. We should form a circle and put Sissy and TJ in the center."

Sinclaire followed his instructions. Her face was swollen and flushed from her agony.

Tears mixed with praise for hours as the friends pleaded with God for mercy and grace.

As their voices weakened, the banging on the door grew louder. Sinclaire leaped up and raced to open it. An officer stood in the doorway.

Sinclaire's body seemed to drift to the floor. Jude rushed over and picked her up.

"Is this about Carlton?" Jude asked.

Removing his hat, he nodded. "May I come in?" He kept his voice low when he spotted the other children. "I'm Officer Eastern, and I'm sorry to inform you that Harrison Wakefield Sr. has been shot and killed after exchanging gunfire with police. A call to 9-1-1 earlier regarding Mr. Wakefield and Carlton Oliver led us to this address."

"What?" Sinclaire shrieked.

Jude pitied Harrison's judgment, but his concern was for the child. "And Carlton?"

"He has been transported to the hospital."

"Is my son alive?" Sinclaire's voice trembled as she stirred back to consciousness.

The officer didn't answer right away. They held their breaths, waiting. Jude could hear his heart pounding.

Sinclaire screamed. "My baby! He's my oldest." Covering her face with her hands, she bawled. Omega and Tally wrapped their arms around her.

"Your son did suffer injuries, shot at close range, but is alive amazingly since he became entangled in a crossfire between his father and an officer who pulled up beside them in a patrol car."

"Thank You, Jesus," Jude yelled to the top of his lungs for all heaven and earth to hear. God had spared Carlton. The Lord had not come to take him away but had protected him.

Safe.

When the officer relayed the hospital information, Jude grabbed TJ. Randall heaved Sissy into his arms, and the sisters-in-law looped their arms through Sinclaire's. They hurried out the door.

Chapter Five

Even the very hairs of your head are all numbered. Fear not therefore:
ye are of more value than many sparrows. —Luke 12:7

*G*od has been so good to me, so why is this happening? Sinclaire wondered.

She knew Harrison resented her for having the courts garnish his check for back child support, and she was okay with his attitude, but to take out his frustrations for her on a child—one of his sons—was unfathomable.

The day was surreal. A routine parental visit went wrong. What made Carlton's father snap? Pastor Rodney gave one sermon and told the saints to love their enemies, not hate them. That emotion should be directed at the forces of demons that controlled people.

Hate.

Sinclaire couldn't slap the devil like she could Harrison. She despised the demon that overtook Harrison's sanity and…hated Harrison for yielding to it.

Head pounding, she sniffed even though her tear ducts were empty. Her son—her oldest baby—was alive. She thanked God that Jude had come to visit and taken charge. At the moment, Jude was her strength.

Unable to reach the pastor, he had called Mother Kincaid from his church. She was one of the intercessory prayer leaders and treated Sinclaire like a granddaughter. Mother Kincaid began to pray for Carlton to pull through. "I'll meet you at the hospital and take Sissy and TJ home with me," she had said to Sinclaire while Jude held the phone and her hand.

Without parents and siblings, these church members had filled the gap. Sinclaire glanced in the backseat at her two healthy children. Their father, Tyler Sr., didn't seem unhinged—yet—just irresponsible, but Sinclaire had to face reality. Demons had been unleashed on the earth, and she had to protect her children and not let them out of her sight.

She and the children rode with Jude while the couples trailed them in one vehicle. Tally had been a godsend and befriended her first. When Tally had briefly moved to New York for a job opportunity, she passed the sisterhood torch to Omega to make sure Sinclaire lacked nothing—from a job to childcare and getting a car. Even Jude provided companionship and a welcome presence in her children's lives.

Church members were her family.

"Lord, please let my son be okay," she prayed softly but loud enough for Jude to hear. He reached over and squeezed her hand with strength and tenderness.

Although she lived about thirty minutes from Children's University Hospital, and Jude drove as fast as he could without asking for a ticket, the ride seemed like an hour away.

When they arrived at the emergency room, Mother Kincaid had beaten them there, waiting outside the door. Her gray hair was brushed up in a neat bun on top of her head. Her eyes were misty, but she had a ready smile for Sissy and TJ.

Sinclaire wanted to race inside and see Carlton, but she feared what she would find.

Mother Kincaid held her arms out, and Sinclaire collapsed in them. She boohooed, afraid of what news awaited her inside. Carlton was alive, but was he conscious? On life support? His body was too small to withstand a bullet close range.

She sniffed, and Mother Kincaid squinted, looking into her eyes. "All it takes is faith the size of a mustard seed to impress the Lord. Now, go in there and see about our baby," Mother Kincaid ordered and took TJ in her arms and held on to Sissy's hand.

Tally and Omega came to her sides, and the trio entered the ER. The men walked behind them. "We're all here for you, Sinclaire," Jude said.

Sinclaire took a deep breath and commanded one foot to move and the other to follow. She jumped when an ambulance with blinking lights and sirens pulled to the hospital's entrance. How could she look at an emergency vehicle again without feeling a certain way, knowing one had brought her son there to save his life?

Surprisingly, the same police officer who came to her house was there and escorted her to the information desk. "I'm Sinclaire Oliver. My son Carlton Oliver came by ambulance..." Tears fell.

"Yes." The woman stood. "This way." She ushered Sinclaire through locked doors. "The rest of you can have a seat."

The hall seemed like a maze to the triage rooms as they passed the nurses' station. The floors were white. The walls were white. It seemed lifeless. *Lord, please let my son have life in him.*

The nurse pulled back the curtain, and Sinclaire sobbed. Carlton's eyes were closed. Her son, perfect since birth, was bandaged and bruised.

His small face was puffy. He no longer looked like her sweet, innocent, and respectful little boy.

Carlton's right shoulder was bandaged, and his arm was in a sling. "He's alive. Thank You, Jesus!" Sinclaire quietly moved closer to the bed. How long had he been here? She'd never known emergency rooms to work so fast.

"Yes. Thank the Universe." The nurse gripped her hands and smiled. "Little fellow came in in shock and bleeding from the bullet wound. The doctor can tell you more."

Her badge read Nurse Ruby Fields.

"Since the Lord created the universe, I'll thank Him," Sinclaire said, resting her hand on her son's. "Carlton, it's Mama, baby. I'm so sorry for what happened."

Grabbing a chair, Sinclaire scooted closer to the bed and sobbed. She blamed herself. "I'm so sorry." She almost lost her son because she had forced Harrison to pay child support, and in turn, he demanded parental visits that he didn't want with their son. Harrison did it out of spite. Sinclaire cried harder.

A soft touch on her shoulder stilled her tears.

I allowed this. Satan wanted Carlton's soul, but I wouldn't allow it, God whispered.

Sinclaire opened her eyes and looked around. No one was there. Even the nurse had slipped out.

Carlton stirred and moaned. "Mom?"

"Yes, son." Sinclaire rubbed his cheek.

"Mommy, I was afraid." Carlton sniffed.

Mommy. Sinclaire mustered a smile. Her son hadn't called her that in a long time. He said he was too old for that. She stood and leaned forward to kiss the side of his head. "God showed Sister Omega that you were in danger, and I was scared too. Minister Jude was upset, too, but we all prayed."

The curtain opened. Officer Eastern walked in. "How's our brave young man feeling?"

"My arm hurts." Carlton tried to lift it but winced.

"Easy now. Your mom is here, and she'll help you get better." He pulled out his pad. "Can you tell me what you remember?"

Sinclaire watched her son's lips quiver. The fear in his eyes revealed the horror he'd witnessed.

"Will he hurt me again?" Carlton asked.

Officer Eastern kept a straight face. "No, he won't. Your dad didn't survive." He looked at Sinclaire. "We didn't want to tell him without you being here. It's still under investigation, but a cruiser began pursuing the vehicle when Harrison ran the red light. The statement from the officer said when the officer saw the weapon fire, he returned fire, striking the suspect and causing the truck to crash. We didn't know your son was inside until he searched the vehicle."

"How horrific. How is the officer?" Sinclaire felt faint but had to be strong for Carlton. *Lord, give me strength.*

"He was transported to the hospital with serious injuries, but he is in stable condition and will be okay."

Sinclaire exhaled—senseless drama.

Carlton bowed his head. "My dad hated me and my mom."

"No, son," she told Carlton, then looked at the officer. "I took him to court for child support." Sinclaire shook her head. She would carry the blame for life that her decision caused her son harm.

I protected him! God thundered.

Forgive me, Lord. Sinclaire patted her chest. "I'm thankful my son is alive."

"Dad seemed to turn into a monster. I thought he was going to eat me. God whispered to me 'though I walk through valley' before Dad pulled out the gun, and God told me to duck," her son rambled as Officer Eastern took notes. "He pointed the gun at me and fired. I heard sirens, and then I heard gunshots all around me. I was afraid, so I kept my eyes closed."

"Thanks for your statement. You get better." He patted Carlton's good arm.

Sinclaire tried to stifle her cries, but hearing what her son had endured made her feel guilty. What-ifs began to haunt her. She should have noticed the red flag—how Harrison talked to Carlton.

"I could have lost you…I could have lost you." More tears spilled from her eyes. Seeing her son bandaged was her undoing. In Carlton's nine years of life, he had never been in an emergency room with a scrap, sprain, cut, or…bullet.

⸺ ∽ ⸺

My dad is dead? Carlton sniffed. *Maybe I didn't love him enough, or I wasn't good enough. That's why he hated me.*

Carlton wanted to cry, but that would upset his mama, who was still crying, so he closed his eyes.

"Miss Oliver, can you step out with me for a moment?" Nurse Ruby whispered.

On the other side of the curtain, Carlton could hear the nurse. "Your son was very lucky today."

"No. He was blessed."

"Yes, alright, and your son will recover," the nurse said in a hushed voice. "Although his body went into shock from the trauma, he's alive. Poor thing kept mumbling, 'God is with me.'" She chuckled. "If God were with him, this never would have happened. I mean… The things I see happen to children who come into this hospital will shake anybody's faith."

"I still trust God, even though this happened. God kept the bullet from killing him—I'm sorry about Harrison and the officer," Sinclaire said. "I'm crying and worshipping God for the horror that my son survived. However, if the Lord had taken my son…He still would have been in the presence of Jesus. Now, are there special instructions I need to know about his care so we can go home? He can go home, right?"

"Oh! We're waiting for the doctor to talk to you before we can discharge him. It shouldn't be much longer."

"Mama," Carlton called with all his strength, and she peeked from the other side of the curtain.

"Yes, baby?"

"Is Minister Jude here?"

Sinclaire smiled. "Yes, he sure is. So are the Addamses and Franklins and other saints from church."

Carlton grinned, then frowned. "Where are my sister and baby brother? Are they okay? Their dad didn't try to hurt them, too, did he?"

"Oh no." She shook her head. "They're with Mother Kincaid. They're fine. I'll go get Minister Jude."

Other children were there too. *Did their dad hurt them too?* Carlton wondered.

Minister Jude pulled back the curtain and stepped into the room with his mother. He was big and strong and wouldn't have let anything happen to Carlton. He was always happy, but not now. Had he been crying too?

"You okay, buddy?" Minister Jude's voice was low as he came closer and rubbed his head, looking at his bandages.

"Yeah." Carlton grinned. He was feeling better already. "God protected me."

"Yes, He did, and we've been praising the Lord for His mercy." He looked sad. "You know I love you?"

Carlton nodded. "You would never hurt me like that."

"Never." He frowned. "Ever."

"Can you be my dad?"

Minister Jude stared, and his mouth seemed stuck. Mama was quiet too. Did that mean yes or no?

Did a nine-year-old just propose to me? Jude patted his chest. Choked with emotion, Jude couldn't speak.

Breathe.

"I'm going to need a new dad now," Carlton said with all innocence in his expression, then turned down his lips.

Jude was speechless. He would give the boy anything within his power. Jude wanted to be a husband and father, but with God's judgment, he didn't know if that was still possible.

He glanced at Sinclaire to rescue him. Blushing, she didn't meet his eyes. She looked at the IV drip, the heart monitor, and even a speck in the corner. Sinclaire finally cleared her throat and smiled at her son. "Carlton, we'll talk about all that later, okay?"

Carlton didn't seem satisfied.

There were more pressing matters. God was coming for the children. Was Harrison's attempt to murder his son part of God's judgment?

Pastor Rodney couldn't come home from his pastor's leadership conference in Minnesota soon enough. Hopefully, he could interpret God's message.

Jude was spared giving an answer when a Black doctor with a thick mustache appeared. He seemed to do a room check. First, to Sinclaire, Carlton, and then Jude. He nodded, stepped inside the room, then introduced himself as Dr. Anderson.

He extended his hand to Sinclaire. "I'm his mother." Then to Jude, expecting identification. "I'm Jude Morgan, a family friend."

"Nice to meet you both." Then he turned to Sinclaire. "Your son is going to be fine despite being shot at close range. He sustained a gunshot wound that entered and exited his upper left arm. That's a good thing, so we treated the bleeding, and no surgery was required. An x-ray showed he suffered a contusion to his right shoulder, probably due to the impact of the crash. With any child trauma, we always suggest speaking with a counselor, but his pediatrician can make that determination when you follow up with them. His vitals are good, so there's no reason to keep him overnight. I'll prepare your discharge papers with instructions for homecare."

Dr. Anderson smiled for the first time when he looked at Carlton. "You're a brave soldier. God was watching over you. That means He has work for you to do. Get well." He took Carlton's hand, patted it, then pulled the curtain back to leave.

Jude sat on the other side of Carlton's bed and wanted to squeeze him tight for what he had endured. The doctor wasn't the wiser because God spared Carlton's life to fulfill a mission. "I'm here for you—always."

Carlton nodded as the nurse reappeared from the other side of the beige curtain, waving papers in her hands. "Look what I have. You get to go home," she said in a singsong tone.

The nurse gave Sinclaire the prescription for pain medicine with the physician's instructions to follow up with his pediatrician.

Jude spied the boy's bloody clothes in a clear bag marked *Belongings*. "Do you have something that he can wear home?"

Sinclaire rubbed her forehead when he pointed to the soiled clothes. She looked like she was about to faint. Jude stood and maneuvered about the bed to give her strength.

The woman with red hair and large red glasses seemed to just notice him. "It's up to the family to bring a change of clothes for discharge."

"We weren't aware," Jude said.

Sinclaire shook her head. "The only thing on my mind was getting to my son."

"Target's around the corner," Jude suggested, having seen it en route.

The nurse bobbed her head. "Yeah. We have families who order from them all the time. Their delivery service is faster than shopping yourself."

Jude pulled out his phone. "Sinclaire, what size clothes does Carlton wear? I'll place an order for underwear, a shirt, and shorts."

"Really? Then that will work. Thank you. Can he stay here while we wait for his clothes to be delivered?" Sinclaire asked the nurse as she removed the needle from his IV. She wrapped gauze around his hand and taped it.

She gnawed on her lips and scrunched her face while efficiently and carefully removing the stickers on his chest that monitored his heart rate. "Ahh…We need the room because we have more children coming in than we can handle. Serious injuries."

Jude watched Sinclaire squeeze her lips to keep from responding.

"What I mean is today has been a bad day for our little ones."

God, what is Your judgment? Jude silently pleaded for insight. He was also annoyed at Nurse Ruby. Wasn't a gunshot victim serious, if not critical? Jude held his tongue and placed the order.

After all, as a Christian and minister, he needed to remain approachable for prayer. Snapping at the woman wouldn't look good as his phone chimed with an alert. "Delivery time: twenty-four minutes. Wow." He was impressed. "Can he at least keep the hospital gown so we can sit in the waiting room until our delivery comes?" Jude asked.

"Mama," Carlton said, looking fearful, "I don't want to be naked around a lot of people."

Nurse Ruby seemed to have a change of heart. "You know what? I'll see what I can do."

Sinclaire dropped her head in her waiting hands. "Thank you."

Jude had restrained himself as long as he could through this ordeal, but Sinclaire needed comfort, so he squatted and hugged her. She didn't protest his embrace, and Jude hid his smile.

His mind drifted to when he had been interested in Tally when she was a new saint at church, not knowing that her former ex—now her husband—had her heart. Carlton had tagged along to brunch that Jude had invited her to. Instead of being the third wheel, the boy had endeared himself to Jude. They bonded, and he began to mentor Carlton as a role model in Christ and a Black father figure since his dad was not in his life then.

"I'm going to pray like you one day, Minister Jude, and I'm going to share my lunch at school if anybody is hungry too."

An indescribable emotion had welled up in Jude. Carlton was easy to nurture, causing Jude to crave a son of his own. "Amen. I believe God will use you for great things."

What happened today wasn't great. The child could have died.

The scenario added to Jude's confusion.

Mitchell texted him from the hospital waiting room, pulling him out of his reverie. **Is Carlton okay?**

Jude had forgotten about them. **Yes. Praise God.** Jude sighed and continued typing. **He's been discharged, but I ordered him some clothes because he can't leave with the bloody ones he came in with.**

Gotcha.

As soon as the delivery comes, I'll let you know.

Oh, Mitchell sent another text. **We overheard nurses discussing a multi-vehicle crash with fatalities, mostly children. What is going on?**

God's judgment. But Jude didn't know if the warning was to be shared until he spoke to Pastor Rodney. The Lord had taught him when to speak and when to remain silent.

While waiting, Sinclaire and Jude let Carlton talk about anything he wanted without prompting him to share his feelings about what he had endured.

"I want to go home and play with Sissy and Baby Brother."

Sinclaire smiled. "You will, son."

The clothes arrived minutes before Nurse Ruby said they had to go.

Despite Sinclaire's attractiveness, the scare had aged her—weariness and hopelessness seemed to drape her like a shawl before he stepped out to give them privacy.

In the lobby, a mini-congregation awaited Carlton. They worshipped God for the good news until the security guard ushered them outside.

"I listened to your prayers," the security guard mumbled with watery eyes. "I needed them."

When Sinclaire walked outside the ER with Carlton in a wheelchair, friends cheered and hugged Carlton, careful of his bandages.

Sinclaire looked exhausted when Jude helped her in his vehicle. "You okay?" he whispered. She nodded, then he assisted

Carlton in the backseat, careful of his injuries. Before Jude left his side, Carlton hugged him and kissed his cheek. Jude choked as he slid behind the wheel.

He loved that boy. Jude rejoiced that Carlton was alive as he overheard whispers that other patients transported to the emergency room hadn't made it.

Sinclaire faced him. "Do you mind taking me to get Sissy and TJ?"

"You didn't have to ask." He started the ignition, waved at some saints getting into their cars, then drove toward Mother Kincaid's senior living residence.

"Thank you," Sinclaire whispered and closed her eyes.

"Minister Jude, I had a dream last night that my dad wasn't going to be nice today because the devil was after him, so I prayed really hard, but the devil got him anyway." His voice faded.

Sinclaire's eyes popped open, and she whipped her head toward the backseat.

Jude looked in the rearview mirror.

"Carlton, I don't want to hear anything about Harrison right now. Your father tried to kill you." Sinclaire shook her head, turned around, and stared out the window.

"I know," Carlton said calmly, "but God told me He's coming for His children."

This time, Jude jammed his brakes. His heart pounded. Did Carlton have an understanding of the message that he didn't? Remaining silent, Jude waited for Carlton to say more as he continued to drive. He exchanged glances with Sinclaire who looked exhausted and bewildered.

Jude checked the rearview mirror. Carlton dozed. Jude had barely parked at Mother Kincaid's place when Sinclaire released her seatbelt. "Sit here while I get Siss and TJ." He rested his hand on hers.

"No, I'll get them." She slipped her hand from under his. "Plus, I want to hear Mother Kincaid pray for me."

Jude conceded and stepped out to help Sinclaire as she was already getting out. He stayed behind with Carlton and waved at the church mother when she opened her door to Sinclaire. Both women seemed to cling to each other before Sinclaire disappeared into the house.

"Minister Jude," Carlton said, stirring from the backseat, "I'm not going to be in trouble for making Mama sad, am I?"

"No." Jude chuckled. The mind of a child was simplistic. Their objection in life was to stay out of trouble. "She loves you and is glad you're okay."

When Sinclaire reappeared, he stepped outside his SUV and watched her walk toward him with the children. Jude lifted TJ out of her arms, opened the back door, and secured TJ in the booster that he left in his vehicle, then did the same for Sissy. Sinclaire waited for him to help her inside.

TJ and Sissy were full of questions about why their big brother had bandages.

Surprisingly, Sinclaire didn't intervene to sugarcoat the truth to the younger children and allowed Carlton to give his version. "My dad was mad and hurt me, and then the police hurt him."

It was not the version Jude would have given, but it must have satisfied his siblings because they asked no follow-up questions. "You want me to stop and get dinner?" Jude offered.

"I have leftovers. I want to go home and rest."

Thirty minutes later, Jude escorted them to her apartment and reluctantly said his goodbyes, but not before hugging and kissing the children, then giving Sinclaire a brief hug. She was the one who had to send the signals that she was interested in more.

Jude had learned the hard way at church if the sisters didn't send him signals, keep the relationships strictly brothers and sisters in Christ.

Moments after he stepped foot through the door of his house, he dropped his keys on the counter, walked to his bedroom, and slid to his knees. The emotions he held in check all afternoon, Jude now released five hours later. "Lord, thank You for sparing Carlton's life!" Tears streamed down his cheeks as he praised the Lord for His mercy, then pleaded with God to reveal His purpose.

"Satan, I rebuke you and your army in the name of Jesus, who has all authority over man, beast, and spirits. All souls belong to God. You can't have them…"

But many will die, the devil had the nerve to taunt as the Lord opened Jude's spiritual eyes to see the dark creature in front of him.

Jude continued his rebuke, "In the Book of John, is it not written that it's the will of God that Jesus shall not lose any of those God has given Him? Now go in the name of Jesus." Jude blinked, and the darkness evaporated before his spiritual eyes.

This wasn't a game. The battle of children's souls was at stake, and Jude prayed until he lost his voice.

Chapter Six

And thou shalt teach them (the law) diligently unto thy children, and shalt talk of them when thou sit in thine house, when thou walks by the way when thou lies down, and when thou rises up. —Deuteronomy 6:7

On Sunday morning, before the congregation gathered for service, Jude was in Pastor Rodney's office to hand off the burden God had given him. His leader listened to Jude without interrupting. Jude was in tears, recalling all the details while his pastor remained calm. "God had given me the prophecy, Omega the vision, and Carlton was shot by his father." Jude patted his chest.

Pastor Rodney nodded. "God has spoken, and His judgment has begun. The first five minutes of the news last night involved crashes, shootings, house fires, or boating accidents where children were among the fatalities." A slight frown crossed his face.

He was silent as if God were whispering in his ear, then stood. "Minister Morgan, it's time for us to enter the sanctuary. God has delivered His message for today. Now, I need to translate it to the saints."

Jude stood, too, composed himself, and trailed Pastor Rodney out of his office. He could feel the presence of the Lord.

The pastor prayed briefly, then began to praise the Lord, and an explosion of praise filled the sanctuary. It was as if God was walking in their midst.

"Saints, we have a reason to praise Him. As many of you are probably aware, we almost lost our precious Brother Carlton yesterday, but God spared his life."

"Hallelujah! Praise the Lord and Thank You, Jesus" were shouted throughout the congregation with hearty applause.

"Yes, yes. We praise Jesus for His mercy. Sister Oliver and Brother Carlton, if you're watching online, know we're praying for you. Unfortunately, sadly, Brother Carlton lost his father."

Gasps and "oh no" filled the sanctuary.

He waved Jude to the podium with him. "Minister Morgan and I had a meeting, and the Lord spoke to him. This is a rebuke, saints. God is not pleased with us. Minister Morgan, please share God's warning."

After Jude greeted them, he began. "A few nights ago, the Lord woke me with this message: 'I'm coming for the children' three times. Just this morning, on my way to church, I heard an earthquake in Africa yesterday killed two hundred schoolchildren…. Pastor told me about the senseless killing he heard about last night. I don't have any children biologically, but I love children. God is rebuking parents for not teaching them God's truth but creating their own truth, then showing children how to hate, bully, steal, and kill. The Lord has given us children and released them into the wild for the wolves to devour."

An eerie quietness was around Jude as all eyes were on him. He choked. "My mind can't paint the images Jesus described to me." Still traumatized from what happened to Carlton, Jude handed the microphone back to the pastor.

"God is angry, and we deserve His punishment, but He is also merciful. We can't change the Lord's judgment, saints," Pastor Rodney said, "but we can pray for His mercy."

He flipped the pages of his Bible and referenced 1 Chronicles 21, when King David sinned and brought judgment on Israel. "Verses eight and nine say, *'David responded to God, "I sinned greatly by behaving this way. But now I am asking you, please remove the guilt of your servant since I have acted very foolishly. So, the Lord responded through Gad, David's seer. Go and tell David, 'This is what the Lord says: "I'm holding three choices out for you: pick one of them for yourself, and I will do it to you.'* King David admitted his wrongdoing and knew how to repent. This world doesn't know how, so no wonder our children don't fear the consequences of their actions. We need to repent first, then teach our children!"

Pastor Rodney continued and read verses eleven through thirteen aloud, word for word, leaving nothing out. *So, Gad came to David and said unto him, 'Thus saith the Lord, Choose thee: Either three years' famine; or three months to be destroyed before thy foes, while that the sword of thine enemies overtakes thee; or else three days the sword of the Lord, even the pestilence, in the land, and the angel of the Lord destroying throughout all the coasts of Israel.*

Now, decide what I am to answer to the One who sent me. So, David replied to Gad, "This is a very bad choice for me to make! Let me now please fall into the hand of the Lord because his mercy is very great, but may I never fall into human hands!"

"God, have mercy on us!" someone yelled from the congregation.

"Yes, have mercy." Pastor looked up at the ceiling as if God were staring down at him. "We know God rains on the just and unjust, so it's fasting and prayer time. No slackers will be tolerated, saints. We will fast three times a week for those who can, and we will go before the Lord, repenting and praying."

The service was solemn. Pastor Rodney made it plain that souls were at stake, and it was serious business.

After the benediction, Jude tapped on Sinclaire's number as he walked to the car. "Good afternoon. Want me to bring Sunday dinner?" he asked.

"Praise the Lord, Jude." She sounded tired. "We watched the church service. So that's why you acted strange when you called me a couple of days ago, wanting to hear our voice, and you came over yesterday, even though you knew Carlton would be gone? You could have told me. Maybe I would have been more prepared."

"Or not." Why was she stalling? He could be on his way with dinner and to see Carlton with a one-word answer. "Sinclaire, I'm not a prophet but one of many intercessors. Our job is to pray relentlessly. I was too close to it, and you were even closer with three children."

She was quiet as Jude became impatient. *Don't break my heart, woman. I want to see the Olivers.*

"So, do you want me to bring dinner?" he asked again.

"Thank you, but I'm already preparing dinner," she said, and Jude waited for an invite that never came before the call was disconnected.

"Seriously?" He looked at his phone. "Fine, I can get a homecooked meal at my parents' house."

Chapter Seven

*In the last days, God says, I will pour out my Spirit on all people; your
sons and daughters will prophesy, your young men will see visions,
your old men will dream dreams. —Joel 2:28 and Acts 2:17*

Carlton couldn't sleep again. He didn't want to tell his mama
because she would worry, climb into his bed, and fall
asleep like she had the first night in the room he shared with his
baby brother. The second night, she slept in a chair near TJ's
bed, watching him.

Tonight, when she peeped into his bedroom, Carlton acted
like he was asleep, and she closed the door.

Sinclaire wanted to treat him like a baby, but Carlton was
nine. When he told Mama that he kept remembering his dad
being angry at him and aiming a gun at him and firing, she said
she was going to make him an appointment to speak with a
counselor.

"But I've already talked to Pastor Rodney, and he prayed for
me, Mom," Carlton said. "Minister Jude calls me every day.
Why do I have to talk to someone else?"

Sinclaire struggled to explain. "Well, son, it's what parents
do when their child goes through something really bad."

"Okay." But Carlton still couldn't sleep without the dreams
coming to wake him up. The man he called Dad didn't look the
same. A demon, a dark shadow, possessed him.

His dad's voice sounded like a growling dog about to attack.

But Jesus spoke to Carlton like He was right inside the truck with them.

Closing his eyes, Carlton sniffed softly so his mom wouldn't hear. He would never get to know his dad now. His tears dampened his pillow.

He felt movement on his bed, then a touch on his shoulder. Carlton opened his eyes and blinked.

He turned around, expecting his mother, but no one was there.

Carlton. It was God's voice.

Alert, he sat up and listened.

I'm coming for the children, God said. *There is a remnant who has not been contaminated by the sins of their mother and father. Those children are fighting for their spiritual lives, and I will redeem them from the enemy.*

Tears ran down Carlton's cheeks, and he lifted his arms, worshipping God.

A bad time is coming. Worse than what you have experienced. Children are wicked like their parents. They are taught to be murderers, thieves, disrespectful, liars, and full of hate. I will destroy them! God whispered.

"What about my friends at school and church? My brother and sister?"

Pray that they will repent and turn to Me. I will stop forming babies in women's bellies. I will keep their souls with Me. I have spoken.

The sound of heavy footsteps like that of a dinosaur faded as God left his room.

"I'm going to tell everybody about Jesus." Carlton's eyelids became heavy, and he fell back on his pillow and drifted asleep.

Jude was still mad. Satan hadn't succeeded in taking Carlton's life, but he was responsible for the aftermath—fear.

The entire church fasted every three days for eight hours and prayed for three hours daily. Jude could only hope for mercy as the Lord carried out His punishment. Carlton was alive but struggling emotionally.

Jude sent flowers and toys for the children to Sinclaire's job. Small tokens to show her how much she and Carlton, Sissy, and TJ mattered to him.

Sinclaire's faith was shaken. Plus, she was angry with him after seeing the Sunday service where Jude told the congregation the message God had given him.

"You could have warned me what God revealed concerning my son," she still fumed on Thursday.

"Sister Oliver," he said, addressing her as he did when he had something important to tell her, "how could I tell you a revelation I didn't fully understand? Why would I instill fear in you when God had not named names? Trust me, I was scared enough for both of us—for all children."

She became quiet over the phone. Jude felt bad for checking her.

He was about to apologize when she whispered, "I'm sorry."

"I accept." Jude grinned and spoke on the phone for at least an hour until the children vied for their mother's attention.

Jude was on his third and final fast period for the week, and he prayed. *Jesus, I know that Your Word says You change not, so please have mercy on Your people. Turn hearts back to you.*

Afterward, he ordered sandwiches and called Sinclaire. "How are you doing?"

"Carlton is healing and—"

"I asked about you first, Sinclaire. Carlton will overcome this and, hopefully, one day testify to others." He checked the notification when his food would be delivered.

"Jude, I'm not okay." She was quiet, and he waited. "I blamed myself, and I blamed you after watching the service. I'd blame God if I didn't have good sense."

He chuckled. "We are in this together if you let me be. Please don't shut me out. You know you can talk to me about anything, and since we're being honest..." he grinned and prepared to tease her. "Because you didn't invite me to dinner, I crashed my parents' Sunday dinner, and my mother had prepared gizzards and gravy. Yikes. It was torture trying to make a meal around that."

When she laughed, so did Jude, then Sinclaire cleared her throat and whispered, "What do you think about taking him to see a psychologist?"

"I think it's a good idea. Whatever it takes to make Carlton whole."

"I guess." Sinclaire sounded unsure. "I don't want it to seem like we're not trusting God."

"To take medicine doesn't mean we don't trust the Lord. All healing comes from God, whether it is through medicine or miracles."

"Okay." She sighed. "You're right. I'll talk to you later."

The following Saturday, Jude arrived at Shade and Fade Barbershop at the same time as Randall Addams. There were only two barbers, and they mainly took clients by appointment only on Saturdays.

"Where's Cortez?" Randall asked.

Derek shrugged and continued clipping his client's beard. "Don't know. He's usually here by now. Take a seat in the lounge." Derek nodded to the waiting area outside the barbershop's suite in a modern building that catered to individual entrepreneurs. Two chairs were on both sides of the door.

Randall sat next to Jude. Both men were interested in the same woman at one time, but Randall and Tally had a history. Even after her salvation and steadfastness to walk with Christ, the two had each other's hearts.

Once God showed Jude that, he backed off.

After Randall surrendered to the Lord and realized Jude wasn't a threat, the two developed a cordial friendship based on a Christian brotherhood.

"I hope Cortez gets here soon. I promised Tally I would take her to an exhibit at the Missouri History Museum. She loves going to those, and whatever makes my baby happy makes me happy." He grinned, then sighed. "You know, I thought about what happened to Carlton last weekend and what you shared at church on Sunday."

Resting his elbows on his knees, Randall bobbed his head. "I guess it makes sense why Tally hasn't gotten pregnant." He sighed and stared at the blank wall in front of them. There were no accents to hold their attention.

"We want a baby so bad… We lost one before either of us surrendered to the Lord, then my sister and Mitchell lost their baby without knowing Omega was expecting. It's too much, man. Too much."

"But God…" Jude began. "He raised you from the dead in the morgue, proof that God is merciful, even as His judgment begins on earth."

"You're right. Randall nodded as their barber walked down the hall towards them. The dazed expression on his face put Jude on alert.

Something was wrong.

Jude and Randall stood at the same time.

"You alright?" Randall asked.

"I need a minute." He opened the door to the shop and seemed to drag himself inside.

Derek glanced up and frowned. "Man, what happened to you?"

Cortez dropped into his barber chair, covered his face, and sobbed.

What was going on? Jude wondered.

"I just saw a truck hit a woman and her child in the crosswalk, and the driver kept going. He never slowed down."

"What?" Derek and his client said at the same time.

"Are the woman and child okay?" Jude jammed his fists into his side, mad at the demons carrying out their assignments.

Shaking his head, Cortez shrugged. "They weren't moving." His shoulders shook with silent tears.

"That's wrong, man. Just wrong." Derek stopped clipping and stared at his coworker. "Think you should be here?"

Cortez sniffed and pinched his nose to trap further tears. "Sorry." He took a deep breath. "We're small business owners. No work, no pay...but I can't get that image out of my head. They hurried across the white stripes meant for pedestrians. She was pulling her child along, who was playing...their screams...the thud. He sped by me and stared me in the eyes with a 'What you looking at' expression. Some witnesses ran to help, but they weren't moving. Man, I froze. I can't remember blinking or breathing as I stared. The ambulance and police came in no time, but with the force of that impact, I don't see how..."

"Bro, I was a dead man," Randall spoke up, "but God restored my life."

Jude could tell by the expression on the customer's face that he didn't believe Randall.

Cortez was quiet, but his hands were shaking. There was no way his clients would get a precision cut that day.

"Do you mind if we pray for the mother and child—and you?" Jude asked.

"I could use some prayer myself," Derek's customer said from his chair.

Jude nodded to Randall, and they approached Cortez and laid their hands on his shoulders. Derek and his client bowed their heads.

"Father, in the mighty name of Jesus, we come to You humbly with thanksgiving for dying on the cross for our sins. Forgive us, Lord, for our selfish ways that have led to these evil days. In Matthew twenty-four, verses twelve and thirteen, the Bible tells us, 'And because iniquity shall abound, the love of many shall wax cold. But he that shall endure unto the end shall be saved.' Cortez has witnessed a cold-blooded act. Jesus, fight our battles; send Your angels to protect us; bind the demons ready to attack our minds, bodies, and souls…"

The harder Jude called on Jesus, the more he had to tug with spiritual forces to leave their presence. Then Jude felt God's hand holding evil back. He opened his eyes when he heard whispered voices.

Derek's client began to chant repetitious phrases that sounded dark and threatening. It wasn't heaven-sent. Jude called on Jesus to rebuke that unclean spirit while heavenly tongues pushed through Jude's mouth, and immediately, the atmosphere changed, and the demons growled in agony and backed away until the peace of God surrounded them.

This time, Jude shed tears of joy and thanksgiving as he praised the Lord for doing what Jude had asked.

"Brothers, make a choice today. Repent of your sins and be baptized in water in the name of Jesus Christ and allow the Holy Ghost to give you the ultimate protection."

Cortez had calmed down, but it wasn't business as usual. Jude pulled Randall aside. "I'm going to give him a love offering and skip a cut until next week."

"I'll do the same. My wife will think I'm just as handsome, haircut or not." He grinned.

"Shameless plug." Jude snickered.

The two gave Cortez what they would have usually given him for his services, plus a tip, and parted ways until church in the morning.

Behind the wheel of his vehicle, Jude phoned Sinclaire. "Praise the Lord. Can I stop by?"

"Praise the Lord, Minister Morgan. For sure."

Why so formal? He frowned but didn't question her. "I'll bring lunch. See you soon."

Something didn't sound right. Jude stopped by a sub sandwich joint, ordered sandwiches and chips, and headed toward her apartment.

Soon, he stood at her door and knocked. Sinclaire opened it with a worried expression. What had happened since the short phone call twenty minutes ago and now?

She mustered a smile, but it didn't fade away the worried expression on her face. "Minister Jude is here," she yelled to the children, who raced from their bedrooms. He squatted to receive their hugs.

"Minister Jude, I like the doll you sent me." Sissy kissed him on the cheek, then acted bashful.

TJ hugged Jude and showed him his toy car. Jude stood and studied Carlton. His eyes were bright, but the grin Jude was accustomed to seeing was absent.

"How you doin'?" Jude asked, rubbing the top of his hair.

Carlton shrugged.

Sinclaire pointed. "That's what I want to talk to you about. Children, wash your hands. Minister Jude brought us sandwiches."

While the children were eating in the kitchen, Sinclaire sat on the sofa with him. She seemed to look at Jude for the first time. "I need advice."

"Okay, but why the formality on the phone? I've never stopped being a minister, but I preferred you call me Jude."

She bowed her head. "I need godly advice, so you're it."

Jude squeezed her hand and smiled. "I'll be your 'it' anytime. What's up?"

Sinclaire took her hands back and fumbled with her fingers. "Harrison's funeral is on Monday, and Carlton wants to go after his grandmother called and requested he be there. Why? To torture him?" Sinclaire gritted her teeth as if she was holding in a scream. "Unbelievable."

"Hey." Jude's voice was gentle to calm her down. "This is about what Carlton needs and how we can best help him through this."

She peered at him. "I also signed him up for counseling. His first appointment isn't until after the funeral. Is he ready for this? I don't know what to do, Jude."

Flustered, Sinclaire massaged her temples. "I did not sign up for my baby to go through this trauma. I regret ever forcing Harrison back into our lives. If I knew he was…deranged," she said, struggling for the right words.

Jude removed her hands from her face to look at her. He didn't let go. "Lord, give Sinclaire rest and confidence in Your will. You spared Carlton while others were taken, and we ask for confidence in Your Word, in Jesus' name. Amen."

He looked up at her teary eyes. "Breathe." He demonstrated. "We have hope in God's mercy. Trust the process." He continued to breathe with her.

Sinclaire's lips curved into a smile, and her eyes sparkled when she laughed. "That's why I needed Minister Morgan. Do you think it's healthy for Carlton to attend, knowing his father wanted to kill him? I wouldn't want to be reminded of that day if it were me."

Jude observed her torn expression as he waited for the Lord to send him the right words to comfort her. But in all honesty, Jude shared her sentiments.

"I mean, I would prefer for him to have a counseling session first…"

The Lord was silent as Sinclaire rambled on.

When Jude was about to speak, God whispered, *If Carlton wants to go, let him. The image of Harrison lying peacefully in the coffin will replace the one that torments him.*

"I believe the Lord would want Carlton to go for closure. His father's remains looking peaceful will distort the last moments with Harrison."

Relief seemed to flood Sinclaire's face. She smiled as she leaned over and kissed his cheek, then stood.

Whew. Jude had to calm his breathing.

"You are a keeper! Now, let's eat."

Jude touched his face, where it still tingled. He got to his feet to follow her into the kitchen. Talk about bad timing to explore his feelings and hers. Jude's mind snapped back into the present before it drifted to where everything was alright in the world.

Chapter Eight

Jesus said to Thomas, "I am the way, the truth, and the life. No one comes to the Father except through Me." —John 14:6

Harrison M. Wakefield Sr.'s funeral was in the Symthe-King Mortuary chapel. There were a lot of black limousines and a lot of people inside them.

Carlton only met his grandmother and aunt a few times because his dad didn't take him around them often. Usually, Harrison took him to the park or for a hamburger. Minister Jude drove Sinclaire and Carlton to the funeral home. Sinclaire opted to leave Sissy and TJ with a sitter.

Many from Christ For All Church came, including Brother and Sister Addams, Brother and Sister Franklin, Pastor Rodney, and Mother Kincaid.

Grandma Pearline, Harrison's mother, nodded to Sinclaire, then patted him on the shoulder. "Carlton, you walk in with the family, sugar."

Am I family now that my dad is dead? Carlton wondered.

He looked to Sinclaire for permission since his grandma hadn't given his mother an invitation. Carlton hesitated, not wanting to sit alone with people he didn't know.

Sinclaire nodded and stepped back as the family processioned in.

Carlton craned his neck to see the front where all the flowers were set up. He was relieved the coffin was closed.

How many people are in his family? he wondered as he scanned faces as they processioned down the aisle as a woman sang "When I See Jesus."

Carlton sat a couple of feet from a big, shiny black casket on the front row with another boy. The boy's mother sat with him beside Grandma Pearline and Auntie Anita. Carlton scanned the front of the program. The picture of his father was handsome, and he looked nice, not like the monster he'd turned into before he shot Carlton.

Reading the obituary, he learned about his father's education and accomplishments. Plus, there were photos where he looked happy with big smiles. Carlton recognized the boy from the photos as his dad's other son. Harrison never took pictures with Carlton, although he had said a few times, "Yeah, I guess you look like me."

There was a lot to read about his dad. Carlton re-read one part of the obituary:

Harrison leaves to mourn his memories: mother, Pearline Wakefield; sisters Anita Wakefield of St. Louis and Shana Bryant (Dennis) of Memphis; sons Harrison Wakefield Jr. and Carlton Oliver; two nephews; and a special fiancée Laney Jordan and their unborn child.

That had to be the pregnant woman on the front row with them. She reminded Carlton of his mother, but Sinclaire Oliver was prettier.

Harrison Jr. appeared to be about the same age. Curious, Carlton whispered, "How old are you?"

"Nine and a half." Harrison Jr. frowned. "How old are you?"

"I just turned nine," Carlton answered, thinking they were almost like twins.

The minister, Reverend Neal Ransom, read Old and New Testament scriptures, and then the soloist sang "Take Me to the King."

His grandmother, aunties, and the pregnant lady wailed. Carlton was too numb to cry and perplexed at his lack of emotions. Harrison Jr. and his mom sniffed, and Carlton felt compelled to shed a tear too.

The preacher began the eulogy and described Harrison Sr.'s character. Carlton was amazed. He learned things about his dad after his death that he never knew while he was alive.

"Harrison was a good man and father to his children. His fiancée adored him, and they were expecting their first child together." He paused. "Remember, Harry and Carlton, that your father loves you, and he's in heaven watching over you."

"No, he's not!" Carlton leaped to his feet. "My daddy tried to kill me. There aren't murderers in heaven. That's a lie. The Bible says a soul that sins dies, and he's dead…"

An uproar followed. People popped up and shouted mean things at Carlton, but he told the truth. Ushers came to his side behind his mother, who reached for his hand. He looked up at her. "Mom, you taught me to tell the truth."

His grandma and aunties wagged their fingers at him, and Carlton even heard some curse words.

"That's what Jesus said." Sinclaire shooed the ushers away, scooted Carlton over to sit beside him, then wrapped her arm around his shoulder. "You did what the Lord told you to do."

Harrison's fiancée stood. One fist was on her hip while she wagged a finger at Carlton. She was mad, but Carlton wasn't afraid. "You don't get to judge him."

Sinclaire stood and defended Carlton. "You and your unborn child didn't take their father's bullet. Don't disrespect my son who is mourning more than the death of his father but his absence in his life too." Then she pointed her fingers from her eyes to the preacher who seemed frightened. "God is listening. Don't lie."

As his mother sat again, Carlton saw a large hand, like that of a giant, holding a sword at the man. Reverend Ransom trembled. For the rest of his sermon, he talked about the good things Harrison did for others but not about him being in heaven.

Carlton didn't want to see a final viewing at the close, and his mom didn't force him. From what Carlton could see, his dad wore a suit and tie.

Others processioned to the casket, then consoled everyone on the pew. Brother and Sister Addams and Sister and Brother Mitchell Franklin looked at his dad's remains and gave the Wakefield family their sympathies.

Carlton couldn't stop the tears when Brother Franklin hugged and kissed him. Besides other church members, no one else had embraced him.

"We're praying for you, Brother Carlton," Pastor Rodney said.

Minister Jude stood before Carlton and hugged him like a real dad without hurting his injured arm. He kissed the top of Carlton's hair. "I love you. Never forget."

"Yes, Sir." Carlton nodded as Minister Jude wiped the tears from his face. "I love you too." He wrapped his arms around Minister Jude's waist.

After the procession out of the chapel behind the casket, Minister Jude steered Carlton, his mother, and siblings to his car and joined the line, following the hearse and limos to the cemetery.

Carlton thought he would be in trouble for interrupting the service because his mom said it was impolite to interrupt adults, but the mood was somber.

Harrison Jr. got Carlton's attention at the burial site and waved him over to sit in the row of chairs facing the casket, which was about to be lowered to the ground. His grandma lifted a brow at him and pinched his elbow that remained in a sling. "Now, you behave."

"*Ouch.*" Carlton rubbed the spot.

The reverend recited words from a small book as the morticians placed flowers on the casket. "We therefore commit this body to the ground, earth to earth, ashes to ashes, dust to dust in sure and certain hope of the Resurrection to eternal life."

One of the morticians faced the family. "This concludes the homegoing service for Harrison Wakefield Sr. Feel free to take some flowers and return to your cars."

Carlton stood and walked away. He didn't need any flowers to remember his father. He would never forget. One shoulder was getting better, but the other still hurt.

As he walked toward his family and Minister Jude, his dad's pregnant fiancée blocked his path. "You rude little—"

Sinclaire stepped in front of Carlton. "Don't even think about calling my son out of his name or laying your hands on him. He is a child of God, and the Lord's payback is greater than two women fighting."

His mother didn't back down until the woman stomped away, mumbling, "Rude and untrained…"

Minister Jude came to his side and took his hand. Sinclaire rubbed his back. "Mom, do I have to go with them and eat? Those adults don't like me to tell the truth."

"You do not. You paid your respects, and don't worry about that rude woman. Once she becomes a mother, I hope she'll act better," Sinclaire said.

"She's too mean to become a mommy," Carlton said, relieved.

When Carlton returned to the apartment, he went straight to his room. He wanted to talk to God—the only father he had now.

Chapter Nine

*And every spirit that confesses not that Jesus Christ has come
in the flesh is not of God: and this is that spirit of antichrist,
of which ye have heard that it should come; and even now
already is it in the world. —1 John 4:3*

"Miss Oliver," the caller on the phone said.

"Speaking." Sinclaire put aside the design she was creating for a company promotion.

"This is Madison Miller from Child Counseling Services of St. Louis. Sorry for the delay in getting back to you. We are inundated with calls for appointments."

Lord Jesus, help each child get help like mine to make them whole again. Sinclaire took a deep breath.

"We've had so many children lately who have been traumatized that we've brought in other providers outside the state to assist. We had a last-minute cancellation for an evaluation tomorrow. Can you—"

"Yes." Sinclaire didn't have to think about it.

Although her son seemed to be okay and was excited about returning to church and his friends, she wasn't sure if he was suppressing his trauma and if it could resurface later from undiagnosed triggers.

Sinclaire cleared a half a day on Friday, and Mother Kincaid offered to babysit Sissy and TJ. Before surrendering to Christ, Sinclaire was a struggling single mom with no support system. Now, she had brothers and sisters in Christ on speed dial.

Surrendering to Christ, Sinclaire had gained more than she could imagine. This situation was no exception, as the church brought the children food and toys. Mitchell, Randall, and especially Jude had been on stand-by for Carlton. Jude's flowers, texts, and lunch boxes constantly reminded her of his presence. Jude not only made her heart flutter, but his texts and voicemail prayers gave her mental and spiritual boosts like energy drinks.

Working alongside a saved, practicing Christian was also a perk. She and Omega had often prayed for each other if they were having a bad day. Knowing someone had her back was invaluable. When Omega confided that she had miscarried without knowing she was pregnant, it was Sinclaire who prayed for her friend and encouraged her that God makes no mistakes.

That was before Harrison's madness. It was hard for her to swallow that this unthinkable crisis wasn't a mistake from Christ. Carlton became indifferent about seeing a counselor.

"Son, you'll miss summer camp on Friday because you'll meet with someone to talk about what happened."

"I already know what happened, Mom. My dad tried to kill me, but God saved me." He shrugged as if it was no big deal.

God, help me help my son. Carlton's attitude worried her.

"But Fridays are fun days at camp." He twisted his lips and folded his arms, then unfolded them. The pediatrician said the bullet wound was healing. If he stayed active this summer, he wouldn't need physical therapy, but make sure Carlton didn't overdo it.

"Carlton, there will be many more Fridays. Camp just started. You'll only miss one." Sinclaire lifted a finger.

"Mom, I told you I'm okay. I prayed. Pastor Rodney and Minister Jude prayed for me, too, and they talked to us together about what happened. God has talked to me too." He sounded more irritated than convincing.

Stubborn child. And that was out of his character.

"As your mother, I am responsible for ensuring you're okay today and in the future. This is not a request, young man." She was firm but compassionate.

One thing she didn't want to do was to convince her son he wasn't okay.

"Yes, ma'am." He walked back into his bedroom and closed the door.

Maybe it was Sinclaire who wasn't okay, and Carlton was actually okay.

On Friday, Carlton wished none of the bad stuff had ever happened to him. Otherwise, he would be at summer camp.

Minister Jude's name flashed on the caller ID while Mom was driving, so she answered through the speaker. "Praise the Lord!"

"Hi, Minister Jude," Carlton yelled from the back seat.

"Hey, buddy. Praise the Lord to you too."

"Mom is taking me to a doctor, but I don't want to go." Carlton frowned.

"If it's okay with your mother, maybe I'll take you to the baseball diamond and throw you some pitches on Saturday after you go to the counselor today."

"Yes!" Carlton bounced in his seat. His dad was supposed to take him to the park that day, but he didn't. He looked at his mother for permission.

Sinclaire nodded with a smile and kept driving.

"Thank you, Minister Jude."

"Do as your mother says and let the Lord and the doctor heal you."

"Yes, sir."

"So, did you call to speak with me?" Sinclaire chuckled.

"Nope," he teased. "Just to check on my buddy."

"You're wrong for that. Hey, we're here. See you tomorrow." Sinclaire ended the call and parked. She looked at Carlton. "If there's something you want to tell the doctor but not me, it's alright because it's confidential unless you're in danger. The most important thing is to share whatever you feel."

He jumped out first, walked behind the car, and opened his mom's door. Minister Jude had taught him to take care of his mother.

"Thank you, son." She kissed his forehead, locked the car, and then they walked into the office.

The receptionist greeted them with a smile and handed his mother a clipboard. "For privacy purposes, I'll have you wait in a private room until Dr. Abbott, the counselor you're meeting with, is ready to see you."

The area, the size of a walk-in closet, was colorful and had a lot of toys in the corner. Sissy and TJ would love to play in there. His mom filled out the forms, and minutes later, the door opened, and a woman led them to an office at the end of the hall.

After the introductions, Sinclaire was given the option to stay or leave during the evaluation.

"I'm okay, Mom," Carlton said as he sunk into a chair that reminded him of a bean bag with legs.

"Are you sure?" Sinclaire studied him and lifted a brow.

"Yes." He tried to reassure her that he was fine.

When Carlton was alone, he faced the lady. She wore big glasses on her little face. Her hair was long, and it reminded him of Sissy's yellow crayon. She folded her hands and smiled. "How old are you, Carlton?" When he answered politely, Dr. Abbott asked many questions about his siblings, favorite sports, and plans for the summer.

"I like being a big brother." Carlton puffed out his chest. "I get to help with my little sister and brother."

Dr. Abbott smiled. "Sounds like you're a great son."

He nodded. "Yep. Minister Jude let me help with the smaller children at church too. I like camp because I learn cool stuff, but…" Carlton thought about what happened.

"It's okay, Carlton. Take your time, and we can talk about whatever you want." Instead of watching him, Dr. Abbott squeezed a ball on her desk.

Carlton exhaled. "Did you know my dad shot me?"

She nodded.

"That's why Mom says I should talk to you. Why? It makes me sad to think about it."

"Well, I'm here to help you work through this. The important thing for you to know is that you're not responsible for someone's actions."

Carlton gripped the chair and bowed his head. "I'm still sad. I wish the devil didn't kill him."

"The devil?" Dr. Abbott *hmphed.* "You're so young to think this way. Your father was responsible for his actions. We can't blame others."

"All good things come from above," Carlton said respectfully. "The Bible says the devil comes to kill, steal, and destroy, and Satan destroyed my dad's mind."

Dr. Abbott was silent as Carlton waited for her response.

"My training is to help you recover mentally like the doctors who help you get better physically. Let's not talk about angels and demons—things we can't see." She smiled, but it wasn't genuine.

But intercessors can see them like Auntie Omega. Carlton began to pray silently, *Lord, can Dr. Abbott help me?*

You need to help her, God whispered.

"Have you ever seen a monster, Dr. Abbott?"

The woman tilted her head as if she had to think about it. "yes, in the movies."

"I saw a real one."

She tapped on her tablet. "Can you tell me about this monster or draw a picture?"

Carlton shook his head. "I can't draw something so ugly and mean. It went in and out of my dad." Carlton started to replay every image his mind captured. He frowned. "I think it was more than one monster that attacked him before Dad pulled out the gun." Carlton closed his eyes. "I don't want to talk about it anymore."

"That's alright. Let's do a role-play exercise," Dr. Abbott suggested. She placed three miniature figurines on the desk before Carlton. "What do you want your little brother and sister to do when you're upset about something?"

"Leave my room."

She took two figurines away. "Now, you're alone. What would make you feel better?"

Carlton shrugged. "A hug."

Dr. Abbott challenged him with different exercises until she thanked him for visiting her.

"You're welcome." Carlton was glad it was over.

She stood tall like a basketball player. "I'm going to speak with your mom." The counselor opened the door. Next, Carlton heard their voices.

"Miss Oliver, my initial assessment suggests that Carlton is suffering from hallucinations triggered by post-traumatic stress disorder and may benefit from medicine."

"I will not medicate my child." Sinclaire peeked through the doorway and motioned for Carlton to come. "If you want to help my son, do it with compassion first and textbook second."

Once they were in the car, Sinclaire said, "Son, I'm sorry I brought you here against your will. You do not have to come back."

"No, mom. It was cool. She needs to know about Jesus," Carlton said. "Maybe we can help her."

His mother frowned. "That's not how it's supposed to work."

"God is sending me," Carlton pleaded with her. Minister Jude would understand and convince her if she didn't believe him.

Sinclaire nodded as if she agreed and drove home in silence.

❧

On Monday, while Sinclaire was dropping off the children at summer camp, Carlton said, "Mom, that's my brother."

She looked where her son pointed. "Huh?" *What are the odds of two half-brothers going to the same camp?*

"Can I go speak?" Carlton said seconds before he yelled, "Harry!" He waved.

The boy turned around and squinted. His slow gait met Carlton's hurried steps to meet halfway.

Harrison Jr. was as excited as Carlton was at the camp. "How long have you been coming?"

"This is my first year," Carlton said.

It was unsettling to come face-to-face with another woman who also had a child by Harrison—his firstborn. Being petty, Sinclaire sized her up as if she were the competition, which she wasn't. Sinclaire had a brown skin tone and was slightly taller than the woman by a couple of inches.

Harrison Jr. and his mother were fairer and had dark hair. The woman had large, expressive eyes. They looked nothing alike, so she wondered what drew Harrison to them. Sinclaire must have been the side chick since the other woman's son was older and carried his father's name. Scoundrel.

Stop! What does it matter? Sinclaire chided herself.

"Hi. I'm Zanetta Erving, Harry's mother. I don't think we've formally met."

"Sinclaire Oliver, Sissy, and TJ," she said as her younger son turned her arm into a swing.

"It truly is a small world," Zanetta said with a smile as she watched their sons chat as if they had known each other all their lives. "I'm glad they have each other. What do you think about the boys getting to know each other?"

She interrupted her son's chatter. "Carlton, would you like to spend time with Harry?"

Carlton twirled around, and his grin was his answer, but Sinclaire wanted to make sure it wasn't lopsided. "Harry, what about you? Do you want to get to know Carlton?"

"Yes, ma'am." His smile resembled his half-brother's.

Polite. That was a plus. "Let's exchange numbers, and I'll get back to you," Sinclaire said.

Zanetta smiled as if it was a done deal. "The universe must have aligned for our sons to meet despite the tragic events."

Universe? Sinclaire's heart dropped. What did the universe have to do with it?

Praise Me, God's whisper thundered.

"Since the Lord created the universe, I will always bless God for the good and the bad that happens in my life."

Zanetta tilted her head and stared at Sinclaire. "That's an interesting declaration."

Witness for Me, God whispered.

Sinclaire stepped closer to keep Carlton from overhearing. "I'm sorry that Harrison lost his mind and soul and a chance to bond with Carlton, but I'm thankful that Jesus spared my son's life."

"I can't imagine that." Zanetta patted her chest. "Well, if you decide it would be good for the boys to spend time together, please call me."

"Okay. Carlton, give me a hug." Sinclaire didn't care if she embarrassed her son with affection. She had learned the hard way that every moment could be her last. Careful of his shoulder, still on the mend, Sinclaire gave him a slight hug, then pressed a kiss on his cheek and did the same to Sissy. TJ, who recently turned four, was one year too young for summer camp.

"Bye." TJ wrapped his arms around Carlton's body, not wanting his big brother to leave him.

"Sometimes I wish I had given Harry a brother or sister," Zanetta said.

The woman's expression was unreadable as Sinclaire walked away, dragging TJI away from his older siblings. Was that regret or blame? Sinclaire didn't know if Zanetta's intentions were innocent. *Lord, help me not to judge.*

Chapter Ten

*Beware of false prophets, who come to you in sheep's clothing,
but inwardly they are ravening wolves. —Matthew 7:15*

On Sunday morning, Carlton was up and dressed for church. He helped his siblings and gave Sinclaire the biggest smile and hug.

At that moment, Sinclaire knew everything would be all right in her world. Despite all the preparedness at home, Sinclaire and the children arrived at church later than usual.

Pastor Rodney approached the podium in the pulpit after the singers finished. "Praise the Lord, saints, and welcome friends. Look around us, outside your front door, even on the streets." He paused and turned side to side. "Sin is all around us, and it's on the rise. Evil is spreading. This weekend alone, St. Louis experienced gun violence in three neighborhoods. That is why our prayer life should be increasing too."

He opened his Bible and flipped through the pages. "Go to Second Timothy, chapter three, verses one through five. I want you to read along with me so you can see what you're up against: *'This know that in the last days, perilous times shall come. Men shall be lovers of their own selves, covetous, boasters, proud, blasphemers, disobedient to parents, unthankful, unholy. Without natural affection, trucebreakers—that means you don't believe a word they say—false accusers, incontinent, fierce despisers of those who are good. Traitors, heady, high-minded lovers of pleasures more than lovers of God.'* Does this sound familiar to anybody? Do you know anyone who would fall into one or more of these categories?"

The congregation responded with shouts of "yes."

Pastor Rodney nodded. "These aren't strangers the Bible is talking about. They're our family members, neighbors, or friends. People in churches—even in this church—could not be serious about their salvation. They're undercover hypocrites."

"Sho 'nuff, Pastor," a woman shouted rows behind Sinclaire and got some "Amens" to echo nearby.

"Why did I have you read this text? So that you will be on the lookout for imposters. Verse five says, *'Having a form of godliness, but denying the power thereof: from such turn away.'* Witness to them about the love of Jesus and His salvation from hell because of His cross. If they rebuff you, it does not lessen your mission from the Lord."

He closed his Bible. "Your soul is at stake. The devil knows the Word of God better than some of you. Shame on you! That has to change, saints. Last week, Minister Jude Morgan delivered a message the Lord gave to him. That's called a warning. There is no recess. Keep fasting, praying, and reading God's Word...."

"Sinclaire never imagined the world could get so bad, but she never imagined her ex would try to murder their son, either. "Lord, help us."

***

The following week, God gave Sinclaire peace despite His judgment on the world and the harm to Carlton. She couldn't understand it. Her son was almost murdered.

It was mid-week, and Sinclaire stopped to treat herself to a cup of coffee before going to Hathaway Health Management. She almost bumped into a woman on her way out of Morning Brew Cafe. "Oh, I'm sorry."

"Sorry. Say, you look familiar," the pretty woman said with a frown, trying to place her.

Sinclaire had never seen her before.

"You were at Harrison Wakefield's funeral." The stranger snapped her fingers.

Sinclaire didn't know if that was a good thing or bad that the mourner had remembered her.

"I'm Nikki Baxter. I didn't know Harrison. I was there to support a friend of one of his friends. Your son was brave to stand up and set that lying preacher right. Ministers always lie at funerals."

Although this woman was a chatterbox, Sinclaire was touched that someone benefitted from Carlton's conviction. "Ministers at my church have nurtured my son. They're genuine and really love God."

Nikki didn't look impressed, reminding Sinclaire of herself with her hesitation about church folks. After all, her children's father attended church. "I would love to invite you to Christ For All Church to see the difference."

"Nah. I'll pass. I don't think the church would want me after the things I've done." She paused. "Let's just say I chose not to be a single mother. No-good..." Nikki mumbled profanity that Sinclaire didn't want to hear.

Abortion, Sinclaire thought. "We're not here to judge. Sin is a sickness, but Jesus died on the cross to cure the diseases. Sinclaire checked the time. She had fifteen minutes before she needed to be at her desk. "Here's my number. Text me if you want to talk or come to church."

"I will," she said as they turned to go their separate ways, then she turned back. "Oh, did you hear that Harrison's fiancée lost her baby?"

Sinclaire gasped. "What?" Time seemed to stop as she considered God's judgment.

Nikki shrugged. "Maybe it was too much stress on her at the funeral. I'm sorry to hear about that, but with Harrison gone, she's better off, huh?"

Numbed by the news, Sinclaire had no words. She felt sorry for the woman. If she loved Harrison, their unborn baby would have been all she had left of him. *I'll say a prayer for her even though she wanted to attack my son.*

At the office, Sinclaire relayed the bad news to Omega. They both paused in their thoughts. Her friend knew firsthand about the loss of an unborn.

"But I have somewhat of good news."

"I'll take it after hearing that." Omega waited. She was still shaken.

"I witnessed for the Lord to the same woman who told me that." Not that she hadn't told anyone about Jesus since her salvation, but she understood Nikki's cynicism concerning the church. People at Christ For All Church didn't give up on Sinclaire. She wouldn't give up on Nikki. "I invited her to service, but I'm going to follow up with a phone call."

Omega exchanged high-fives with her. "That's what it is all about in life, to win souls for the Lord, and they'll thank us for them escaping hell. Everything else in life is perks from the Lord." She paused. "With the Fourth of July this Sunday, she might go out of town, so don't be too disappointed if she's a no-show."

"I won't." But Sinclaire would not be discouraged.

"In the meantime, don't forget Mitchell and I are hosting a barbecue, and you and the children have been invited."

"We'll be there."

Sinclaire wouldn't call herself an intercessor like the Addamses or Franklins because she couldn't do the all-night shut-ins with her children. Yet, Sinclaire had learned to cry out to the Lord before His Throne and teach her children, but she looked forward to wearing a crown.

Second Timothy 4:8 was her morning Scripture before she left the house: *Henceforth there is laid up for me a crown of righteousness, which the Lord, the righteous judge, shall give me at that day: and not to me only, but unto all of them that love his appearing.* Now, she would have to add Nikki to her prayer list.

Back in her office, Sinclaire admired the flyer she'd designed for an upcoming community picnic. Omega and the other Hathaway Health Management reps would pass out information to seniors and others with disabilities about transportation services to doctor appointments.

She knocked out one project after the other. Before lunch, she texted Jude. **I'm so excited. I witnessed to a woman today who reminds me of myself. She might come to church on Sunday. Pray she will!**

Jude called her. "Praise the Lord, Sinclaire. She must be as special as you. I can feel your excitement! Good work in the harvest for the Lord."

They chatted a few more minutes, then said goodbye so he could attend a video meeting. Sinclaire exhaled. It was exhilarating to share the good news. Her church and ever-expanding circle of friends were priceless.

On Friday, the Fourth of July barbecue was in full swing with water games for the children, plenty of light-hearted talk for the adults, and food for everyone.

As she shared her news about possibly winning a soul for Christ, Omega turned her head and stared at about a dozen children, including hers, running through a water sprinkler game.

Sinclaire watched her. God had given Omega a special gift to see angels in spiritual warfare. She seemed in a trance.

Omega's husband tapped her arm. "What is it, babe?"

"Angels," she whispered. "They're tall, circling the children as if they were building a fence around them, and their swords are drawn. They're protecting them."

Tears staining Sinclaire's cheeks went unchecked.

"Hey, are you okay?" Jude asked, standing over her. He never seemed far away from her.

Realization hit Sinclaire. "Those children are spared. What about the others?"

Jude shook his head. "We can't interfere with God's business. The Lord's will be done on Earth as it is in heaven. Heaven has no foolishness or wickedness, so we are subject to God's judgment on Earth." He placed a wad of tissue in her hands.

Sinclaire had a sinking feeling. What was God going to do next?

Chapter Eleven

My sheep hear My voice, and I know them, and they follow Me:
And I give them eternal life, and they shall never perish, neither
shall any man pluck them out of My hand. —John 10:27–28

Nikki was a no-show at Sunday's church service, even though Sinclaire texted her on Friday, Saturday, and again that morning.

Nothing.

No replies.

Sitting on the same pew between Omega and Tally and their spouses, her friends tried encouraging her as TJ scrambled off her lap and onto Tally's, who spoiled him. Some mornings, he couldn't wait to go to youth church. Today was not one of them.

Tally and her husband's longing for a child was tangible and torturous, whereas Sinclaire was single with three children and never had a husband.

Omega rubbed her back. "Nikki is in God's hands. Remember, you planted a seed. Someone else will water it."

"And God will cause them to come willingly to Christ," Tally said, raising her hand, "because that's how Jesus dealt with me."

"Right. If the Lord Jesus doesn't call them, they won't come and stay," Omega said.

Sinclaire agreed and closed her eyes to dismiss her disappointment and absorb the worship atmosphere, and her spirit seemed to flutter in excitement. She opened her eyes as all movement in the sanctuary stopped.

No music.

No chatter.

No crying babies.

Angels? She blinked. Was it a vision like Omega saw? she wondered.

She had never seen an angel before, but they weren't humans. Their form was magnificent, standing taller than two men stacked on each other. They marched without their feet touching the floor.

Sinclaire squinted. There was a small person who moved in step between them.

A child.

Yet angels surrounded her.

Last week at the barbecue, Omega mentioned seeing angels protecting the children.

Now, there was a stillness in the sanctuary, and it appeared everyone saw them—angels heading toward the pulpit. Speechless, Pastor Rodney stepped back as the girl turned to face the audience.

"My name is Jazmin, and I'm eleven years old. I was snatched by bad men who took me to hotels where I was ordered to have sex for their money. The last man hurt me, and I cried…" The girl's voice cracked, then she sniffed.

Sinclaire's breakfast turned sour in her stomach at the thought of what that child endured.

"B-man," she shrugged, "I don't know his real name—told me to shut up, or he would go after my family and get ready for the next customer. Then we were going to another place. I cried inside and asked God if He was listening to help me. The room was dark, and when the next customer opened the door…a bright light seemed to come through the window and burned his face like fire. Two angels walked in and told me to follow them out of the hotel."

"Praise God," Omega mumbled.

"Three other girls were outside too. The same thing happened to them, but we didn't know where we were."

"God responds to prayers." The angel on the left spoke for the first time. The monotone voice was powerful. "Many prayers have ascended to heaven, and the Lord heard them all."

"I thought about ways to kill myself, but one night, God spoke to me and told me to pray. My soft prayers couldn't be muffled. I didn't know more people were praying."

Sinclaire covered her mouth with her hand as if to trap her emotions. Her vision blurred. *Jesus, save us from this wicked world.*

"Please pray for us. We're children. God sent me here to tell you He's coming for the children—good or bad." Jazmin paused. "Please tell everyone about Jesus while there is still time." She walked off the pulpit and didn't stop as they exited the sanctuary.

Pastor Rodney was quiet for a moment before he stepped to the podium. "The Lord is trying to wake us up, saints of God. Romans the thirteenth chapter and verse eleven says, *'knowing the time, that now it is high time to awake out of sleep: for now, is our salvation nearer than when we believed.'* Let us fall on our knees and pray."

What is the world coming to? Sinclaire wondered but did as Pastor Rodney instructed them.

Maybe God is coming to rescue the children, Sinclaire thought.

Jude thought he had figured out what God was up to after the angels escorted the little girl to their church. He hadn't.

Your thoughts are not My thoughts, God spoke. *My judgment has been set.*

Prayer and fasting three times a week were still in force as news outlets released more stories about children's fates, whether violence, hunger, or abuse.

Jude was in overprotective mode concerning Carlton. Although Sinclaire had him in weekly therapy, Jude wanted to have an active role in helping him recover.

That's what families did. Jude's heart pounded as he watched Sinclaire re-braid one of Sissy's ponytails. Jude had invited her and the children to an outdoor Friday movie night at a neighborhood park. He brought the blankets, and Sinclaire prepared snacks.

"Do you think we'll have another angel visit our church?" Sinclaire asked as they sat on the blanket in Wintergreen Park.

"God sets the agenda at church." Jude shrugged and chuckled as he watched TJ stuff crackers in his mouth.

"In the two years since I surrendered to the Lord, I've never experienced a spiritual encounter like I have these past few weeks." Sinclaire lowered her head. "I have so much to give thanks for—sparing Carlton and rescuing that young girl and others from human trafficking. I saw on the news that FBI agents did a sting, made arrests, and recovered more than one hundred girls. Those poor mothers. I can't imagine if someone molested Sissy like that."

Jude balled his fist. Physically, he could beat down a man taking pleasure in violating a girl or woman, but Christians had to be strategic in battle. Evil was in the spiritual realm that manifested itself in the flesh to willing participants. His job as a minister was to do the work of an evangelist to free those who were lost in sin. But the collateral damage was unthinkable.

"God said he was coming for the children. Did that mean rescue the innocent and punish the guilty?" Jude shook his head and crossed his legs at the ankles.

Sinclaire's phone alerted her of a text. She read it and grinned. When she looked at him, her face glowed with happiness. "Nikki says she will see me Sunday."

"Great." That was still two days away, Jude thought. Satan was an expert on how to distract people from coming to Christ.

Anything could happen between Saturday and Sunday morning to cause Nikki to change her mind. "Let's pray nothing stands in her way."

"I'm on it!" Sinclaire crossed one leg over the other.

The way she stated it and the look of conviction on her face made Jude's heart flutter, and he stole a second to admire her colorful sleeveless top that showed off her toned arms, faded jeans, and the recent pedicure Tally and Omega had insisted she needed. Good for them.

As if she sensed him staring, she glanced over her shoulder and blushed.

What was she thinking as her eyes danced with happiness? Did Sinclaire know where his mind was wandering? She leaned closer and whispered, "Look at Carlton. He's enjoying himself and making new friends. I was concerned after what happened, he would become withdrawn."

"Hey, we're doing all we can to ensure he feels safe."

"I like the 'we' part."

"Me too," Jude said but tore his eyes from her to monitor the children.

"You know, summer camp seems to be the best therapy for Carlton because he talks about his half-brother nonstop. Dr. Abbott stated the two boys might be helping each other heal and suggested more time together outside the camp."

Sounded good to him. "What do you think about that?" He waited for her to look at him.

Sinclaire shook her head and lowered her lashes. "I'm not feeling it." She stared into his eyes. He recognized uncertainty. "Can I be transparent?"

"I've never asked you to be anyone but Sinclaire Oliver."

"Okay." Her shoulders slumped. "I don't trust Zanetta's motives, and it could be my insecurity knowing that I was Harrison's side chick while he was with her."

"Sinclaire, you are the most beautiful, confident, and loving woman I have ever met. You will always be the main attraction in any relationship. Don't let the devil intimidate you otherwise."

He had never seen her speechless. It was hard for him to keep a straight face. She glowed when she blushed, like when he opened doors for her, complimented her on her growth in Christ, or how nicely she and the children were dressed.

"Jude, I can't tell if you're teasing, flirting, or being nice, but thank you for saying that." She whipped her head around when Sissy called them to watch her do a cartwheel.

"You're welcome." He looked away without giving her the answer she wanted. Although he was attracted to her in the flesh, the immediate need was the spiritual battle for souls, and he, of all people, a minister of God, had to stay focused.

After the movie, Jude helped Sinclaire pack their things and round up the children. He watched Carlton rub his arm. It was a reminder that he had overdone it. There would always be a scar, but it was healing.

"Come on, buddy." Jude patted his back and steered everyone to his vehicle in the parking lot. Minutes later, he headed toward Sinclaire's apartment for drop-off, then to his place to end the night.

On designated Saturdays, the older brothers at church had set up a schedule to mentor Carlton. Randall planned to take Carlton to a St. Louis Cardinals baseball game, so Jude decided to use his free time for personal grooming.

Jude had confirmed with his barber that he could receive an overdue haircut. A few times during the week, Jude had checked on Cortez, who still seemed traumatized after witnessing the hit-and-run where the mother and child had died.

"I'm good," Cortez said after Jude had prayed for him. "I just got to man up to take care of business. See you in a few hours."

When Jude strolled inside Cut-and-Fade, Cortez seemed to be back to his usual self, but Jude saw a glimpse behind the mask—fright, uneasiness, and confusion. His barber was not okay.

After the two exchanged a fist bump, Jude sat in his chair. *Time to get to work in God's harvest.* "Bro, I had to walk up in church with this." Jude patted the half-inch new growth. "You've never accepted my invites to Christ For All Church. Now is as good a time as any. The Lord knows how to give us rest for whatever is troubling our souls."

His barber was quiet.

Jude waited.

"Man, I don't want to join anybody's church and expect to be there every Sunday. I may have other plans," Cortez finally said.

"Church is a place of fellowship. God expects you to spend time with Him daily without excuse, whether reading a couple of Scriptures to encourage you, praying for five minutes, or downloading a Bible app. Better yet, I'll challenge you to this: There are thirty-one days in most months. Read one chapter in Proverbs daily, and you'll be finished in a month."

Cortez grunted. "Too much work. I'll visit on Sunday. The key word is *visit.*"

Jude wanted to nod and smile, but Cortez was lining his forehead, so Jude remained still.

At home, Jude sat in a small room off his bedroom that he used as his quiet place to pray and talk to the Lord. He sat, closed his eyes, and asked, "What more, Lord, can Your people bear? Hit-and-run, shootings, rape." Tears streamed down his cheeks. He covered his face and petitioned Jesus until his stomach growled for attention.

Prayers were answered on Sunday when Cortez showed up for church, and to Sinclaire's delight, so did Nikki.

Sinclaire's guest was attractive, with short black hair and polished facial features. The two stood about the same height.

The service was lively when the Spirit of God filled the sanctuary. Pastor Rodney finished preaching, "Today is your day of salvation…come to be set free of torment."

Cortez stood, stepped out of the pew where he sat, and walked down the aisle to the altar, where he lifted his arms in surrender to God. His barber repented and was led to a dressing room to change for the baptism in Jesus' name.

Jude nodded at him from his perch on the side of the pulpit where other ministers sat. Cortez gave him a thumbs up.

Surrender wasn't the case for Sinclaire's friend as Jude glanced at where they sat. Nikki wasn't budging. After service, Jude planned to introduce himself and maybe water the seed Sinclaire had planted.

That didn't happen as Cortez walked back into the sanctuary half an hour later, speaking in a heavenly language that had his barber in awe. Those remaining in the sanctuary rejoiced for a soul the devil had lost, and Jude saw Sinclaire's sorrow as Nikki walked out.

God gained one soul; the devil kept one. Jude prayed the Lord would break the tie if the woman came again.

Chapter Twelve

*Jesus said, "I must work the works of him that sent me, while it is day:
the night comes, when no man can work." —John 9:4*

Summer camp was the only time Carlton saw Harry. Whenever they did the same activities, they had fun and talked about many things—except their father.

Maybe Harry felt terrible that their dad tried to kill Carlton. His mother thought it would be good for Harry to see a therapist, too, since he had violently lost his dad.

The boys compared notes about their counselors.

"Dr. Abbott said I could talk about whatever I wanted, but I think she really wants me to talk about what happened with our dad," Carlton said as they ate lunch at a picnic table under a big tree.

Harry bit off from his sandwich. "Dr. Nixon says that it was okay to be angry with my dad because he was sick…"

Carlton had been ill before, and so had his siblings. But their dad wasn't sick. He had turned into a monster with glassy eyes and fangs for teeth, and he even growled when he yelled at Carlton. That was a fact. He hadn't imagined it. And when he told Dr. Abbott, she said that monsters weren't real and there was nothing to fear.

She wasn't telling the truth. That's when he told Dr. Abbott to read her Bible because Behemoth and Leviathans were mentioned, and everybody knew the dragon was mentioned in Revelation. His counselor acted like she didn't know that.

He couldn't wait to tell her at his next weekly appointment, but Dr. Abbott had to reschedule because she was sick.

"Carlton!" Sissy called, snapping him out of this musing. Her group at summer camp was on the swings and sliding boards in the playground area.

He grinned and waved. Harry waved at her too.

Harry was a good brother, and Carlton liked him a lot. Sometimes at home, when Carlton looked into the mirror, he saw Harry's expression and similar features. Because they played in the sun all summer, Harry became darker than Carlton.

They finished eating and lined up for the next activity, which was fishing. "I wish I were a big brother like you," Harry said as they sat beside each other at the lake.

"Since you're older than me, you're my big brother." Carlton wanted to cheer him up.

"I guess," Harry said, swinging his legs as he stared at the water, "but only when we're here. I don't have a brother or sister living at my house, and it's lonely."

"You can visit me." Carlton thought about what else he could do. "The older brothers at my church are like uncles who take me places on Saturdays."

Harry was quiet. "I don't have any uncles. I wish I could go home with you sometimes." His brother looked so sad.

Did I not tell you to witness to the children? God scolded Carlton.

"Maybe you can come to my church to meet Minister Jude— my mom calls him Jude—and Brothers Mitchell and Randall. They are like my uncles. They don't have any children yet, but they like me, so they'll like you too."

Harry's line began to jerk. The group leader hurried to them to help.

"Hold it with a steady grip, Harry," Dave coaxed him.

Carlton watched until his line began to jerk too. He reeled it in to see a blue gill. Seconds later, Harry lifted his pole to reveal a bigger fish.

The brothers smiled at each other as they followed their group leader's instructions on unhooking them and throwing them in a bucket.

Become a fisherman of men. Convince your brother to come to Me, God whispered.

As they were about to clean and gut their fish, Carlton turned to Harry. "This is what Jesus used to eat. In the Bible, He fed a crowd with a few fish and loaves of bread, and there was some left over."

"God made sure that my mom had food to feed us. That's how we met Sister Tally Addams in the store when my mom didn't have enough money for extras. Sister Tally paid for it and left the change for my mom. We needed gas to get back home."

Harry's eyes got big. "For real?"

"Yep." Carlton nodded. "God does a lot of miracles…"

"All right, time to pack up," Dave yelled to the groups around the lake. "If you didn't catch any fish today, plenty is still in there for next time."

The fun was over when Carlton and Harry had to return to their assigned vans to head back to the lodge with their group leaders. It was a strict rule that children couldn't swap vans. Everyone had to leave and return with their group.

The day program ended at one-thirty. Carlton kept Sissy by his side as they waited for their parents. Harry's mom arrived first.

"Do you think your mom will let you go to church with us on Sunday and meet my friends?"

"Let's ask her." Harry seemed excited as his mother parked her car, then walked up to them seconds before Sinclaire.

"Hi, Miss Zanetta," Carlton spoke.

"You don't have to call me Miss, Carlton. Zanetta is fine."

"Addressing an adult by his or her first name is not fine," his mother said to Harry's mother and then gave Carlton a knowing look that he understood to mean "don't you dare."

Humph. "I was not offended. You did nothing wrong," she said to Carlton, putting him in the crossfire between the two moms.

"It shows respect." Sinclaire reached for Sissy's hand. "Come on. Let's go."

"Wait, Mom." Carlton stopped her. "Can Harry come to church with us on Sunday?"

He and Harry watched as his mother and Harry's mom looked at each other. Neither could guess what they would say.

"You and your son are always invited to visit Christ For All Church." Sinclaire smiled. "We don't hold long, and we even had classes for the children their age."

"I go to Sister McKnight's class," Sissy volunteered.

"Can we, Mom?" Harry looked at his mother, hopeful as he and Carlton crossed their fingers.

"Maybe some other time." Zanetta shrugged. "Say goodbye to Carlton and his family, son."

"See you tomorrow, brother," Harry said.

"Okay, see you." Carleton hugged him. So did Sissy, then they waved goodbye until camp the next day.

The longing Carlton had for Harry tugged at Sinclaire's heartstrings. Could she convince Zanetta to visit their church for her soul's sake? Sinclaire didn't realize how exhausting it was to witness for the Lord when the person wasn't willing. Had she been that stubborn, too, with Tally?

"Mom," Carlton said, snapping her back to the present, "since Harry and I don't see each other except at summer camp, God wants me to bring my brother to Christ."

Sinclaire was quiet. It sounded off for Carlton to refer to anyone besides TJ as his brother. They both had spiritual assignments: Harry was Carlton's, and Zanetta was Sinclaire's. It made sense for Carlton to want to see his half-brother surrender to Christ with all the things happening in the world affecting children.

There's a war going on. Choose sides, God thundered. Either you will do My will, or someone else will take your place to work in My harvest.

Immediately, Sinclaire was convicted and remorseful. She owed God everything for sparing her son's life. Instead of waiting for Zanetta to reach out to her, Sinclaire needed to be proactive. "I'll give her a call."

"Yay, because Jesus wants to save Harry, and I don't want the devil to kill him."

"Me either, son." She nodded, then continued to Mother Kincaid's house to pick up TJ.

Twenty minutes later, as they walked through the door, Jude's ringtone made Sinclaire smile. Even the children recognized his chime.

"Minister Jude," the children sang in a chorus before Sinclaire answered.

"Well, praise the Lord, our favorite minister." Her children weren't the only ones who got excited when he called. In her opinion, he was the epitome of a spiritual God-fearing man—not only him but her close friends' husbands. She was in awe of men who genuinely surrendered their pride to God.

Sinclaire had clarity on the difference between Harrison and Tyler. Her children's fathers were hypocrites, mocking Jesus' grace and preying on her, swaying her faith to believe in them— her first mistake.

"Praise the Lord back to the best mother of three," Jude teased. That accolade made her blush.

"What's going on?"

"I just wanted to hear everyone's voices," he said casually.

Sinclaire suspected it was more to that. What was he not telling her?

Her heart dropped as she walked away from the children into the kitchen and kept her voice low while they got ready to bathe after a day at camp. "Something happened, didn't it?"

"Yes." Jude huffed but was quiet. Sinclaire waited him out as she washed her hands to start dinner. "A father in California is accused of killing his three children, then turning the gun on himself."

It was a Harrison nightmare all over again. Sinclaire gasped, then covered her mouth with a shaky wet hand. "I'm so sorry for those children's mother and family. It makes me appreciate the Lord's protection over Carlton even more. I could have been burying my firstborn son…"

"Sorry. I didn't mean to alarm you, but I'm keeping my natural and spiritual eyes open. Witchcraft is deteriorating people's minds. I'm fasting and praying, and although I know your children are safe, it makes me want to hug them when I hear horrific stories like this."

"You're welcome to come at any time." Sinclaire smiled, then chatted a few minutes before they ended the call.

It's a race against time, God whispered. *Tell people of My goodness so they will repent.*

Jude was in his office the next day when his phone sounded an alarm. It was an Amber Alert. He read the details: a non-custodial mother had taken her two small children. Immediately, Jude began to pray for mercy and the children's safe return. At the same time, most of his colleagues ignored the alert on their phones or read it and continued working.

Since God pronounced judgment on Earth, Jude didn't take any news regarding children lightly. After work, he called Sinclaire and asked if he could stop by with dinner. He didn't want to wait for the weekend.

"No need. You're invited if you don't mind settling for leftovers—smothered chicken, mashed potatoes, green beans, and corn muffins."

"Yummy." He rubbed his stomach. Not too many women he knew could cook like his mother and Sinclaire, where their leftovers tasted just as good. "You're a great cook. Save me a seat."

He ended the call with a smile. The Olivers held a special place in his heart. Although Sinclaire was a single mother, pride wasn't part of her personality, and she didn't accept help when offered.

Jude's good mood vanished when he got home. Never a news junkie, he now absorbed it as if it were water so he could see God's Word come to pass as a reminder that it was real.

When he heard the new mention of an Amber Alert, Jude assumed it was an update from the local news.

It wasn't.

This was a world news headline: "Authorities are investigating missing children reports in several countries across continents that activated the Amber Alert in the U.S., Canada, Europe, and the Child Rescue Alert in the U.K. This is not a prank. It appears this was a well-coordinated terrorist attack to steal children. This is a developing story…"

Jude sent Sinclaire a quick text, then fell to his knees and prayed. He would miss dinner. She understood when Jude had to work overtime for God's cause. "Lord, where are these children?" Jude hoped it wasn't more human trafficking rings.

Chapter Thirteen

For we wrestle not against flesh and blood, but against principalities, against powers, against the rulers of the darkness of this world, against spiritual wickedness in high places. —Ephesians 6:12

Thursday morning, Sinclaire drove past the business that performed abortions. The protesters didn't catch her eyes, but what was on the building.

It was the most heinous creature she had ever seen on the movie screen or read in a horror book. The sight was spooky as the thing jumped up and down on the roof, piercing it with long swords and pulling them out, dripping with blood. Its actions were so ruthless. Sinclaire feared the building would implode. She wouldn't want to be trapped inside it.

How could pedestrians and motorists not see this? The thing was like a dark, ugly, and thick cloud-like substance against a sunny and cloudless blue sky, except for a mass she couldn't describe that hovered over the beast as if giving it power. Sinclaire could feel in her spirit something was off around her.

A scream lodged in her throat as she blinked as motorists honked behind her. Sinclaire moved forward. She sneaked a peek in her rearview mirror to see if that was her imagination. It wasn't. The sunny sky behind her seemed to illuminate the dark cloud-like creature.

She shivered. "Lord, save us from self-destructing decisions." Sinclaire thought about Nikki again. She couldn't afford to give up on her—or anyone, including Zanetta and Harry— just because she came to church and left without surrendering.

There was always next time, but their souls could be in danger. Then she saw what appeared to be an angel in a tug-of-war over the outline of a body.

What she saw was real. Her spirit felt its authenticity, even if no one else saw what happened. It was real.

Her hands were shaking. Instead of treating herself to a cup of coffee, she headed straight to work without any more detours. Sinclaire made a beeline to Omega's office and collapsed in her chair. Thank God she was alone.

"What's wrong?" Omega didn't hide her concern as she reached across her desk and rested her hand on Sinclaire's. "You look like you've seen a ghost or something…" Her words trailed off.

Nodding, Sinclaire swallowed to gather her words. "I did see something alright. It makes the computer-generated images on TV look cartoonish." She shook her head in disbelief. "It was stomping on the top of the building where abortions are performed and puncturing it with a sword like a magic show. I was so scared. I thought the creature would jump off the building and attack me."

In a calm tone, Omega coaxed her to breathe by inhaling and exhaling.

Sinclaire did.

"Believe it or not, it's beneficial to discern spirits that mingle around you. They play tag with sinners' and saints' minds and souls, hoping to spark a conflict. As saints of God, we can't take the bait. Right after surrendering to the Lord, I saw something similar on a building roof where two friends lived. They were sisters. It was a fierce battle going on. The devil wanted April and Caylee's souls badly and tried to take them out with suicide, murder, and who knows what else was planned, but God said no." Omega closed her eyes, lifted her hands in the air in silent praise, then looked at Sinclaire again.

"*Hmmm*. I don't know what was going on. One moment, this creature appeared to rip the building to shreds with a dark cloud above, feeding its power. *Whew*." Sinclaire blinked. "Then the next thing I knew, two demons, creatures, animals—I have no words in my vocabulary to describe anything that's not human, but it tugged on what appeared to be an outline of a body from a crime scene." Sinclaire rubbed her forehead.

"It wasn't the building, but who was inside. The demon was clawing his way to get to somebody. Since it was an abortion clinic, it could have been the baby or mother." Omega paused. "Without the Holy Ghost fighting for us, people wouldn't stand a chance of overcoming sin. The hope of any mother who succeeds with an abortion is to repent. All is forgiven."

Sinclaire shivered. "Seeing the angels enter the church was awesome, but this ominous glob of darkness in bright, sunny skies was scary."

Omega's phone rang. "God is calling you to be an intercessor, Sinclaire. It's not a gift to be taken lightly or ignored. People in distress are depending on our prayers to get them through, and it could be a matter of life or death. When you see things in the spiritual realm, begin to pray God's will to fight the battles," she said, then answered her phone before it dropped into voicemail.

Standing to leave, the realization hit Sinclaire. Intercessory prayers were made on Carlton's behalf.

"Yes, Lord, send me the dreams or visions, and I'll pray."

⸻ ⧜ ⸻

Sinclaire was as productive as she could be after the morning fright. She texted Nikki a friendly message. **Hope to see you Sunday at service, or we could get together over the weekend...**

Although she didn't get a response, her phone showed her message was delivered. There was an urgency for souls that Sinclaire couldn't ignore.

During her lunch break, she drove to the camp lodge to get Sissy and Carlton. They were standing on the sidewalk talking to Harry and his mother.

"Hi, Mommy!" Sissy shouted with a wave.

Carlton turned around and smiled. He seemed in no hurry to leave Harry's side.

Zanetta stepped in her path and smiled. "Hi, Sinclaire. The boys and I discussed them doing something fun together this weekend. I'm all for it if it's okay with you."

Sabotage. Sinclaire sensed a setup. She had two options: Go along with their plans or be the bad guy. Neither sounded appealing.

As they waited for her answer, Sinclaire made a counteroffer. "This Saturday, Carlton is spending time with his mentors from church. They provide positive role models for single mothers like us with sons. I'm sure they won't mind Harry coming. On Sunday, we have morning service. It's an inspirational environment where all are welcome to learn more about Jesus and His plan of salvation. You two are invited to that as well."

Please say yes. Sinclaire smiled.

"I've already instilled faith in my son. If we think positively, God will give us what we want. There's more than one way to heaven besides attending church." She jutted her chin as if she had the upper hand.

Did the woman have this spiel memorized? Lord, give me the words to say to be an effective witness about Your redemption. "Zanetta, the Bible proves that theory wrong. We are told to repent because whether we try to or not, we hurt people's feelings, do things we know we shouldn't, and we think things…" Sinclaire tried hard to convince Zanetta to accept the invitation, but she didn't know if she was winning.

Zanetta tapped a finger against her lips. "How about a movie on Saturday evening? Then we'll see if we're inspired to attend your church on Sunday?"

Is she countering Sinclaire's counteroffer? This woman wanted to play chess with her soul. Why was God having her cross paths with another stubborn person? Nikki was hard enough.

You, too, were stubborn, God whispered. *I have loved thee with an everlasting love: therefore, with lovingkindness have I drawn thee. Read Jeremiah 31:3.*

"Okay, Zanetta."

Harry and Carlton shouted, "Yeah," in unison.

"Can I go, too, Mommy?" Sissy pouted.

"Of course, sweetie." Sinclaire agreed on a time and location.

With her two oldest children by her side, Sinclaire said her goodbyes while Carlton and Harry hugged. The two loved each other. Sinclaire would do everything she could to extend kindness and win Zanetta over.

Carlton watched as Dr. Abbott entered the room. She smiled at him as she took her chair across from him.

It felt odd to see her on a Friday afternoon instead of the usual mid-week. She had missed their last appointment, and Carlton had to see her colleague as Mom called him.

"Carlton, how are you feeling?"

"Good."

"And your arm?"

Carlton rolled his shoulder to test it before answering. "Good. My doctor says it would be sore, but the hole is healing really good." He grinned. "That's because Minister Jude and everyone at church have been praying for me."

Twisting her mouth as Carlton did at times, Dr. Abbot nodded, then changed the subject. "Any plans for the upcoming weekend?" she asked.

He couldn't smile any wider as he wiggled in his chair. "Yep. I get to spend time with my mentors *and* my brother. He might come to church."

"You mean your half-brother...." She tapped her nail on the desk. "Harrison—Harry—right?"

"Don't say half-brother." That made him mad. "We have the same father—or we did. Harry and I like to do a lot of the same things, and some kids even thought we were twins. Please don't call him my half again. I ask this respectfully."

Sissy and TJ had different fathers from Carlton, but to him, they were his brother and sister. And nobody was going to call his big brother half-anything. Now, Carlton was ready to go home. He sighed.

"I apologize." Dr. Abbott nodded, then tapped on the keyword on her tablet. "How is your brother, Harry, doing?"

Carlton perked up. "We talk a lot but not about bad things that happened because we're happy to be together. He might come to church with us on Sunday. I hope he comes. That way, we'll see each other more."

Dr. Abbott let him talk about the fun stuff he and Harry were doing at summer camp.

"You should come too. It's a lot of demons out to get us. Have you ever been saved?" he asked but didn't give her a chance to answer. "Everybody should get saved..."

She cleared her throat. "Carlton, you are here to talk about whatever you want, and I'm here to listen and get you on the road to full recovery. Me coming to church or getting saved," she used air quotes, "isn't part of your treatment plan."

Twisting his lips, Carlton squinted. "If you almost died, wouldn't you be talking about Jesus too?"

Dr. Abbott never answered him.

Chapter Fourteen

Be sober, be vigilant, because your adversary, the devil, as a roaring lion, walks about, seeking whom he may devour. —1 Peter 5:8

God whispered, *Pray*, into Jude's spirit, and he jolted from his bed as if a trumpet had blown.

Without a clue for who or why, Jude obediently slid to his knees. "Lord, I don't know what to pray for or what demons to bind, but I know you know everything, so please intercede on someone's behalf...."

After an hour, he crawled back into bed, adjusted his alarm for an extra thirty minutes, and drifted off to sleep. He still might be sluggish at church in the morning.

When he arrived at Christ For All Church, Pastor Rodney's car was missing. Jude frowned. Their pastor never missed Sunday service unless he was out of town for a conference. He walked inside, greeted fellow members, then opened the door to the sanctuary.

His pastor wasn't missing as he first thought. Pastor Rodney stood on the pulpit and worshipped God with one arm in a sling.

What had happened to him?

Jude planned to find out, but first, he slid to his knees in front of the chairs reserved for the ministers on the pulpit. He thanked the Lord for being in His house, then stood and spied the sanctuary where Sinclaire sat with Omega, Tally, and their husbands.

Nikki was there again, sitting next to Sinclaire. He also recognized another woman who was at Harrison's funeral.

It must be the mother of Harrison's other son that Sinclaire had mentioned.

He smiled to himself, doing a touchdown dance in his head. Sinclaire was witnessing for the Lord. Bliss radiated from her being.

Praise God.

When the singers held the note on their last song, the sanctuary broke out in thunderous applause, and then Pastor Rodney greeted the congregation.

Nikki and Harry's mom appeared uncomfortable when he asked visitors to stand to be acknowledged. Jude prayed that they could feel the peace of God around them and be reminded how much Christ loved them.

"Praise the Lord, saints," Pastor Rodney shouted. "Even with an injured arm, I can lift my other one to praise the Lord." He paused. "So, to answer the question many of you might have, last night, as I left a store, robbers carjacked me at the gas pump. It was a coordinated effort. I thought I was about to lose my life, but God told me someone was praying for me. Hallelujah!" he shouted and danced in place. "The thugs didn't want my wallet or phone, just my car."

Pastor Rodney chuckled despite the seriousness of the situation. "I wonder how they will respond to the many phone calls I received from folks asking for prayers. Someone might end up witnessing to them."

Jude and others snickered.

"But seriously, I am standing here because God spared my life so I can complete my assignment on this Earth."

Jude choked with emotions to know his prayer last night mingled with others to keep their pastor and countless others safe.

"We are in what the Bible calls perilous times." Pastor Rodney paced the pulpit before standing at the podium. "I know

I preached from Second Timothy, chapter three, not long ago, but it's wise for us to revisit this passage." He pointed to the exit doors. "It is a war zone out there. Let's read verses one through four: *'This know also, that in the last days perilous times shall come.'* Hold it right there. If you didn't know it, these are the last days, and we don't know how long it will last, but the ingredients are there. Verse two says, *'For men shall be lovers of their own selves, covetous, boasters, proud, blasphemers, disobedient to parents, unthankful, unholy. Without natural affection, trucebreakers, false accusers, incontinent, fierce, despisers of those that are good. Traitors, heady, high-minded lovers of pleasures more than lovers of God.'* No wonder God is coming for the children."

Jude watched the expressions from Sinclaire's guests. Zanetta gasped in horror, which he could understand. He was horrified when God told him that too.

Nikki appeared indifferent as she sat with her arms folded.

Pastor Rodney shouted, "Although the world will not get any better, as saints of the Most High God, we have hope in Jesus for salvation, protection, and redemption in His blood. So today, I appeal to you to repent of your sins, surrender your will, and consent to the baptism, in Jesus' name, and the baptism of the Holy Spirit will keep you. This is your time to make the decision."

The sanctuary was still, then suddenly, there was an explosion of noise followed by a mad dash to the altar. Nikki was among them.

He had never seen Sinclaire praise the Lord as she was doing now. Omega and Tally had to hold her up as she worshipped for the soul she wanted to see saved.

⸺ ❦ ⸺

Sinclaire thanked the Lord for sparing Pastor Rodney's life and for Nikki calling her at the last minute to say she wanted to attend church again.

Plus, she had no idea that her son was talking to Harry about convincing his mom to bring him.

Surprise.

Surprise.

Sinclaire hoped the sermon would be a wake-up call for why they needed to surrender to Jesus and get under His protection from the enemy.

"Don't place your hope in this world," Pastor Rodney said. "Put your hope in God."

"See, that's why I don't like churches. That's negative energy." Zanetta shook her head.

Compassion. That's what the woman needed. "Churches that teach the Word give you more than good music and entertaining preachers. It's about where do you want to spend eternity—heaven or hell? The Bible says the truth will make us free..." There was so much more Sinclaire could have said, but she conceded to the pastor.

"Will you come today and confess your sins to the Lord and consent to baptism, in Jesus' name, where He will wash your sins away?" Pastor Rodney asked.

"Baptism is optional," Nikki mumbled, but Sinclaire heard it. The next thing she knew, Nikki hurried to the altar with the others. It was an unbelievable sight.

Zanetta looked ready to run out of the door in the opposite direction. The woman might be in the parking lot if it weren't for Harry in the children's church with Carlton.

While some returned to their seats after receiving prayer, Nikki followed others to the dressing room.

Yes. Jude was one of the ministers assigned to baptize converts that Sunday. Sinclaire stood when Nikki walked into the pool, which could be seen through a clear glass behind the pulpit. With tears streaming down her face, Sinclaire prayed quietly, *Lord, You know her heart. Please add her to Your kingdom today, in Jesus' name. Amen.*

Omega and Tally stood with her and squeezed her hands, whispering, "Thank You, Jesus."

"My dear sister, upon the confession of your faith and the confidence we have in the blessed Word of God concerning His death, burial, and Grand Resurrection, we now indeed baptize you in the name of Jesus for the remission of your sin, and you shall receive the gift of the Holy Ghost, Amen."

Nikki was submerged and came up swinging as if she was drowning. Jude steadied her as she began to speak in another language.

Usually, when someone received the evidence of the Holy Ghost by speaking in heavenly tongues in the water, the minister in the pool would rejoice with them. Jude didn't.

"I think God filled Nikki with His spirit," Sinclaire said.

Her friends said nothing.

After all the candidates were baptized, Pastor Rodney praised God for each soul, then blessed the congregation for dismissal. "Be watchful. Keep your spiritual antennas alert for the devil's tricks until we meet again, saints, in Jesus' name. Amen."

"*Whew!*" Zanetta looked relieved and scanned the sanctuary for Harry, but he and Carlton hadn't returned from the educational annex where the Sunday youth classes were held. "I've never been so depressed as I was today. God is about uplifting. I didn't get any of that."

"Maybe not today, but you've been warned about what you need to survive in a world that could care less about you, your child, and what you have. If it weren't for God preparing Carlton for what to do when Harrison lost his mind, my son might not have survived," Sinclaire said.

Omega added, "Zanetta, God loves us like you love your son, and He wants to save us like you want the best for Harry.

Whether you want to recognize it or not, Second Timothy, chapter three, verses twelve through thirteen says, *'All that will live godly in Christ Jesus shall suffer persecution. But evil men and seducers shall wax worse and worse, deceiving and being deceived.'* The devil is real, and so are God's angels. I have seen them with my spiritual eyes."

"We both have." Omega's husband, Mitchell, joined the conversation.

"Mom!" Harry ran up to them, smiling. His face glowed with excitement. "I like this church. Carlton has some cool friends, and they're going to the Game Room next week. Can I go?" Her son was breathless.

Harry exhaled and waited eagerly for his mother's okay.

"*Ahhh...*" Zanetta stuttered. "Let me think about it."

Sinclaire touched her hand. "You're always welcome to come. This is good not only for the boys but also for you. Remember, you were all for them getting to know each other outside of camp."

"Yes, well—" Zanetta started. The poised, confidant woman she saw at the summer camp was gone. Zanetta was flustered.

"Come on, Mom," Harry pleaded with her, and Carlton mimicked his brother's expression. "I've made friends here already. They're not like some of the bullies at camp."

"What?" Sinclaire and Zanetta said in unison.

"Why didn't you tell me?" Sinclaire frowned.

"I will speak with the director." Zanetta huffed.

Before Sinclaire could say more, Jude approached the group. "Praise the Lord, everyone. Zanetta, it's nice to meet you. Carlton has shared great things about you. I hope you will come back."

Maybe it was Jude's velvety voice or handsome features, but Zanetta blushed. "I might."

Yeah. Jude had that swoon effect on women in and outside the church walls. His usual warm smile didn't reach his eyes.

"Mother Kincaid wants you in the prayer room," Jude said quietly.

"Zanetta, let's talk about this later. Our sons are brothers. We can be friends," Sinclaire said politely. "I'll be back. Carlton, stay with your aunties."

Mother Kincaid was the designated church pillar for praying and worshipping with newly baptized believers. She had the pleasure of witnessing the Lord fill them with His spirit. "Is anything wrong?" Sinclaire asked as she followed Jude.

Omega, overhearing them, invited herself. As an intercessor, she must have sensed something.

Is that a good or bad thing? Sinclaire wondered as she walked into the small prayer room. It was empty except for Nikki, Mother Kincaid, and Mother Vincent. Where were the other converts?

Then she heard thunderous voices lifting praises to the Lord in a heavenly language down the hall.

Mother Vincent frowned. "You aren't clean, honey," she spoke to Nikki. "You must completely surrender all your sins for God to dwell inside you. The devil and Jesus can't share the same space."

Confused, Sinclaire stepped forward, but Jude restrained her and whispered, "Listen and pray."

When Nikki began to speak in another language, Omega rebuked her. "Those are chants. Stop that, in the name of Jesus. Who are you?"

It's Nikki. Sinclaire wanted to answer the obvious question, but Omega already knew that. Something else was happening here. Sinclaire had spoken in heavenly tongues when she prayed, and they sounded different than other saints in the church, but there was something about what Nikki spoke that made her feel uneasy.

"I am Deceiver." The voice that came out of Nikki's mouth sounded nothing like her.

"Deceiver, in the name of Jesus, I command you to let Nikki go!" Mother Kincaid roared.

Whatever possessed Nikki seemed to shake her before it released her. Mother Kincaid helped her to a seat.

"Young lady, did you repent before you were baptized?" Mother Kincaid's voice was gentle but firm.

Jude, Omega, and Sinclaire sat in a row of chairs across from their guest.

"Yes, ma'am." Nikki was polite.

Mother Kincaid nodded. "You're not clean, sweetie. You need to confess your faults to God for Him to dwell inside you. Whatever you're holding on to, you must willingly give it up." She opened her Bible and flipped back and forth until she located the passage she wanted. "Matthew six and twenty-four reads, *'No man can serve two masters: for either he will hate the one and love the other, or else he will hold to the one and despise the other. Ye cannot serve God and mammon.'* That's two gods."

Nikki was quiet as she bowed her head, and Mother Kincaid patted her back. "Keep coming to church, read your Bible, and God will reveal what has you in a stronghold."

"Yes, ma'am." Nikki stood, gathered her things, and walked out of the room without a glance at Sinclaire.

"What just happened?" Sinclaire asked Mother Kincaid, then looked to Jude and Omega.

"Demons are real and are not to be played with. Whatever Nikki's been dabbling in, doesn't want to let her go," Jude said.

"Be careful, Sinclaire, to let your light shine to encourage her to crave holiness. Otherwise, the Bible asks what fellowship light has with darkness. And in that dark place, witchcraft is real, and the devil plays for keeps," Mother Kincaid said as she gathered her purse and Bible, and all of them walked out of the prayer room together.

Chapter Fifteen

I must work the works of him that sent me while it is day:
the night comes when no man can work. —John 9:4

*T*his has been the best summer vacation ever! Carlton thought as Sissy skipped beside him as he walked her to craft class at camp.

Two weeks. That's all Carlton had, and he didn't want to think about the end of summer camp. He would miss doing fun stuff and seeing his new friends and brother Harry. But Carlton had been praying that God would save the bullies.

At first, Carlton was ashamed to be there after overhearing some of the boys repeat what they heard from their parents, "That little boy's father tried to kill him." And when their mom or dad came to pick their children up, they would look at him and whisper.

The day an older boy picked on Carlton because his T-shirt didn't hide his bullet wound, Harry came out of nowhere to his defense. Carlton was glad. Minister Jude and his other mentors had taught him and the other youths at church how to de-escalate situations to avoid violence. It was the same advice Dr. Abbott told him, except she didn't mention praying for his enemies.

Since the shooting, Carlton knew the Lord was always present with him, or he would be dead.

Harry's backpack hung loosely from his shoulder as he joined Carlton on the path to their groups. "Hey, baby brother." He had begun to tease him whenever they were alone.

Didn't matter. Carlton loved the endearment.

"I liked the young people's church yesterday. It was as much fun as a summer camp." He grinned.

"Cool."

"But I don't think my mom wants to come back." Harry's shoulders slumped.

What? Carlton was too old to cry like a baby because he didn't get what he wanted. "If you don't come, we may never see each other again." He and Harry exchanged sad glances. "I'm going to pray really hard that your mom changes her mind. You have to come to church. Jesus loves little children, even though we're big."

"I want to." Harry grinned. "But I don't know how to convince my mom. Something spooked her at your church, and she refuses to go back. But she's taught me about positive energy, and I felt it while I was there, so I don't understand."

"Brother, you felt God."

Harry nodded as if he was considering what Carlton said. "If we don't do something, we won't be able to do things together anymore."

Lord, I don't want my brother to die without Christ, Carlton pleaded.

After the camp ended each day, Miss Zanetta avoided Sinclaire for the rest of the week.

The Lord visited him on Thursday night while Carlton was in bed. *I'm coming for the children. I have My arm of protection around you so you can draw others to Me. Time is running out.*

Carlton didn't realize he cried out in his sleep until his mother rushed into the room. She sat on the bed and hugged him. TJ hadn't moved in his bed across the room.

"It's okay, son. It was only a bad dream. Dr. Abbott said you might have nightmares sometimes, but you're safe."

He sniffed and wiped his eyes with the back of his hand for traces of tears—none. "But my brother may not be. Mom, please pray for Miss Zanetta to return to Christ For All Church and for God to save my brother."

"God has to draw her, sweetie. I know how important Harry has become to you, and I'm glad, just like I have Omega and Tally as my sisters since I surrendered to Christ." Sinclaire sighed and rocked him in a hug as if he were sick.

Shaking his head, Carlton wanted his mother to understand. "But Harry isn't *like* my brother. He *is* my brother."

Do not be discouraged. Be about Your Father—My—business, God whispered.

"Mom, let's have a contest!" Carlton scooted back out of her embrace.

Sinclaire laughed and gave him the side-eye. "What are you up to, my firstborn?"

"Let's see how many souls we can win for Christ."

His mother lifted her hand for a high-five, and Carlton smacked it with his. "Okay. Now," she kissed his forehead, "go back to sleep."

Carlton snuggled back under the cover and smiled. Soon, he and Harry would be on the same team, working for the Lord.

❧

Leave it to a nine-year-old to put Sinclaire on notice. Winning souls for Christ had to be a priority. People were doing what they wanted without blinking at the consequences.

Like in the days of Samson, when there was no king in Israel, every man did what he judged was right. God whispered, *Judges 21:25.*

Sinclaire needed to refocus and be the light God expected of her and all the saints. Not only should she be persistent with Nikki but flexible with Zanetta too.

During the Friday morning drop-off at camp, Sinclaire had hoped to see Zanetta, but the woman was running late, and Sinclaire had to get to work.

She texted Nikki while she waited because she hadn't heard from her all week, and Sinclaire was concerned she might get discouraged.

Sinclaire crossed paths with Omega in the office break room as she filled her water jug for the day. "You've been bummed all week, sis. Everything okay?"

"Yeah," Sinclaire said, shrugging. "I didn't realize how much determination it takes to win a soul for Christ. Witnessing, invitations to church…what else could I do?"

"Prayer—a lot of it. The results may not be seen right away."

"But I still don't understand what happened with Nikki last Sunday."

Resting her jug on the counter, Omega leaned against it and folded her arms. "Sis, I've been walking with the Lord for a few years and still don't understand why God does certain things. Whatever Nikki is involved in, she's not letting it go easily for the Lord to dwell in her soul. When I walked into the prayer room, God revealed a shadow-like figure with arms around Nikki so she couldn't move. When some people come to Christ, we have no idea what demons they are fighting, so we can't judge how easily it will be to win a soul for Christ."

"Why would God give me two hard cases for me to be a witness?" she asked Omega. "I think Zanetta is frightened of the Gospel and prefers just to believe and it will happen. Nikki came, but it looks like she's fighting demons."

"Then you wonder whether she surrendered—really? Repent—really? I can tell you one thing," Omega said, picking up her jug and taking a sip, "when some people are released from prison, they will do whatever it takes never to return. Others don't want to put in the effort or work and are comfortable in prison. Sin is prison. We'll chat later. I've got to jump on some conference calls."

When Sinclaire returned to her desk, the Lord dropped Jeremiah 31:3 into her spirit. *"Yes, with lovingkindness, Christ has drawn me."* She had been overthinking things.

To her surprise, later that day, Nikki texted. **I know you've been reaching out to me. Sorry. I'm just not sure I'm a good fit to walk with God.**

Nonsense, Sinclaire texted back. **Let's get together and talk.**

I would like that. Never can have too many friends.

They exchanged texts until they agreed to meet at a place close to Sinclaire's. She was in a better mood when Jude called her. "Praise the Lord."

"Praise the Lord, stranger. Believe it or not, I have to come into the office in the morning, but afterward, how about I stop by and bring lunch for you and the children?"

"That's sweet, but…" Sinclaire pouted. "I've already made plans to spend time with Nikki. She finally called me back."

Jude was quiet. "*Hmmm.*"

Had she hurt his feelings? "How about Sunday after service? You're invited to my place to babysit while I cook."

"I can multi-task—help while playing with my little friends. No way do I call that babysitting."

Sinclaire laughed. "Okay. They're going to wear you out."

"Hey, I'm up for the challenge, but…remember, there's a reason why Nikki didn't receive the Holy Ghost. Sometimes people just aren't ready, so ask God for guidance on how to draw her."

"I will, and I have."

"One last thing." He paused.

She waited.

"It's a fact that hell was enlarged because of unrepentant sinners. No matter how strong our witness is, everyone won't be saved because they don't want Jesus. Many are called, but few are chosen."

"All right. I get it." Sinclaire ended the call and then stared at the design mockup on her desktop that needed tweaking. She enjoyed perfecting her graphic design skills at Hathaway Health

Management, where Tally and Omega helped her secure the position.

One of the many benefits of walking with God. New friends. New everything. Before her surrender, Sinclaire wanted to go to heaven, even when she didn't attend church.

She also wanted to win souls for Jesus as her gratitude for the Lord saving her. Despite the setback, Nikki seemed eager. Zanetta, on the other hand, seemed afraid of God's truth.

Chapter Sixteen

Elisha went to Bethel. Little children came out of the city, mocked him, and said unto him, "Go up, thou bald head; go up, thou bald head." Elisha turned back, looked at them, and cursed them in the name of the Lord. And there came forth two she bears out of the wood, and tare forty and two children of them. —2 Kings 2:23–24

Jude was resting comfortably when God's thunder shook his bed.

Start praying!

Minutes later, his burglar alarm blasted. "Front door."

Fully alert, Jude jumped out of bed and called 9-1-1.

He didn't want to die tonight. Neither did he want to kill someone in self-defense. While he waited for his call to be answered, he hurried into his closet, which also served as his backup prayer space when he had to drag himself out of bed in the wee hours of the night. He eyed his 20-gauge shotgun he used for hunting small game. Jude last used it a year ago when he hunted with his dad.

"Nine-one-one. What's your emergency?" the male dispatcher answered.

"Someone has broken into my house through the front door." Jude was frantic while the dispatcher spoke calmly. He lived in a quiet cul-de-sac tucked away from the main street with young families and professionals as his neighbors. *This was not supposed to happen here, or so* he thought.

"What's the address?" the dispatcher asked.

After Jude gave him all the details, the man said, "They're on their way. Stay on the line with me."

"I hear gunshots and yelling." Were they inside or out? They could be downstairs. The sound was so close.

More noise.

More voices.

He had to investigate, so he grabbed his shotgun. *Lord, help me and the criminals.* "I've got a gun, and I will use it," he shouted over his banister downstairs as a warning.

There was no response, but there was the noise of what sounded like an automatic rifle.

His heart pumped faster as he raced back to his bedroom and reached for the metal case under his bed that held the bullets, all the while praying. Jude stretched out on the floor on the second floor and squinted through the scope for movement.

Suddenly, his house seemed to shake with a force that slammed the door against the wall. There was a thump. A body fell to the floor, and Jude hadn't fired yet. Two more entered his house. What did they want? *Lord, please don't let them come up these stairs.* Everything was happening so fast.

Sirens grew louder in the background, but they weren't there yet. Jude recognized the outline of semi-automatic weapons in the intruders' hands. He placed his finger on the trigger. Any movement toward him and Jude would have to fire.

"Officers are on the scene," the 9-1-1 dispatcher said, reminding Jude that he had stuffed his phone in the pocket of his boxers but stayed focused on the entrance. "I will end the call."

When Jude blinked, he heard gunfire, and the pair turned around and were shooting at someone else. Another body slumped in his foyer.

"We have two juveniles in the front entrance," an officer said outside on his front porch. "Send EMS." He then yelled inside. "This is Officer Patton. I need you to come outside with your hands up."

Jude left his weapon on the floor and walked down the steps. He glanced at the bodies on his floor. A young black male with his pants cupped under his underwear. The other boy had on a hoodie, blood soaked through his chest.

Some parents' children had gone astray. He looked away, but the image was already seared into his memory. This was the trauma Carlton was exposed to at his father's hands. Jude couldn't help himself as he collapsed on his stairs and sobbed, something he never remembered doing as an adult. Shedding tears, yes, but this uncontrollable wailing weakened him.

Officer Patton stepped forward with another man. "Sir, do you mind stepping outside so we can get a statement and give access to EMS?" It wasn't a question as he helped Jude to his feet. "Take deep breaths."

Tears flowed as Jude thought about the dead's mothers, fathers, and siblings. Some of his neighbors had gathered on the sidewalk in front of his house. One of them, Cameron, to the right of his house, brought Jude a robe and shower flip-flops. He looked at his lack of decent attire for public viewing.

"Thanks, man," Jude said as he slipped on the robe. With a gun pointed at him, Jude hadn't been concerned about what he was or wasn't wearing.

"This one is already gone," the female paramedic said. "We got a weak pulse on the other young man. Prepping him for transport now."

Taking a deep breath, Jude angled his body so he wouldn't see the victims on the stretchers.

"We'll do a thorough investigation, but it looks like a car was joyriding and shooting at random homes in another block. Why your house was targeted for them to enter is anyone's guess at this time," the officer, whose name tag read Miller, said.

"Lost souls," he mumbled, then swallowed. His heart ached for them. One died in his sins—no chance to repent.

No chance for a second chance.

Gone to eternity.

They lived by violence, and violence was their end, God whispered. *Their judgment has been set.*

Jude took a deep breath and rubbed his eyes. "What time is it?" he asked Officer Miller.

"Four in the morning. While most of us would rather be in bed, these youngsters are wreaking havoc." He walked away.

Two of his neighbors came to comfort him.

"Minister, you can wait at our house until they finish the crime scene," Draper offered from across the street.

Crime scene?

His modest house in a quiet middle-class neighborhood was now part of crime statistics.

"Thanks." Jude was about to follow Draper when Officer Miller returned with a sheet of paper torn off a pad.

"Here is a list of companies that handle biohazardous waste after a shooting, and I scribbled the name of the company that can board up your front entrance until your door is repaired."

Great. Jude accepted the paper but was annoyed that he would have to spend Saturday taking care of business instead of enjoying his day off. It wasn't forgotten that he was out half-naked. He pulled his neighbor's robe tighter around his waist.

At Draper's house, his wife made him coffee and warmed two bagels. The white couple had two teenagers spending the summer with their grandparents in Florida.

"I'm still stunned this happened…here." Sarah, Draper's wife, said as she stared out the front window at Jude's house. "I'm glad you weren't hurt, Minister. What happened?"

Jude took a sip of coffee first. He had to be careful how he retold the story because he didn't know how it would be gossiped around the neighborhood. "The Lord woke me up to pray before my alarm went off. I thought I saw three of them, but there were only two bodies, so I don't know."

"I wonder why they targeted your house." Draper frowned.

Jude shrugged. "Me too. I feel sorry for their parents. One was dead. I hope the other one survives, and he will turn his life around." He paused when he saw the sheet of paper and called the number, surprised that Bio-One offered 24/7 services.

"We'll be there within the hour," the tech said after Jude gave his address and what to expect.

The Drapers made him comfortable in their front room as they watched the activity in front of his house. The police had yellow tape around his property, and small yellow tents marked the shell casings across his lawn and sidewalk.

He would have to call his parents and brother and give them the news but ensure them he was okay. Jude slapped his forehead. "I'm supposed to be going into the office this morning."

"Doubt you're doing that now," Draper said.

"Exactly." Jude shook his head. That also meant he might have to cancel on Sinclaire and her children for a fun activity.

The bio-clean team arrived as promised. Once the officers cleared the scene of the investigation, the team moved in and began their work while Jude dozed on his neighbor's sofa.

His body was drained, but his mind still processed the devastating events until he could get back into his house.

It was mid-morning when Jude woke in his bed. Not that he had gotten much sleep once he could lay his head on the pillow. Jude sighed. He called his supervisor first and left a simple voicemail. "Hey, Todd, I had a break-in at my house early this morning. It was bad, so I have to take care of the damage."

There was no need to go into further detail. Next was his pastor, who prayed for them, reminding Jude that what happened was part of the devil's mission. "I'll reach out to a few brothers at the church, and we'll be on standby to assist you with whatever you need, Minister Morgan."

When the call ended, Jude closed his eyes and rubbed his face. Lastly, he dreaded calling his parents. His mother was ready to rush over.

"Mom, I need to rest—please. Maybe later," Jude said, reassuring Camille Morgan that he was unharmed.

His father, Douglas, on the other hand, was glad Jude had a shotgun to defend himself. "Minister or not, you are serving God's purpose while hoodlums are answering to Satan. Proud of you, son, for being prepared."

He couldn't reach Sinclaire, then recalled she planned to go out with Nikki. Jude's first impression of Nikki was the lady wasn't ready to surrender to the Lord, and when he heard her chanting in the prayer room, his spirit was uneasy. Sinclaire had her work cut out to win Nikki, but he preferred she stepped back and let a seasoned female minister work with the woman.

Early afternoon, Jude was back in his house. There was no trace of blood or body fragments on his floor, walls, carpet, or ceiling in the foyer. It was cleaner than he had ever gotten it.

The only telltale sign was the boarded-up space that once was his front door. Exhaustion overpowered him, and he stretched out in his bed.

Then he heard a knock at his door. "What now?" he whined, getting up. Without a door with a peephole or windows, he yelled, "Who is it?"

No answer.

There was another knock.

Get to Sinclaire's apartment—now! God's voice was crisp.

One name made his heart leap with fear. What was going on? When she didn't return his call, Jude wasn't concerned.

As he pulled out of his garage, he saw another neighbor staring at his house and shaking her head.

Her house was next last night, God whispered. *She would have been killed.*

The magnitude of that information made Jude praise God as he waved at her and drove off.

"So much violence!" Jude hated the devil even more.

He couldn't get across town to Sinclaire's apartment fast enough, but God gave him help with the traffic lights. His heart pounded as he prayed. First, the devil tried to take Carlton out. What now?

Jude barely put his car in park when he arrived at Sinclaire's apartment village, located in a safe area with a park and a small strip mall within walking distance. His neighborhood was safe, too—until last night.

He hiked the stairs and was almost at her door when he heard Carlton shouting and a gun go off.

"No, no, no!" He banged on the door and banged again, yelling. He was about to recall all the karate kicks he had ever seen on TV as a child when Carlton opened it with tears in his eyes.

"What's going on?" He yanked Carlton out of harm's way.

The fright on the boy's face was genuine. "Sissy found a gun, and she pointed at me, but I hid."

A gun? Where did a gun come from? Just then, Jude spied Sissy playing with the pistol.

"Sissy!" Jude shouted.

She turned toward him. He tackled the girl, and the gun slid across the floor.

Adrenaline rushed through Jude's chest. He crawled to the pistol and removed the magazine, then cocked the chamber to make sure a bullet wasn't stuck inside. He ran into the kitchen, wrapped the weapon in a towel, and then put it on the refrigerator.

Safe. Everyone was safe.

Jude grabbed her and squeezed her tight. "A gun is not a toy," he said more forcefully than he should, and she began to cry. "*Shhh.*" He kissed her tears. "You're not in trouble."

TJ? Where was he? Jude hurried to the bedroom. The boy was asleep with a slight snore, uninjured. Praise God. He exhaled and walked back into the living room. "Where's your mother?"

"She went to the coffee shop with Miss Nikki," Carlton said, shaking.

Still holding Sissy in his arms, he squatted and pulled Carlton in a tight embrace. "Are you okay?"

He nodded, but Jude wasn't convinced. "Listen, son, you don't have to be afraid of guns. You must respect them like cars, fires, or tools. My dad taught me how to game hunt when I was about your age. I have a shotgun to hunt for wild animals, not to shoot people. You understand? Hunting is a fun sport."

"Can you show me?" Carlton seemed calmer.

"Maybe later if your mom says it's okay, but no time soon." Jude frowned. "Now, why did your mom leave you alone?"

"Miss Nikki said I was old enough to babysit my siblings."

And how would Miss Nikki know that? Did the woman know what Carlton had experienced earlier in the summer? "What!" Jude knew that didn't sound like something Sinclaire would do—ever. So why did she?

"But Mama asked Mrs. Edwards down the hall to watch us until they came back," Carlton said.

"Where is Mrs. Edwards now?" Jude had to reign in his frustration.

"She had to go to her apartment for something."

Suddenly, a short, petite woman rushed through the door, out of breath and patting her chest. "What happened? I thought I heard gunshots. Whew." She looked from Carlton to Jude.

"You did." Jude frowned. "While you were gone, Sissy found a gun."

Mrs. Edwards gasped. "Where did it come from? And who are you?" She squinted.

"He's Minister Jude from my church and our friend," Carlton was quick to answer.

"That's correct, but I have no idea where the gun came from, but I'm about to find out." He called Sinclaire.

She answered in a light-hearted tone that usually made him smile. Not this time. He was hot!

"Hi, Jude. I saw you called earlier, but I forgot to call you back—"

"I'm at your place," Jude cut her off. "Come home—now." He balled his fists, mad at the devil's shenanigans.

"What's wrong? Are my babies okay?" Her voice shook with alarm.

"Yes, but how fast can you get here?"

"I'm leaving now. What's going on? Where's Mrs. Edwards? Why are you there?" she rambled off one question after another.

Jude scolded himself for being so forceful with her and had passed on his fears to her, and he needed to calm her down. He slowed his breathing. "The children are safe. Your neighbor had to run to her apartment for something," Jude was not about to blame the woman who looked like she would pass out any moment, "The Lord had me come to check on them. How close are you?"

"I'm turning the corner now!" She huffed. "I can see your car in the parking lot."

"Good." Jude nodded. "I'll see you in a few."

Ending the call, Jude paced the floor with Sissy in his arms. The girl had no idea the fear she had caused. Eight minutes and counting, Sinclaire rushed through the door. She looked from him and Sissy to Carlton. "What's wrong?"

"Your daughter had a gun and shot at Carlton." Jude was trying to rein in his temper. Did this woman know how much he loved these children—and her? Jude released Sissy, who ran to her mother, then walked into the kitchen and retrieved it from the top of the refrigerator.

"Oh, dear." Mrs. Edward's hands shook as she covered her face. "Sinclaire, I'm so sorry. I had no idea there was one in the house, and I was only gone for minutes."

"A gun? Where did she get that?" Sinclaire examined Sissy, then did the same to Carlton. She didn't respond to her neighbor.

"TJ is asleep," Jude said, knowing she would check anyway.

Nikki walked through the door at an unhurried pace where Sinclaire had sprinted to get here in record time. "What's all the fuss?"

Jude saw the dark figure in the spiritual realm that had Nikki in a trance-like state. Her eyes were opened but closed spiritually. God showed him the name of the demon, Deceiver, who had disfigured hands wrapped around her head. Either she was deceived or conditioned to deceive others. Did the woman understand the magnitude of what could have happened?

Nikki's eyes were glazed over, and her lips were curved into a mocking grin. "Thank goodness you were here."

"Here for what?" Jude squinted. "How do you know what the emergency is? As Sinclaire gathered her babies, Jude stepped forward. "Demon, what is your name, and why are you here?"

"Tisad." The voice that responded didn't sound like Nikki or anything human. "The God of heaven and earth is taking the children to paradise. I am commanded to destroy them."

Like the young people who broke into my house. "By the authority in the name of Jesus Christ, I command you to release Nikki and cancel that assignment—now!"

"Go, in Jesus' name," Carlton echoed behind him and pointed.

The dark mist withdrew as if it was being sucked away, and Nikki blinked. She seemed confused.

Sinclaire was physically shaken as she spoke to Sissy. "Sweetie, where did you get that gun from?"

Sissy pointed to a tote bag behind the oversized chair by the door, and Sinclaire pushed the furniture aside, lifted the navy tote, and searched inside. She faced Nikki. "This is yours because it's not mine."

There was no way this woman was getting the gun back, Jude thought as he called 9-1-1.

"Yes, it's mine. I left it and planned to get it when we came back."

"It has a gun in it," Sinclaire screamed.

"It's for self-defense." Nikki shrugged. "The crime is up everywhere."

"There was almost a crime scene in my apartment because of you." She pointed and stepped forward. "My daughter found the gun and shot at her brother, not knowing it wasn't a toy."

Jude had never seen Sinclaire so mad.

Upset, yes. Jude had to nudge her away from her "new" friend before she assaulted the woman, and the police would arrest her.

When an officer arrived, he slipped the gun in a plastic bag as evidence before asking what happened, then questioned Mrs. Edwards and the children before interrogating Jude, Sinclaire, and Nikki.

Nikki was arrested for allegedly endangering the welfare of minors and improperly storing her firearm.

Sinclaire approached Nikki with balled fists. "I'm praying for your soul, but this will be our last time together. I hope I have made myself clear."

The woman didn't respond as she was led away.

Sinclaire was shaking, so Jude guided her to her sofa and sat with her. "Carlton, get your mother a glass of water."

Jude covered her hands with his. "Breathe," he coaxed her, and she followed his instructions until Carlton brought her a glass of water.

"Why is this happening to me and my family?" Her voice trembled.

"It's happening everywhere. God's judgment has been set to remove the children from the world's dangers." He didn't mention his drama from earlier this morning. Jude felt it was best not to add to her trauma. "You heard that demon say they want to destroy them."

Jude ordered takeout, then as if he was about to tell a bedtime story, they gathered around him as he read from the Bible.

On the way home, Jude was about to turn off the radio when the national news said there had been a record number of child deaths from violence in major cities in the past two days.

"Carlton and his siblings could have been added to the number!" Jude choked with emotion. He wondered if the intruders at his house were included in the list of deaths. What was coming next?

Chapter Seventeen

Trust in the Lord with all thine heart; and lean not unto thine own understanding. In all thy ways acknowledge him, and he shall direct thy paths. —Proverbs 3:5–6

The what-ifs plagued Sinclaire after Jude left. She was mad at herself for letting her guard down, believing she could make a difference to convince her new friend—who really wasn't—to surrender to Christ.

The water baptism in Jesus' name was void if Nikki hadn't repented, and it appeared she hadn't.

It was her fault that she'd invited Nikki into her apartment because she was around the corner, and Sinclaire wasn't ready to go yet. How had Nikki easily talked Sinclaire into something she would have never done?

Nikki was under the influence of witchcraft, God spoke, *if you let your guard down, Satan will try to tempt you. Stay alert!*

She sat at the kitchen table with only the stove's night light on. A tear fell. The devil's mission was to take out her children, but God said no. How many times would she have to tell God thank you? Nikki purposely left the bag with the gun inside behind the sofa.

Sissy was her busybody child, and she could treasure hunt in the garbage. She always found something that Sinclaire had forgotten about.

"Lord, this is hard." A tear fell down her cheek onto the table. There was no sense in wiping it away. More were coming. "Jesus, I can't lose my children. They are all I have."

Her shoulders shook in agony of what could have been.

You have Me, Sinclaire, God whispered. *Listen to My voice, and I will guide you to feed My sheep, whom I call. Zanetta and Harry.*

Sinclaire paused. Zanetta? In Sinclaire's opinion, the woman was a harder sell on Christ's salvation than Nikki.

You picked the wrong team. Satan sent Nikki to deceive you. Zanetta needs things you cannot see. I'm looking at her heart, God whispered.

The wall clock ticked the time in her kitchen, and Sinclaire sat there reflecting on what God had said. Mother Kincaid came to mind. Since it wasn't too late, she called her.

"Praise the Lord, daughter," Mother Kincaid answered.

With her parents dead and having no siblings, the term was endearing. "Praise the Lord. I hope you're still up."

She chuckled. "Of course I am. I may be old, but I don't go to bed early. How did your day go?"

Sinclaire bawled as she told her what had happened with Nikki and how Jude had shown up in time.

"Minister Morgan?" Mother Kincaid was quiet. "With all he went through early this morning with the burglars, he is faithful."

"Huh? Someone broke into Jude…I mean, Minister Morgan's house? Oh no." Sinclaire gasped. When interacting with others, she tried to use his title.

"Yep. Unfortunately, all he told us was two thugs shot up his house. One died. He didn't know about the other one. And dear, I know you two are on a first-name basis." She giggled.

Sinclaire didn't. All she registered was Jude's house, a gun, and a dead person. "He looked fine to me and didn't mention anything."

"When you're an intercessor for others, their crisis is the priority. I know what happened because I spoke with Pastor Rodney when Jude called."

Lord, I want to be a prayer warrior for other people, Sinclaire prayed silently.

Zanetta Erving is your assignment.

"The devil's been busy today. He sends demons to kill, steal, and destroy, but as saints of God, we have to be strong in the Lord and the power of His might. When we put on the armor of God, we're suiting up for spiritual warfare." Mother Kincaid went on to tell her she was almost robbed coming out of a grocery store where she confronted juveniles up to no good. "But a police officer was nearby. I had never laughed so hard. Neither plot to harm me was successful."

"Well, there has been nothing for me to laugh about this summer. Whew. I guess I'm not praying enough." Sinclaire felt like a failure, especially after today when she couldn't see through Nikki's motives.

"It's not how long we pray, but how we pray. In Matthew, Jesus told us to acknowledge Him. We are to earnestly pray for the Lord's will to be done on earth as it is in heaven. People are wicked because our flesh is tainted from birth. The Bible says we are born in sin and shaped in iniquity, even these children like the ones who tried to rob Minister Morgan and a group of them I overheard plotting to shoplift—the little demons were coordinating which aisles to hit."

"Where are their parents?" Sinclaire shook her head.

"Chile, some of their mammas and daddies are barely grown themselves. I walked over to the next aisle to disrupt their plans. The girl got sassy with me, and the boys called me names they only could have picked up from the bottom of hell."

"Weren't you afraid?"

"The flesh was concerned, but my secret weapon, which isn't a secret, is that every knee shall bow at the name of Jesus. They won't be able to help themselves."

"And every tongue confess," Sinclaire said. "So, what happened?"

"Since they cursed me, I *returned* their curses to them."

"In what way?"

"There were about six or seven of them. Two of them suddenly had nose bleeds, one became plagued with a severe headache, and he had to sit down. The others seemed frozen with fear. I went about my business and shopped. They were laid out on the ground when I passed the aisle again. The manager called the police, and the paramedics came too. I overheard a cashier say they had stolen merchandise on them, so they got caught red-handed."

"Mother Kincaid, thank you for sharing your experience and what happened to Jude. I was starting to feel the devil was only targeting my family." She rubbed her face, removing any remnants of makeup from earlier.

"He is. Satan's job is to destroy the saints of God, so be encouraged. I'm alright, and so are Minister Morgan and your babies. I'll see you tomorrow at church."

When she ended the call, Carlton walked into the kitchen. "Mom, why are you sitting in the dark?"

"I have the light above the stove on. Plus, I was talking to Mother Kincaid." She circled his waist and pulled him closer. "You know how much I love you?"

Carlton nodded. "Yep. Mom, can I go to Harry's house after church tomorrow?"

Saying no should have been on the tip of her tongue after the day she had, but God had given her an assignment. "Sure, son."

He hugged her tight. "Mom, don't be sad. God loves us more than anything," he said, racing back to his room as if knowing she needed the hug and words of wisdom.

Chapter Eighteen

Two are better than one because they have a good reward for their labor. If they fall, the one will lift up his fellow: but woe to him that is alone when he falls; for he hath not another to help him up.
–Ecclesiastes 4:9-10

Sunday morning, Sinclaire saw Jude step out of his car in the church's parking lot.

"There's Minister Jude," Carlton yelled and waved as Sinclaire pulled into an opening.

Jude walked to their car and opened her door. "Well, praise the Lord, my favorite family." He smiled.

Instead of a cheerful greeting, Sinclaire frowned and mumbled as she stepped out, "Why didn't you tell me what happened yesterday at your house?"

"Something else happened, Mom?" Carlton asked.

"Stop eavesdropping, young man, or you won't see your other brother today," Sinclaire threatened.

"Yes, ma'am."

That was wrong. Sinclaire didn't want to get in the habit of using Harry as a bargaining tool. "Son, you'll always be able to spend time with your brother, but you need to exercise good manners."

"Sorry, Mom."

Jude closed her car door, then helped TJ and Sissy out of their booster seats.

"When God speaks, Sinclaire, I listen." He lifted a brow and waited for her to have a comeback.

"Are you okay?" She didn't hide her worry. She wanted him to see how scared she was for him. "The next time something like that happens to you, I want to be on speed dial." She could pray and worry later. "Are we clear?"

Jude lifted his hands in surrender. A slight smile crossed his handsome face. "Yes, ma'am."

She turned away so he wouldn't see her victory grin. Sinclaire cared about him.

They said nothing more as they entered the foyer. Jude veered right where the ministers entered the pulpit. Her children made a beeline to the left for the youth church.

Sinclaire walked ahead, speaking and waving at church members she had come to love, then walked into the sanctuary to sit with her friends, Omega and Tally, and their husbands.

The place seemed to be on fire with praise and worship, and Sinclaire stood to thank God for protecting her family. She whispered to Omega, "I can't wait to tell you and Tally what happened yesterday."

"Whatever it is, I know you have a testimony. God told me to pray, and I stopped doing laundry and pulled Mitchell off the couch, and we called out your name and the children's names in prayer until peace settled over us." Omega scrunched her nose playfully. "I can't wait to hear your testimony."

Sinclaire squeezed her friend tight. "Amen."

Before Pastor Rodney preached his sermon, he reminded the saints there was a war going on. "There's a spiritual battle, whether you can see it or not."

"Don't I know it." Sinclaire grunted and crossed one leg over the other. "I've seen a lot."

Omega squeezed her hand and whispered, "The devil tried to set you up. The only thing he did was put you on full alert."

Pastor Rodney pulled them back into the message. "Last week, the devil came after me. This week, it was Minister

Morgan. Mother Kincaid set the devil straight the other day when young kids tried to intimidate her…" He gave a recap of instances Sinclaire didn't know about.

And me. Sinclaire planned to speak with the pastor soon about what happened, but she didn't want her naiveté broadcast to others.

She wanted it to be a lesson learned.

"More now than ever before, we need to intercede for others. When God wakes you up to pray, wake up," he shouted to the congregation.

Sinclaire glanced at Jude, who happened to be looking at her. If it weren't for him interceding on her family's behalf, she could have lost her children.

Jude gave her a slight nod and then refocused on the sermon. The man was incredible. He came to her rescue after he suffered his incident and had the nerve to scold her for leaving the children alone as if he were her husband. She blinked. Husband? They had never kissed or held hands… *Lord, my prayer is to teach me to be an intercessor so I can stop the devil in his tracks.*

"I can't stress enough, saints of God," Pastor Rodney spoke, "as the Lord Jesus reigns down His judgment because of the world's wickedness, we are to be vigilant in fasting and prayer. By the time we wake up in the morning, Satan has already dispatched his demons to torment us with depression, distraction, anger, agitation, fear, suicide, murder, drug overdoses, confusion about who God created us to be… Should I continue?"

Sinclaire leaned over and whispered into Omega's ear, "I guess I can see why this message could be depressing if a person doesn't believe angels and demons are real. Pray that God gives me the words to draw Zanetta to Him."

Pastor Rodney pulled her attention back to him before Omega could answer. "I guess I'm ready to start my sermon." He chuckled, and so did others. "Open your Bible to Second Corinthians, chapter ten, verses three and four: *'For though we live or walk in the flesh, we do not wage war after the flesh. The weapons of our warfare are not carnal, which is worldly. Instead, they are mighty through God to the pulling down of strongholds.'* We got this, saints. Once the Holy Ghost comes upon you, you shall receive power. Use the spiritual power God gave you…"

The inspiration came in the form of a warning, and Sinclaire appreciated that since Satan seemed bent on taking her family out. *The devil is a lie.*

Service concluded after the altar call, to which four people responded and then took an offering to the Lord. Understanding Jude's sacrifice, Sinclaire owed him her thanks.

As her children came into the sanctuary smiling from their activities in youth church, Sinclaire waved for them to follow her.

When she stood in front of Jude, she smiled. "Thank you for being an intercessor."

She admired his brown suit and orange multicolored tie as he towered over her. Not that she hadn't noticed how he dressed, but at this moment, she was enthralled as he looked at her with tenderness compared to yesterday. He was a force to be reckoned with regarding her children.

"I can't take credit for that. It's what prayer warriors do." He smiled back.

Modest.

Not boastful.

Qualities that impressed her. "Although I'm meeting Zanetta at the Bumper Car Zone, can I treat you to brunch for your heroism?"

"Yeah," Sissy said, jumping up and down, not understanding the magnitude of yesterday's events.

TJ grabbed Jude's hand as he often did whenever Jude came around, as if it was the norm, and kept a firm hold.

"How about I treat you and the children to brunch?" he countered.

Sinclaire shook her head. "That deal is not on the table."

He tilted his head and looked at her. "I thought a lady never turns down a free meal? C'mon. You pick the place, I'll treat you, and then you can give the tip."

She rolled her eyes and turned to lead the way out of the sanctuary. "Stubborn."

His hearty laugh made her blush.

Brunch at Breakfast Bar had a festive feel to Sinclaire as her family shared chicken and waffles with Jude despite the weekend events. He seemed fine after the break-in, and Carlton and Sissy seemed unfazed by the gun incident, but only God knew.

Carlton's happiness was contagious. He could hardly eat because of his excitement to see his brother Harry. "I can't wait for school to start so I can tell my friends about my big brother." Carlton grinned, stuffing a piece of waffle in his mouth.

"Don't talk with food in your mouth, son."

"I wish I had another big brother." Sissy pouted.

"You have Carlton, and he's a good big brother," Sinclaire said, and Carlton hugged Sissy and kissed her cheek.

"Minister Jude, are you coming to Bumper Zone with us? You get to drive these cars and have fun." Sissy bounced in her seat.

"Yeah." Carlton's eyes lit up.

"If I'm invited," he said, then gave her an amusing smile, challenging Sinclaire—or maybe it was a flirt. She couldn't tell, but it was fun to make-believe.

Carlton and his siblings looked at her, and she finally agreed.

The children loved Jude as if he was part of the family. In a way, he and members at Christ For All were the village Sinclaire had desperately needed when she surrendered to the Lord's salvation.

"Since we still have time, why don't I trail you home, and then all of us can ride together?" he asked.

At Bumper Zone, Carlton greeted Zanetta, then he and Harry raced to get in line.

"Zanetta, do you remember Minister Morgan?" Sinclaire reintroduced them.

"From your church, right? I do." She turned to him. "Nice to see you again."

He gave her a sheepish grin. "Sorry. I didn't realize that this was a mothers-only outing. If it's okay with you, I'll take TJ and Sissy and get in a bumper car."

"In a suit?" Zanetta asked.

Jude looked down, then nodded. "I think it will hold up."

When Sinclaire and Zanetta were alone, Harry's mother said, "I'm feeling positive vibes between you two."

Sinclaire wanted to roll her eyes at Zanetta's New Age terminology but held her peace. Her soul was important. Christ had a purpose for Zanetta, and Sinclaire's job was to be a light to her.

"So, are you two dating?"

She hadn't had this conversation with Omega, Tally, or Mother Kincaid. Zanetta wasn't a stranger, but they weren't girlfriends either. Maybe this was a way to build a relationship with her. Sinclaire chuckled. "He's in love with the children." She thought Jude was a better father figure to three than Harrison could have been to one.

"That's even a better reason for you to be in love with him." Zanetta wiggled her brows.

"After being in love twice and three children later, I prefer working on my relationship with the Lord," Sinclaire said to steer the conversation away from Jude.

Zanetta nodded. Maybe she picked up the hint. "I see. Can you believe this is the last week at summer camp? Carlton is all Harry talks about at home."

Sinclaire smiled. "Not surprised. Same at my house. Sissy even wished she had a big brother."

"I'm glad Harry has Carlton because it's been me and him for years. Harry was Harrison's firstborn. I learned he was unfaithful while I was pregnant. Instead of confronting Harrison, I channeled my energy to stay positive and work on my personal growth to align with the Universe. I meditate daily to clear my head and use tarot cards for guidance. That gives me peace, and I only have one child—I'm not judging you," Zanetta quickly added. "I didn't know about Carlton until you took Harrison to court for child support. He became angry and irritable, but he never mistreated Harry."

The revelation causes Sinclaire to tear down the wall she has created because she thinks Zanetta has classified her as the "other woman."

"If I had known that asking Harrison for financial support for his son would have enraged him like that, I would have skipped the drama that almost caused my son to lose his life."

Zanetta shivered. "That was scary. Before Harry met Carlton, he asked me why his dad would try to hurt his other son." She teared up and looked away. "I didn't have an answer. I encouraged Harrison to meditate and think good thoughts, but he couldn't grasp that he was in control of his destiny."

Oh boy. Okay, Lord, direct my words. Sinclaire sighed, then spoke in a manner that wouldn't come off preachy. "We're created in God's image, but we are not gods who can control our destinies. The only God Almighty was with Carlton that day. Jesus spoke to him the night before. My son is alive because he listened to God."

"See, that doesn't make sense to me." Shaking her head, Zanetta frowned, then looked toward the bumper cars where their sons were having a ball. "Why would God allow bad things to happen?"

"The Lord is the God of the heavens and earth. Satan and his demons can only do so much. My son was shot but not killed, which seemed to be Harrison's intent that day."

"Hey, Mom," Harry called and waved. His grin was from ear to ear. Zanetta waved back.

"Look, Mom!" Carlton shouted, giving Sinclaire a thumbs-up. Her son had recovered well mentally and physically over the summer, and for that, Sinclaire was grateful when she thought about what could have happened.

"Mommy, Mommy!" TJ yelled from the bumper car with Minister Jude.

He gave Sinclaire a salute. The man was a big kid.

"You sure you two don't like each other?" Zanetta teased.

"We *respect* each other." Sinclaire changed the subject. "What school does Harry attend?"

"Scully Elementary in U. City, where I teach fourth grade."

"*Hmmm.* You're brave. I have three children, and it can be exhausting, but an entire class? Whew. We're in South City. Not close at all. Carlton goes to Clay Elementary."

"I feel your positive energy. I think it's good that our sons are becoming friends. Without a father in his life, Carlton is his only connection since Laney lost her baby. So sad."

"Yes." Harrison left a trail of drama and trauma behind, but Jude ensured Carlton didn't miss anything.

Chapter Nineteen

Be careful for nothing, but in everything by prayer and supplication with thanksgiving, let your requests be made known unto God. And the peace of God, which passes all understanding, shall keep your hearts and minds through Christ Jesus. —Philippians 4:6–7

Jude didn't know who had the most fun at Bumper Zone, the children or him. He was living in the moment where everything was okay in the world, and God was pleased.

It was an illusion because children were in danger at this very moment.

Had time run out? Jude's desire was to get married and have a family. He craved reliving his childhood with his own children.

The only glitch was he had become a third wheel at this outing. It wasn't that he hadn't treated Sinclaire and the children to fun before, but he had become clingy to Carlton since Harrison's attempted murder on his life.

TJ rode with him. Although both were fighting to steer the car, Jude kept a watchful eye on Sissy, who wanted to drive like her big brother. Her car was in front of him.

Harry and Carlton acted as race car drivers in their separate bumpers. They laughed and yelled to move out of the way. The brothers crashed repeatedly into each other anyway.

Despite the threat to his life a few months ago, being around Harry seemed to be Carlton's best therapy.

But what was Harry's purpose in Carlton's life? Was God coming for Harry, or would he be spared? That would devastate

Carlton to lose his new companion. Could he win his brother over to Christ? He doubted it without Zanetta surrendering to the Lord.

Jude spied the table where Sinclaire and Zanetta sat, conversing deeply. He squinted. Zanetta didn't seem to have a hidden agenda. She was honest in her opinion. Zanetta was turned off by the church—period.

The two women seemed to have an unlikely friendship, having sons from one man about four months apart. That was a history that couldn't be overlooked.

Lord, in Your mighty name, give Sinclaire wisdom and discernment, in Jesus' name. Amen.

I called you to pray, not worry. Everything will work out, according to My will, God whispered.

Jude accepted the Lord's rebuke, repented, and regrouped. If Sinclaire made any mistakes in her judgment, God knew how to auto-correct her.

"Is Minister Jude your new daddy?" Jude overheard Harry ask as the boy whizzed by him in a red car with Carlton on his tail.

"Nope. You and I don't have one. Minister Jude goes to my church and likes to spend time with us," Carlton explained. "Mom calls him a special man."

Does she? Jude smirked. It took him to ride in a bumper car to find this out? That was a start, but he wanted more. The church mothers and sisters also described him in that way. That was his label. He had made his interest known to three lovely ladies, but their hearts were taken, and in the end, they married the men God had for them.

Every time, he brushed off the hurt feelings and trusted God to give him the desire of his heart. One day, that special woman would walk into his life and be everything he wanted a wife and mother of his children to possess.

That day seemed a long way off, or maybe she was right in front of him. Would Sinclaire want to fill that position?

When the mothers called for their children, they all complained, making Jude dismiss his wandering thoughts.

"Mom, do we have to stop?" Harry, the oldest of all, feigned a pout. "We're having fun."

Surprisingly, Sissy mimicked him. "Yeah."

"Yes, son," Zanetta said.

Harry turned and hugged Carlton, then Sissy ran to him and wrapped her arms around Harry. So did TJ.

Whether Sinclaire or Zanetta admitted it, the children were a family. They didn't care if they had the same mother or father. They shared Carlton's bloodline.

As Jude and Sinclaire gathered the children, he received a text.

Mr. Morgan, we have an update on the investigation into your home invasion. Click on this link to read more.

As he was about to click, another text flashed.

It was from his mother. **Jude Morgan, we have been waiting to see or hear from you since yesterday. We drove by your house, and the front is boarded up. Don't let me have to track you down. Call me now.**

He huffed as he opened the door for Sinclaire.

"Is everything all right?" He had seen the same concern in her eyes many times when it came to her children.

"My mother," he lowered his voice so the children wouldn't hear. "She hasn't spoken to me since yesterday after the incident, so I better stop by her house after I take you all home."

"Yeah," Sinclaire said, lifting a brow, "I want to talk to you about that too. How far away does she live from you?"

"*Hmmm*, about fifteen minutes."

"Jude, we're in St. Charles County. You plan to take us home to South City and then drive from South City to North County. Sounds like madness to me," she mumbled as he closed her door.

It did to his ears, too, but Jude never minded driving. Yet, his energy waned after yesterday's chaos, church service today, and Bumper Zone. He monitored Carlton, strapping his siblings in their belts and then his. Jude double-checked, then stepped away from the vehicle and called his mother.

"Jude! Where have you been?"

He had to cut her off to get a word in. "Mom, I'm fine, but I'm out with a family from church. I mentor the mother's son, so I was about to take her and the children home."

"Bring them! Since you and your brother haven't brought any prospects, it may be a while before we have grandchildren. I'll check the freezer for dessert. I'm sure we have ice cream. I hope we have cones, or do you think they're hungry? I'll check for leftovers..."

"Mom, Mom. Slow down. Let me ask Sinclaire, and I'll call you back." He slid behind the wheel of his car and whispered, "If you don't mind stopping for a short visit, you can meet my parents, and my mom can see I'm alive and well. Then we can be on our way."

She said, "Of course," then gritted her teeth as if unsure.

"What?" He frowned and pulled out of the parking lot toward Rock Hill, a western suburb of St. Louis City.

"*Ah*, will your mother think we're more than friends?" She gnawed on her lips, then reached into her purse and slipped out her lipstick tube.

"Would that be a bad thing?" Jude's heart pounded and waited for her response. Sinclaire had a natural beauty and had little need for cosmetics. "She knows I mentor young boys at church and your son."

Sinclaire was silent. Was she thinking?

"Although my mother expects her sons to marry and give her grandchildren, she has never tried to play the matchmaker. And I'm grateful for non-meddling parents."

"That's nice, but I have three children and had two fathers to contend with. I doubt I would be on an approved-to-marry list."

Stopping at a red light, Jude snapped as he glared at her. "Don't you ever say that again. You're at the top of—" He wasn't about to show his hands and pressure her. He exhaled and then apologized for raising his voice. "You will soon learn that my family operates in a no-judgment zone."

"We'll see," she mumbled and looked out her window.

Chapter Twenty

Finally, brethren, whatsoever things are true, whatsoever things are honest, whatsoever things are just, whatsoever things are pure, whatsoever things are lovely, whatsoever things are of good report; if there be any virtue, and if there be any praise, think on these things.
—Philippians 4:8

What did Sinclaire expect Jude to say but the truth? They weren't in a relationship, even though she fantasized about marriage. She had to stay focused on her three children.

The suburbs west of the St. Louis Galleria off Manchester Road, which ran through Rock Hill, had the feel of old money and close-knit neighborhoods.

Jude turned on a quiet, dead-end street with modest two-story homes and parked. "Well, this is it." He unsnapped his seatbelt.

The white brick house had charm. The red door and black wood shutters on the four second-story windows and the two on each side of the door were welcoming.

Colorful blooms with diverse floral selections were against a lush green lawn divided by a brick-laden walkway from the curb to the house.

"This is nice." She faced him. "How many bedrooms?"

"Four."

"I hope to purchase my first home within the next year, and this is a perfect size for the children," Sinclaire said and glanced at the backseat but not before noting an odd expression cross Jude's face, then it disappeared,

"They are knocked out." Jude grinned. "I'll carry the small ones and wake Carlton."

Minutes later, the front door opened, and a nice-looking couple stood in the doorway with huge, warm smiles.

"My prodigal son." The woman opened her arms and hugged Jude, even with the children in his arms. She stepped back and admired Sinclaire's babies.

"Sinclaire, these are my parents, Camille and Douglas Morgan."

"Welcome to our home," his dad, an older but still very handsome version of Jude, greeted them with joy in his eyes, then looked at Carlton, who was leaning on Sinclaire, barely awake. Douglas chuckled. "Who do we have here?"

"He's Carlton, my oldest," Sinclaire said. "Another parent and I treated the children to fun at Bumper Zone, which wiped them out. Jude is holding TJ and Sissy."

"See, Mom, I'm alive and well, so let me go and get Sinclaire and her family home." Jude made a motion that he was about to turn around.

Sinclaire could tell by the look on his mother's face that lame excuse wouldn't work, and it didn't when Camille shook her head and ushered them inside.

"Why don't you lay them all down in the sunporch so they can see us through the French doors. I'm sure they will be hungry or want a snack when they wake."

Jude huffed and gave Sinclaire a "sorry" look, then did as his mother said.

Sinclaire stepped inside the foyer and immediately loved the décor. Fresh pastel colors of blues and preaches were in one room near the sunporch. On the other side of the stairwell was an open library with books from the floor to the ceiling on one wall. The other walls were rich, dark burgundy.

"Make yourself at home, dear, while I bring refreshments," she said while her husband helped get the children situated comfortably on oversized sectionals.

They joined Sinclaire in the sitting room as Camille brought out trays of mini-sandwiches, fruit kabobs mixed with cheese, and miniature salad bowls.

"Wow. Preparing for a party?" Sinclaire was amazed.

"You—our guests. Take-out to the rescue when I discovered there was no dessert in the freezer. I couldn't help myself for getting a little of this and that." Camille grinned. Jude had her smile. "Since my son called and said he was bringing guests."

He groaned. "Mom, I said we were stopping by, not staying."

Camille shushed him. He would not win, and it was fun to see the confident minister not in control. Sinclaire hid her smile.

"Since our sons are too busy to visit their aging parents..." All of them laughed at that remark. "Anytime we have guests, it's a party."

"Have a seat so we can dig in," Douglas said as Jude pulled out Sinclaire's chair under his mother's watchful eye. "Son, please bless the food."

"You can use the hand sanitizer in the center of the table." His mother pointed, and all four of them did, and Jude reached for her hand.

"With bowed heads, Lord, thank You for this day that was not promised to us. Lord, please bless and sanctify this food and the hands that prepared it. Help us to be mindful of those who are hungry and feed them, in Jesus' name. Amen."

Amens were repeated around the square table, perfect for cards or a board game. After a few bites, Camille cleared her throat. "Son, we drove by your house yester—"

"Mom, that's out of your way." Jude didn't look happy.

"Don't blame your mother. I agreed. We had to see what God spared our son from," Douglas said, taking a sip of lemonade from his glass. "So what happened?"

Jude stuffed the remainder of a wedge sandwich in his mouth and chewed. He craned his neck to peer through the glass at the children.

Sinclaire was interested in the story too.

"Well, early Saturday morning, the Lord woke me from my sleep to pray seconds before my alarm sounded, and I heard gunshots. I called 9-1-1 and loaded my hunting shotgun, praying I wouldn't have to use it."

"Oh my God." Sinclair was riveted to the details.

"They were teenagers, not adults. Three of them. Two were shot in my foyer, and one died." Jude pushed his plate away.

Sinclaire covered his hand with hers. He was always there for her. She wanted to be there for him.

"Your neighborhood is so quiet." Camille frowned. "I couldn't believe it. We saw other houses with windows boarded up before we turned on your block. What in the world were those thugs thinking? Don't people know there are security cameras to catch them?"

"Mom, criminals don't fear God as He records their deeds with crystal-clear vision, so the door cameras are meaningless to them."

"Even though they risk getting caught." Camille dabbed her mouth with a napkin.

"Sinners risk getting judged by God every day. The devil brainwashed them not to care," Jude explained as he pulled out his phone. "The police texted me an update before I came over here."

"Read it," his mother urged him as she glanced over her shoulder at the children still asleep. "I hope they can eat something before you leave. If not, I'll wrap up to-go bags."

Touched, Sinclaire swallowed. "That's kind of you, but you don't have to do that."

"But I want to." His mother's eyes sparkled as she rested her elbows on the table and folded her hands, waiting for Jude to share the update on the police investigation.

"According to this, 'Hazelwood P.D. responded to calls of drive-by shootings in the 5900 block of Adler and Winston at three-fifteen a.m. Witnesses report a car following a group of young men who split up and ran. The vehicle with four occupants chased one of them, seventeen-year-old Tywan Blade, and he ran from house to house for help in the 1200 block of Rose Haven, where he was shot and killed at 1240 Rose Haven by one of the suspects who followed him to the residence of Jude Morgan. Police arrived at the scene and exchanged gunfire with fifteen-year-old Anthony Townsend, who was transported to the hospital where he died. Three other suspects are still at large…'"

Jude was quiet. He looked up, and his eyes were glazed over as he blinked rapidly. "God told me to pray. I guess it was for the guy they were chasing."

Before he could say more, Sissy yelled, "Mommy!"

Sinclaire stood and hurried in the direction of her daughter. "I'm here, sweetie." She opened the door and squatted to give her a reassuring hug. TJ stirred, too, and then Carlton sat up and stretched. She felt Jude's presence before he spoke.

"Hey, buddy. You hungry?" he asked Carlton.

Jude guided them to the bathroom. "After you wash your hands, my mom has made snacks for you."

"Yes!" Carlton said.

The short visit turned into a couple of hours as Jude's parents entertained them with stories of Jude's youth and his mother doted on the Oliver children.

There was no judgment, just pure respect for her and love for her children.

Before they walked out the door, Sinclaire heard Camille whisper to Jude, "Are you sure about her?"

"Yes."

The ride to Sinclaire's house was quiet as she pondered what Jude was sure about concerning her.

Chapter Twenty-one

A father of the fatherless and a judge of the widows is
God in His holy habitation. —Psalm 68:5

Carlton had a lot to talk about with Dr. Abbott at his session. "I had fun with my brother Harry at Bumper Zone. He's going to be Sissy and TJ's brother too."

"Oh, how's that?" Dr. Abbott asked.

Carlton squinted. His counselor wasn't too smart. "Since Harry's my brother, he's their brother too."

"I see. How is Harry?"

"Good." Carlton grinned.

"So, what else did you do this weekend?"

"I met Minister Jude's mom and dad. They're nice and let us nap at their house. When we woke, they had a lot of sandwiches and stuff. On Saturday, Mom went out with a friend who left a gun in her bag. Sissy found it and pointed it at me but—"

"Wait, Carlton." Dr. Abbott held up one hand. "Did you say someone left a gun at your apartment?"

"*Uh-huh.*" He bobbed his head. "And Mom was mad and called the police on Miss Nikki. No, it was Minister Jude who called," Carlton corrected. "He came and protected me and took the gun away from Sissy. He said guns have to be respected, and he may take me hunting, but not now…he's my hero."

"*Hmmm.* I'll say." She tapped on her tablet. "How did seeing the gun make you feel? Were you afraid?"

"I was scared for Sissy because I've seen a gun before, remember?" He raised his sleeve. "See my bullet wound. But I prayed that God wouldn't let my sister and brother die, so He sent Minister Jude, and I'm praying that my brother Harry surrenders to Jesus so he can be saved too." He paused. "Dr. Abbott?"

"Yes, Carlton?" She smiled.

"Have you been reading your Bible?

Dr. Abbott frowned. "Well, ah, I have read it before."

Carlton scolded her. "Dr. Abbott, you have to know who Jesus is when I talk about Him." He *tsk*ed. "Harry is starting to read his Bible."

The session seemed to end too soon when Dr. Abbott told Carlton to wait in the room because she wanted to talk to his mother before they left.

With the door cracked open, Carlton heard Dr. Abbott question his mother about the gun Miss Nikki had brought into their apartment.

"Miss Oliver, I'm concerned about Carlton's healing process if you can't do more to keep his environment free of guns. Your son may have PTSD throughout his life."

"Dr. Abbott, if you listen to Carlton, he's a happy child who continues to bounce back after the trauma. Let's not place the blame on anyone other than the gun owners. Now, I believe in counseling and that Jesus is a Wonderful Counselor. If you fail to do your job, rest assured the Lord will do His."

Humph. Dr. Abbott opened the door. "Carlton, thanks for coming. Your session is over for the day."

"This early?" Carlton had more to say.

"Yes. See you next time." She gave a slight wave.

"Come on, son. I think we both deserve some ice cream and whenever you feel you no longer want to go to counseling, let me know."

Carlton grinned. "I like talking to Dr. Abbott. I don't think she knows too much about Jesus, so I have to help her while she thinks she's helping me."

His mother laughed. "I'm rearing a smart boy." They walked outside the building and got into her car.

The next evening, at the dinner table, Carlton asked if his mother was planning anything for his birthday.

She touched her forehead. "Sorry, son, I've been distracted. What kind of party do you want this year?"

"Ponies," TJ shouted as corn spilled from his mouth.

"Clowns?" Sissy asked.

"September first is not either one of your birthdays." Sinclaire smiled. "And TJ, don't talk with food in your mouth."

Going into the fifth grade, Carlton thought he was too old for kiddie-themed parties. "Can I have it in the park so there's enough room for my friends from church and Harry to come?"

His mother frowned. "There's plenty of room in the church's banquet hall."

Carlton stared at the uneaten corn and green beans—his favorite—on his plate. The chicken drumsticks were devoured. "But Miss Zanetta probably wouldn't let Harry come." He looked into his mother's eyes. They were sad too. "I want my brother to do everything I do because I'm all he has now."

"*Uh-uh.*" Sissy shook her head.

Sinclaire chuckled when TJ mimicked his sister, and then she reached across the table and touched Carlton's hand. "Well, let's pray that God will soften her heart to say yes to the party and Jesus." She tilted her head as if she was considering his suggestion. "But your idea might work. Most people would probably enjoy the last cookout and holiday of the summer."

"Mom," Carlton began, "I just remembered. This year, I was supposed to spend my birthday with Dad because last year I spent my ninth birthday with you. Do you think the judge knows my dad is dead?"

"I don't know." She rubbed the curls in his hair. "When your dad died, I don't have to share you."

"I know." Carlton nodded. "You explained that to me, but do you think Minister Jude can be my dad for the day?" *I guess he could be,* he thought. Sissy and TJ still had their father, although he didn't come around much.

"I'll call him after dinner and ask." His mother pointed to the food on his plate.

Carlton finished eating in record time at a speed that wouldn't get him in trouble. Then he helped her wrap and put up the leftovers while Sissy wiped off the table. TJ liked using the broom vacuum on the floor because he got a kick out of the noise.

Mom let him, but they all watched him. When it became a toy to TJ, they would have to jump out of his way before Sinclaire took it from him.

"Praise the Lord, Jude." Carlton eavesdropped on his mother's phone call from his room.

She was quiet, listening to whatever he was saying, then thanked him for something. "I'm calling with an unusual request for Carlton's birthday." Sinclaire chuckled at something he said.

Put it on speakerphone, Mom, Carlton silently pleaded so he could hear why his mother thanked him, then laughed.

"My son wants you to be his dad for the day. I guess he's missing Harrison because this was his custody year for his birthday."

There was another long pause. Carlton held his breath, hoping he didn't say no.

"Okay. Hold on. Carlton, Minister Jude wants to talk to you," she yelled.

He zoomed out of his room like he was driving one of the bumper cars again. Minister Jude was his friend, so he wouldn't say no, would he?

Carlton bit his bottom lip.

His heart pounded with uncertainty.

Taking the phone, Carlton walked into his bedroom and closed the door for privacy—in case he said no, Carlton would try not to cry. Maybe he was still a baby at nine, and it was a childish request. "Hi, Minister Jude." He swallowed and held his breath.

"Hey, buddy. How are you doing?" He always sounded happy, except the day his dad shot him and when Sissy got the gun out of the bag.

"Fine." Carlton was afraid he'd say no. "Can you be my dad for a day, like on my birthday?" He repeated the question he'd heard his mother ask him.

"Done. You don't have to ask. Whenever you need me, I am here for you. I think I'll like being your dad for a day."

"Yes!" Carlton leaped, pumping his fist as TJ banged on the door. Grinning, Carlton opened the door and marched out. He gave his mother a thumbs up. "He said yes, Mom! He said yes." Carlton gave her back the phone and ran into his room. Wait until he told Harry that he would have a dad for the day on his birthday.

Summer camp ended a week later, and school hadn't started yet, so Harry and Carlton spoke every day for hours.

"I'm starting to have nightmares," Harry whispered over the phone.

Carlton teared up, but he held them back. *Lord, please don't take my brother.*

He overheard his mom talking on the phone about two children around his age who had died from fentanyl overdoses. Carlton didn't know what that was, but their parents left them lying around, so he guessed it was like the guns. Sometimes, parents were stupid and didn't care about their kids—like his dad.

"Jesus can chase those nightmares away," Carlton said.

"I'm scared because I was with a lot of kids." Harry's voice shook, and he sniffed. "I couldn't see their faces, and I don't know where we were, but someone started shooting. Bodies were everywhere, then I woke up crying. I'm not a crybaby. What do you think it means?"

Carlton shrugged to himself. "Did God talk to you at all?"

"I don't think so. How do you know?"

"I heard His voice in my head, and I could tell I wasn't alone." Carlton would never forget that.

"The only time there's a lot of kids' bodies is when there's a school shooting. Maybe I'll act like I'm sick on the first day. I don't want to die."

"I don't want you to either." Carlton wiped at a tear. *Satan, you will not kill my brother!* He would ask Minister Jude or Sister Omega if they knew what that nightmare meant. "Brother, I know how to pray and will teach you."

"O-okay."

"Do you have a Bible at home?" Carlton asked.

"Nope. Mom says we don't need it since we can meditate and have faith in God to get whatever good things we want."

"Hold on." He hurried across the room and swiped his Bible on the desk he used for homework. Minister Jude had given it to him and other new converts after their water and Holy Spirit baptism in Jesus' name. *Help me, God, to find the Scripture that talks about You are greater than the devils. Please help me.*

Read Romans 10:13–14, God whispered.

Carlton flipped the pages until he found the passage and read verse thirteen. "'*For whoever shall call upon the name of the Lord shall be saved.*' His name is Jesus." He paused at the next verse. "'*How then shall they call on Him whom they have not believed? And how shall they believe in Him of whom they have not heard? and how shall they hear without a preacher?*' First, brother, you must believe in Jesus to save you."

"I do."

Good. Carlton exhaled. "I'm going to teach you how to pray on the phone and every time we see each other, even this weekend when we go to the movies," Carlton boasted.

"Okay." Harrison sounded excited.

Carlton cleared his throat. "In Matthew the sixth chapter, Jesus says to praise Him in heaven and to pray that His will be done on earth as it is in heaven. The devil wants to kill us, but God wants to rescue us. We're supposed to ask for forgiveness for the stuff we did bad and forgive others who did bad things to us."

"Did you forgive our dad?" Harry asked.

"Yeah, because he was my dad, although I still don't know what I did to make him mad at me." Carlton was quiet. "Now I wish I had taught my dad how to pray. We must ask God to keep us from being bad and bad stuff from happening to us. You can start with that. The next time you have a nightmare, whisper or yell for Jesus, and He'll scare the demons away. Got it?"

"Yep. I will, and I'll tell you what happens."

He loved his brother. "Something will happen. Wait and see," Carlton said as TJ and Sissy busted through his bedroom door, wanting to play.

"I've got to go, Harry. See you this weekend."

Chapter Twenty-two

It was the best party ever! Carlton couldn't contain his excitement as all his friends from Christ For All Church showed up to help him celebrate, along with some of the older saints. Classmates from school came, too, and his new brother Harry had come.

During the music, water games, and kickball, God reminded Carlton that He was coming for the children, and Carlton had to tell them about Jesus.

Carlton ran up to Minster Jude. "God wants me to tell my friends about Jesus' salvation. Can you help me pray for them?"

Jude grinned. "Let's do it." He exchanged a fist bump with Carlton.

Lord, I ask that you protect my friends, he whispered as he gathered his friends for prayer. He stopped as two cars slowed down, music blasting louder than the one at his party. They parked, and several older teenagers climbed out and headed toward a basketball court nearby.

Carlton didn't know them, but he sensed something terrible was going to happen. The adults watched them, too.

The guys stopped playing basketball and began to grab their guns. The teenagers pulled out their weapons to return fire.

Carlton and his guests would be in the crossfire. "Jesus!" he screamed from the top of his lungs. "Protect us!"

They mean you harm, but I will confound them! God thundered, and suddenly Carlton heard a loud marching sound but didn't see anyone. Then, in the distance, an army of tall angels—about the height of a light post—carrying swords as they marched toward him.

"Whoa," some of the children at his party said, seeing them.

The bullies saw them, too, and froze with fear. When the angels opened their mouths, a roar was released that made the bad boys turn to run, but they bumped into themselves. Some tripped and fell. The bigger boys left their friends behind as they ran into traffic but didn't get hit.

The angels stayed in place while the cars sped away, and the teenagers on the basketball court scattered as they heard sirens in the background.

Sister Omega came to Carlton's side and laughed. "God's angels spooked them. They'll think twice. Hallelujah." She began to praise God, and others did, too.

Some of his friends yelled, "Yay!" and cheered.

The power of the Holy Ghost fell on them like a mist as the army of angels marched away, disappearing before their eyes.

Carlton felt the Lord's presence. Not only were some of his friends from church praising God in heavenly tongues as the Spirit guided their mouths, but some of his classmates were worshipping Jesus in a heavenly language that seemed to amaze them.

It was like a tent revival Minister Jude had taken them to last summer when he preached in a neighborhood, and five people repented.

Tears streamed down Carlton's face as he began to pray. "In the mighty name of Jesus, we honor You, Lord, because We know You love the children. Thank You for protecting us. God, teach us how to serve You and to live a life pleasing to You.

Please watch over us as we go to school, play, and at home. Help our parents, too, in Jesus' name. Amen."

Everyone shouted, "Amen," even bystanders.

"Wow. You do know how to pray." Harry's eyes were wide in awe. "I wasn't even afraid."

Carlton had hoped Harry had seen the spiritual realm, but he was happy everyone had seen God's power. He hugged his brother. "I want Jesus to save you, brother, and I've been praying real hard."

"Now, I understand how God protected you while you were with Dad. Help me pray that my mom will let us come to church again."

"Yes." The brothers exchanged a silly handshake that they had made up.

The parents who didn't know about the darkness lurking to take the children were dumbfounded about what happened. Minister Jude, Sister Omega and her husband, Sister Tally and Brother Randall began to talk to them about the Holy Ghost.

The party continued with more food and games. His friends said it was the best birthday party they had ever attended.

Miss Zanetta didn't look like she was having a good time. Mother Kincaid walked over to the table to sit with her. She must not have been talking about Jesus because Harry's mother laughed.

His mom and Minister Jude approached Carlton. They looked happy and were having a good time too. Minister Jude patted his back. "You did good, son. Your prayer was perfect."

Carlton grinned. "Thanks, Dad." He was glad Minister Jude agreed to be his dad for the day.

Sister Omega walked toward Carlton, then hugged him. "What a birthday celebration when the Lord shows up at the party. When I started seeing spiritual warfare, angels protected me and Brother Mitchell. I'm glad the Lord let everyone see the spiritual battles angels fight for us daily."

Sinclaire waved Carlton over to the table. "Let's open your gifts and thank everyone for coming, then we have to clean up."

"Yes, ma'am."

Carlton couldn't believe how much money, gift cards, and clothes he received. His three mentors— Minister Jude, Brother Randall, and Brother Mitchell—got him a bike, helmet, knee pads, and more.

As people left, Carlton and Harry sat on a bench, eating another slice of cake. "I'm glad we're brothers."

"Me too," Carlton said.

Too soon, Miss Zanetta was ready to leave. "Time to go, Harry. Carlton, your party was…interesting, but I'm glad you invited us." She shivered and rubbed her arms. "What I felt today was," she looked confused, "I'll say it was a different vibe, for sure."

"Does that mean we can go to Carlton's church on Sunday?" Harry asked with a hopeful expression.

"We'll see. No promises. Goodbye, Carlton. Happy birthday again." As Miss Zanetta was leaving, she stopped and hugged Mother Kincaid.

Lord, I wish my brother and I lived in the same house so he would never go home. Carlton sighed and began to clean up.

Minister Jude drove them home and helped to bring in the leftover hot dogs, hamburgers, and gifts. "Son, I see you had a good time, plus the believers and unbelievers had a chance to see what the power of God can do."

Carlton smiled. "And it was fun you being my dad today."

"Anytime. Any day." He hugged him, and Minister Jude kissed his head and whispered, "Remember, I love you."

"Okay, Dad. I love you too."

Later that evening, Carlton asked Sinclaire, "Mom, do you think I can keep calling Minister Jude, Dad?"

Sinclaire was quiet for a long time, then said, "That's a conversation for another day. Time for bed. Good night."

Chapter Twenty-three

But seek ye first the kingdom of God, and his righteousness; and all these things shall be added unto you. —Matthew 6:33

On Sunday morning, Sinclaire couldn't believe her eyes. Carlton walked out of his bedroom, ready for church, and had gotten TJ dressed too. Sinclaire was still in her house robe. "Mom, is it a good day to talk about me calling Minister Jude Dad?"

Did my son dream about this? She didn't have an answer last night or this morning. Jude would do anything for anyone. She had seen his chivalry with the church mothers—young and old—or whenever they were in public and someone needed help. Afterward, he always explained to her children the importance of kindness to others. But letting a child adopt him as Dad beyond one day was asking a lot. She didn't want Jude to feel obligated.

Carlton waited patiently as he rocked on the side of his shoes.

"Can you give me time to think about it? In the meantime, continue to call him Minister Jude at church. Understand?"

"Yes, ma'am. I wish Harry could come to church with me. I want to be the best witness for Jesus!"

"Me too, son." She patted him on the shoulder. "But we've learned—or rather, I have— that God's timing means everything, and we can't move unless God tells us." Sinclaire's zeal to encourage Nikki to surrender to God's will was a valuable lesson. It had been foolish to get ahead of God's plan and purpose.

Enthusiasm without knowledge is no good; haste makes mistakes. Proverbs 19:2 dropped into her spirit.

Lesson learned. If an eternal place of unrest wasn't important to some, Sinclaire couldn't sway their minds.

"Thanks for being the best son in the world." She kissed his cheek.

"Me too, Mommy." TJ frowned as she kissed him.

Sissy folded her arms and pouted. "What about me?"

Sinclaire smiled at the best gifts God gave her besides the Holy Ghost. "I have the best children in the world!"

While they cheered, Sinclaire told Carlton to feed them, so she got ready.

She dressed in record time in a new gold dress. Grabbing her Bible and purse, Sinclaire gathered her children and headed out the door for service.

Barely inside Christ For All Church, Carlton took off in another direction in search of Jude.

"Carlton Oliver," Sinclaire called him above a whisper. When he stopped in his tracks and twirled around, she frowned. "Did you forget about your brother and sister?"

Embarrassed, her son hurried back and took his siblings' hands to take them to youth church in the annex building. Then Jude appeared. He stopped and gave them his full attention.

Jude glanced up, and his jaw dropped as he looked at her. He practically gawked. She would have felt self-conscious, but she didn't. The twinkle in his eyes made her blush. Sinclaire waved, then walked inside the sanctuary, where she knelt to say a prayer of thanks before squeezing between Omega and Tally and waving at their husbands.

"I got some Word," Omega whispered as the two stood to clap during praise and worship.

"What do you mean?" Sinclaire asked.

"Last night, the Lord showed me a vision of babies floating down from the sky." She grinned and danced in place. "Maybe God's judgment is ending soon." Omega looked hopeful. "Tally and I both can't wait to have babies."

"And our children will be out of danger. That would be wonderful." Sinclaire closed her eyes and sang along to the words of "Lord, You Are Good," a church favorite for years by Todd Galberth.

Soon, Pastor Rodney stood at the podium in the pulpit. "I got a Word from the Lord this morning when I ended my fast. Unfortunately, we're to endure this evil mayhem for seven more months until God preserves His remnants of children who will be His witnesses."

Omega exchanged disappointed sighs with Sinclaire. Wasn't that what Carlton asked about this morning, being a witness for the Lord? She exchanged sorrowful and disappointing glances with Omega.

"Let's face the facts, saints." The pastor huffed and shook his head. "Everyone isn't going to heaven because they don't want to remove the sins from their lives to do what it takes to receive God's promise if they walk with Him. One word: *holiness*. In Hebrews 12:14, the Bible says, *'Follow peace with all men, and holiness, without which no man shall see the Lord.'* We have not seen a lot of holiness in this world, have we? And that's why we are under this judgment. The world doesn't want peace when they can settle disagreements with a gun or any weapon. *Holiness* has become a bad word. Wickedness reigns for a little while, but Satan can't defeat God, so don't let him brainwash you."

Nikki had brainwashed Sinclaire into thinking that she was sincere. Sinclaire loved her church. It was the pep talk she needed to make it through the week.

After service, Jude sought her out while she waited in the sanctuary for her children to come from youth church.

Sinclaire took a deep breath. She braced for the embarrassing conversation that she needed to have with Jude. But when she walked closer, all she saw was his smile, and she couldn't help but curve her lips upward.

"Praise the Lord, Sinclaire. Your beauty today is brilliant like a star, but what's wrong?"

"Oh, you saw me frowning?" She glanced over her shoulder for Carlton. Her son wasn't around.

"Yes." He lifted a brow, and dare she say it was sexy while in church?

"Well, first off, thank you for being Carlton's daddy for a day."

"My pleasure." He nodded but didn't break his stare as he tilted his head. "But I sense a *but* coming."

Sinclaire exhaled through gritted teeth before she opened her mouth. "He wants to call you dad from now on. Jude, I'm sorry. I wouldn't have agreed to this if I had known this would happen. I'm sorry to put you in this position and—"

"You know I'm many things to the young people around the church." Jude gave her a lopsided grin.

"But how many of them call you Dad?" Sinclaire played with her curls, frustrated that Jude wasn't getting the harm it could cause. "Minister Jude," she called him when others passed by them, "what's going to happen when you get married and have your children and—"

Jude took her hand and squeezed. "You worry too much. Carlton has my heart, and if my son wants to call me Dad, I'll answer."

Checkmate. Sinclaire was speechless as she saw her children racing toward her.

The following Saturday was Jude's one-on-one time with Carlton as his mentor. Everywhere they went, people mistook them for father and son. There was nothing similar about their features, but Jude knew it was the connection he shared with Carlton.

Jude bought them a burger and then sat on a bench in Forest Park to watch the ducks.

"Mom says you and Auntie Omega are intercessors. I want to be one too." Carlton looked at him as if he were a superhero.

"That call comes from the Lord, which takes more than saying prayers. You have to stand in the gap for someone who you might know if the Lord drops their name in your heart or for a stranger you may never meet. God expects you to make that prayer request personal. It's agonizing when the Lord shows you what will happen if you don't fast and pray on that person's behalf."

"But Jesus already woke me a while ago and told me to pray for the children. I don't want my brother Harry to be lost."

So, God has already prepped him, Jude thought. "You'll have to do more than read your Bible. You have to study the Scriptures and meditate on them to see how to apply them to situations."

Carlton seemed pensive before he bobbed his head. "Okay. I still read the Bible."

"Great. When you encounter a word or phrase you don't understand, you must research it like you do homework to earn a hundred."

"I'm really smart in school."

Jude rubbed the curls in his hair. He needed to get him to Cortez for a haircut. *Lord, I want a son just like Carlton who loves You.* "Here's the hard part: You might lose sleep. The Bible tells us demons like to lie in wait. And finally, love the Lord with all your heart, trust Him, and be strong, even when evil is ready to attack you."

"God told me not to be afraid before Dad shot me, but I told God I was afraid."

Hugging him, Jude kissed his forehead. "God will help us not to be afraid. Even I get scared until God calms my fears. I'll talk to your mother about having you join the evangelism team so you can learn how to minister to people in our neighborhoods and communities."

"Does that mean I'll be a minister?" Carlton's eyes widened with excitement.

"When we work for the Lord in the harvest, we are His ministers. Come on, let's shoot some hoops and grab takeout for your mom and siblings."

On the basketball court in Forest Park, Carlton showed off his skills. He was intelligent, athletic, and respectful. Any man would be proud to call him son. Born for God's purpose, the devil tried to kill him but failed.

A couple of hours later, back at the apartment, Jude spoke with Sinclaire privately while the children devoured the wings, fish, and fries.

"How was your day?" Jude smiled.

"I spent time shopping with Tally and Omega. Somehow, they buy more stuff for my children than themselves." She chuckled.

"They're waiting for God to open the windows of heaven and shower down souls for new babies."

Jude nodded. "Seems so far away, but we endure the Lord's righteous judgment. I wanted to ask you about Carlton's participation in the evangelism ministry. That way, he can see how we witness and minister. It's more than simply telling people about the Lord's salvation. Some need to be delivered from torment; others need to know God can provide shelter or food."

"If he's with you, then I won't worry." Sinclaire stood and walked toward the kitchen, then looked over her shoulder. "If you're hungry, you'd better come on and eat before it's all gone."

Chuckling, Jude stood. "Did you forget I know how much they eat and brought plenty?"

"Thank you for taking care of us."

He walked to her side. "Thank you for letting me."

Maybe all this was a dress rehearsal, imagining being Sinclaire's husband and the children's father, Jude thought.

Chapter Twenty-four

A thousand shall fall at thy side, and ten thousand at thy right hand,
but it shall not come near thee. —Psalm 91:7

Mid-week at work, Sinclaire reviewed the graphics for an upcoming community day when Zanetta called her on her cell. They hadn't spoken much since the start of the new school year a few weeks ago.

"Zanetta, how are you?"

"I took a quick break while my class is at recess. Yesterday, I got a call from Pearline and Anita Wakefield, Harrison's mother and sister."

"O-okay." What drama should Sinclaire brace for from Harrison's relatives who hadn't contacted her after his funeral?

"Harrison had a one hundred-thousand-dollar life insurance policy that listed Harrison Jr. as the sole benefactor..."

Wow. That was generous of Harrison for his namesake. Sinclaire didn't know how she felt about her son being snubbed, but so be it.

Zanetta continued, "He also had smaller policies he left to his mother and sisters. Pearline didn't say how much..."

What about Carlton? Sinclaire wondered.

"Now, here's the thing. Pearline thinks I should split it with her since Harrison was her son. *Hmmph.* I think I should split it with you since Carlton is Harrison's son too."

A son that Harrison didn't want to acknowledge in life or death. Zanetta's offer touched Sinclaire. She was choked with emotions. "*Awww*. Thank you so much for thinking of Carlton. He has already started to receive monthly Social Security death benefits as Harrison's dependent. That's a nice gesture, but I haven't heard from the Wakefields since the funeral, and I didn't like the way they treated my son. I'm not trying to foster that relationship."

"I know. They are bad energy." Zanetta *tsk*ed. "But this would be between two mothers for their children. Think about a college fund or something for Carlton's future," she pressed the issue.

"My church has a college scholarship fund to assist the graduates, especially those from single-family homes. It won't provide a full ride, but that will help with books and other expenses whenever. I hope to get a salary bump as I soar in my career." Sinclaire tried to convince herself and Zanetta.

Zanetta sighed heavily. "I had hoped you would see the reasoning since our sons have become so close."

"I do." Sinclaire stared out her office window as the fall weather was approaching. "Something tells me those Wakefields are messy. If there were a hint Carlton would get one dollar of that money, they would drag us through court. Zanetta, I'll pray the Lord will help you make the right decision that's less stressful."

Zanetta was quiet. "Thanks, but I stay positive and remove myself from negative energy. It's strange because, on certain occasions and holidays, Pearline wanted Harry around because he carried the name, which is why I'm surprised they want to take anything away from their grandchild."

A bell rang in Zanetta's background, so Sinclaire spoke fast. "We live in an evil world where bad things happen to good and not-so-good people. As you saw for yourself, only Jesus can give us that peace and protection, like at Carlton's party."

"Right." And without a goodbye, Zanetta was gone.

Sinclaire hoped Zanetta wouldn't cave into the Wakefield's demands but prayed for God to give Zanetta wisdom.

She glanced at the time. She had to finish her project so she could leave early to pick up Carlton from school for his appointment with Dr. Abbott. The woman was condescending, and Sinclaire honestly didn't like her attitude, but Carlton enjoyed talking to her so Sinclaire would hold her tongue.

Carlton couldn't wait to see Dr. Abbott today. He had been praying really hard for her. When he told her about how God had protected everyone at his party, she didn't see it as protection at all.

"Carlton, do you believe some people could be in the wrong place at the wrong time?" Dr. Abbott had said.

"Nope. Things happen for a reason." He shrugged as they played games to teach him how to recognize safe places.

Dr. Abbott hadn't liked his answers when he said he could hide under the shadow of the Almighty. "It's in the Book of Psalms," he had said, but she wasn't impressed.

Last night, God had whispered in his ear what would happen at his session and the answers he was supposed to give.

"Carlton," she greeted him with a smile that didn't appear genuine, "tell me what's been going on since our last visit. Anything…" Dr. Abbott didn't finish her sentence.

"Just going to school and playing with my friends and talking to my brother Harry."

She seemed relieved for some reason. "Good. Today, I want us to do a new exercise. When I say a word or show you a picture, please tell me the first thing that comes to mind. This will help me complete your final evaluation for our next session."

"Okay." Carlton crossed his legs on a bean bag and waited.

"Darkness." Dr. Abbott held up a black card.

"God."

She tilted her head and looked at her card, then at Carlton. "Why that answer?"

"In the beginning, God created the heavens and the earth, and He separated the light from the dark."

Dr. Abbott cleared her throat and shifted in her chair. She showed a photo of weapons. "Guns."

"God," Carlton said. Minister Jude taught him to respect guns and to practice safety, but not to be afraid, trusting in Jesus.

"Why?" she asked.

"The Bible says He is a Protector, and He protected me." Carlton grinned, proud that he remembered the answers the Lord had told him.

She huffed. "Something tells me whatever photo I show you, your answer will be the same, but let's try this one more." She shuffled the cards and pulled out a card with four colors. "What color makes you feel calm—blue, red, white, or purple?"

"Blue."

"Finally." Dr. Abbott exhaled. "An answer that aligns with the Journal of Applied Psychology. We might have a breakthrough."

As she jotted her notes, Carlton explained, "Light blue reminds me of the clouds and one day, Jesus is going to split the clouds and come back for the Christians who were redeemed through His blood. You read that in your Bible, didn't you?"

"Ah, I haven't found time," she said as she continued making notes on her tablet.

Carlton sighed. "Dr. Abbott, we have one more session. You're supposed to help me cope. God gave me a job too—tell everyone about Jesus' salvation so they don't have to die in their sins and then burn in hell. Did you know hell will be thrown in the Lake of Fire and Brimstone..."

Dr. Abbott gasped. "Carlton! Now, I'm more concerned about your brainwashing than your trauma."

"I'm not ashamed of Jesus." Carlton had repeated everything God whispered in his ear.

For the remainder of the session, Dr. Abbott had him watch an interactive video, refraining from asking him more questions.

Chapter Twenty-five

If anyone is thirsty, let him come to Me and drink.
Whoever believes in Me, as the Scripture has said: 'Streams
of living water will flow from within him.—John 7:37–38

The next evening, Sinclaire called Zanetta to invite her and Harry to apple picking the following Saturday at Eckert's. "The mentors at my church are taking the children. I'm sure Carlton would love for Harry to spend time with him."

"Sounds like a plan. Harry seems to blossom around his brother and his friends. About spending time, what about a sleepover at my house—"

Sinclaire didn't let her finish. "My children don't do sleepovers."

"Oh." Zanetta was quiet.

"If you don't have any objections, I don't mind Harry spending the weekend with Carlton at your house."

"No offense. I don't allow that either. I have a young daughter and son in the house, and I can't protect them if I'm asleep. I'll rest better knowing my children are safe at home."

"That's a bit overprotective, don't you think?"

"I don't." Sinclaire felt an attitude building but calmed down. As a single mother, someone always had an opinion about how she reared her children. "If I were overprotective, Carlton would not have gone with Harrison that day when he was acting like a jerk."

Use this as a teaching moment, God whispered.

Sinclaire prayed for the right words. "This world is not filled with positive energy. It's filled with evil, wicked people. Because they're a majority, the Lord made room for them by enlarging hell. God sent His protection on the day of Carlton's birthday."

"Whew!" Zanetta said. "That was a wonder to watch."

"Yes. God is amazing. We are living in the last days, Zanetta. Christians must be vigilant. These things are foretold in the Bible to happen. I'm not a Bible scholar, but I do know this scripture, Second Peter 3:8: *But, beloved, be not ignorant of this one thing, that one day is with the Lord as a thousand years and a thousand years as one day.* If you're going to meditate daily, tap into the right source—Jesus, our Father, who created heaven and earth."

Wow. Sinclaire amazed herself with the knowledge that was coming out of her mouth.

At the end of the phone call, Sinclaire's answer to Zanetta was still no.

No to accepting Zanetta's offer to split Harry's inheritance.

No to any kind of sleepovers.

Something was different. Carlton could sense it while he talked to Harry. It was the Friday before they were supposed to go apple picking.

"Brother, I've been praying to God—not the Universe like Mom says—that He gives me what you and the other kids at your church have. I need that power to keep the nightmares away."

Carlton didn't know what to say. Harry was stuck between what his mother had been taught and what God showed him.

"Last night, when I was in bed asleep, something happened. I leaped out of my bed and began to praise Jesus. Then I heard words come out of my mouth as if they were spilling out of my stomach like I was vomiting, but it was only words, and then I couldn't stop. I started crying. My feet danced, and my arms lifted."

As Harry described the evidence of the Holy Ghost by hearing himself speak with a heavenly language, Carlton began to praise God too. "Thank You, Jesus! Thank You, Jesus! Thank You for answering my prayers."

He opened his eyes. Sissy stood in the doorway, banging on her toy tambourine, and TJ jumped in place. His mother clapped, praising God. Did she know what God had done?

When Carlton took a deep breath as the Holy Ghost gave him a reprieve, he shouted, "Harry received the Holy Ghost!"

"Hallelujah," his mother yelled, unconcerned about the noise disturbing the Marshalls who lived upstairs.

Carlton handed his mom the phone to hear Harry's heavenly worship.

Putting the call on speaker, Sinclaire and Carlton encouraged him to keep talking to Jesus.

Miss Zanetta was in the background asking Harry what was wrong. She grabbed the phone. "Hello? Carlton? What is going on with Harry? He's acting strange like some of those children who were at your birthday party."

"Zanetta," his mother said, catching her breath, "this is God's doing. The Book of Acts says, *'This is what was spoken by the prophet Joel: In the last days, God says, 'I will pour out My Spirit on all people. Your sons and daughters will prophesy, your young men will see visions, your old men will dream dreams.'* If you want to understand fully, you must read the Bible. You can search online for the verse in Chapter Two."

"This is too much carrying on in my house at this hour." Zanetta huffed as Harry's praise softened in the background. "Your brother will talk with you later." She ended the call.

"Can I call Dad?" Carlton asked his mother, grinning. His eyes were wide with excitement.

It was six-thirty. "Sure. He might be home from work. She smiled every time she talked to him. His mother was quiet as she listened to whatever he said. "Well, Carlton has some exciting news for you." She handed him the phone.

"Guess what, Dad?" Carlton could barely contain himself.

"You're getting married," he joked.

"No, I'm not old enough, dad. Harry got the Holy Ghost! He shouted so God could hear him."

"That is good news, son. God said He's coming for the children, and I'm glad Harry received the gift God had for him. This calls for a Holy Ghost celebration."

"Yeah." One down, one more to go. How much prayer would Miss Zanetta need to surrender?

Chapter Twenty-six

And let us not be weary in well-doing, for in due season
we shall reap if we faint not —Galatians 6:9

Apple picking at Eckert's Family Farms in Belleville, Illinois, was family-friendly. Fifteen minutes crossing over the Mississippi River from downtown St. Louis was a short trip. The church van carried children whose parents didn't have transportation. It was a highlight for the Christ For All Church children, and Jude loved seeing them smile.

Omega, Tally, and their husbands rode together while Jude drove Sinclaire and her family.

"Mom, Miss Zanetta knows, right?" Carlton asked for the second time since they got on the road.

"I told her, son," Sinclaire said softly. "We'll have to wait to see."

Jude hoped Harry wouldn't miss it. Last year, Jude recalled chatting with Mitchell, who couldn't wait to have his first child so he and Omega could start a tradition of bringing their child to the farm every fall.

But God's judgment interrupted those plans. Jude thought back to when Pastor Rodney said God revealed His punishment would rein seven more months in the world because of sin, but the saints had to do their jobs and draw people to Christ before they spent eternity in hell.

Once they made it to the farm, the church group joined others to begin their exploration.

Jude watched Carlton. The child shared with him that Zanetta now supervised his calls with Harry. Whenever they spoke of prayer, the Bible, or the Holy Ghost, Zanetta made Harry get off the phone. She thought holiness was a cult, even though she witnessed God's army of protection at Carlton's birthday party.

Mitchell and his brother-in-law, Tally's husband Randall, walked up with their hands tucked in their pants pockets.

"Man, I'll be glad when God's judgment ends," Mitchell said, looking around. "There are so many heartbreaking stories about children dying through the week and teenage shootings on the weekend."

"Yep." Randall sighed and frowned. "It's like the Wild Wild West out here."

Jude nodded. "Our children are in danger because of us— adults and their parents. God's anger thundered that night in my bedroom. *Men take innocent babies and use them for sex. They do not teach them about Me. Guns are their toys. They prostitute their children for money, drugs, and evil acts. I have been watching*, then God listed wicked deeds that I can't even repeat because they don't seem real. People are selling their souls to the devil. It's real, and they are giving up their children's souls in exchange for riches and fame."

Mitchell grunted. "Sounds like that Illuminati stuff. Some people think secret societies are a myth or conspiracy, but the Bible backs it up."

"Yep." Jude kept an eye on TJ as Sinclaire, Tally, and Omega filled their baskets with apples and other fruits. "To me, parents need to teach their children Ephesians six as they learn their ABCs. That way, the children will know how to protect themselves. Verse twelve says, *'For we wrestle not against flesh and blood, but against principalities, against powers, against the rulers of the darkness of this world, against spiritual wickedness in high places. '"*

Mitchell walked ahead on the same trail as his wife and friends. "Omega told me about Harry receiving the Holy Ghost. Sinclaire says Zanetta was freaking out. We've been praying for her."

"I'm praying for her to seek God for under—" Jude froze, then blinked. Zanetta was getting out of her car with Harry racing ahead. Carlton must have sensed his presence because he turned around, dropped his collection of apples, and met Harry halfway. The brothers hugged as if they had been separated at birth or reunited after a long time. "Looks like God has answered our prayers. They're here." He pointed. *Lord, give me the words to say to win Zanetta over.*

Ask her about the god she serves, God whispered.

"I'm going to tell Omega." Mitchell took off in the direction he saw his wife go, and Randall followed him.

While Harry ran off with Carlton, Jude took that opportunity to talk to his mother privately. "Hi, Zanetta. I don't know if you remember—"

Her expression was unreadable. "Of course. From Bumper Zone. When my son talks about his brother, your name comes up. You and Sinclaire should get married if Carlton hero worships you. Half the battle is won when single mothers date, and there's a connection between the non-father and her child and vice versa."

Jude refused to get pulled into a conversation with a woman who seemed to be digging for dirt. He was on another assignment. "Do you mind if we talk about something else?"

Zanetta rolled her eyes. "If it's about Harry and his carrying on, save your breath." She squeezed her lips as if the subject were distasteful.

"Actually," he said, nodding at new arrivals from his church, "I would like to ask questions about your spiritual beliefs."

She smiled. "Sure. I feel your good vibes. Before I became pregnant with Harry, a palm reader told me I would meet a man who I would fall in love with, but he would break my heart, but to channel that hurt into self-growth by tapping into my inner self and connecting with the Universe that gives me life and happiness."

Jude didn't interrupt. Practitioners of the New Age movement believed they could use their will or imagination or visualize what they wanted and manipulate God to give it to them. They were idol worshippers who worshipped themselves.

My people perish for the lack of knowledge, God whispered.

"Since my ancestors paved the way for me, their spirits can guide me through life to better myself and warn me about another person's energy. My growth is dependent on positive thought meditations."

"What about tarot card reading and casting of spells?" Jude had done his homework on this subject, but he wanted to hear her thoughts.

Zanetta laughed. "You can't believe everything you hear. Since we were made in God's image, we are mini gods, and we determine our destiny to get to heaven."

Witchcraft, God whispered.

Jude saw two dark figures covering Zanetta's eyes and talking in her ear. The woman was in bondage. He began to pray in the spirit, rebuking demons to release her mind, then uttered, "I believe God created man in His image and a little lower than the angels. I believe Jesus is the only way to Heaven. I believe that every knee shall bow at the name of Jesus.

"I believe that demons cannot pluck one soul out of Christ's hands, which are sealed with His blood from the cross. And finally, Jesus wasn't beaten, bruised, humiliated, and bled on the cross for you or me to come up with our own plan of salvation. Oh, and one more thing: I believe the Holy Ghost has the power over all demons, and your son will show you the way. Every tongue will confess that Jesus is Lord." He crossed his arms.

Zanetta grunted. "I'm starting to feel your negative energy." She walked away, and the two demons followed.

"You know everyone is praying for you, Minister Jude, Brother Mitchell, the pastor, Mom, everybody," Carlton said, sad. He and Harry walked together with their arms around each other's shoulders.

Harry sighed. "My mama is nice, but she's become so different." He stopped in his tracks and stared at Carlton. "Do you think my mama will hurt me too?"

"She can't because God won't let her, but she needs help. Pray that God will show her His power." What else could he say to his brother? Carton didn't think his dad would hurt him either, but look what happened. *Jesus, don't let Harry be afraid, or me, either.*

On the way home, Carlton was quiet as he looked out the window.

"You okay, buddy?" Minister Jude asked.

"Dad, do you think Harry's mom would try to hurt him like my dad did to me?" Carlton asked as the vehicle jolted to a stop.

Minister Jude and his mother glanced in the back at him.

"What makes you think that son?" Sinclaire asked.

"Harry said she's acting strange. She was the best mom ever. He even said he thought about giving God back the Holy Ghost to make his mother happy again."

"No," Minister Jude said firmly. "I'm calling Pastor Rodney. Ain't nobody giving nothing back. The devil is a lie. Harry needs intercessors. Maybe Pastor Rodney will open the church for a shut-in service this Friday."

Sinclaire faced him. "Carlton, I don't want you or Harry to be afraid. Like Jesus pulled you from the clutches of death, I believe He will do the same for your brother."

Trust Me, Carlton, God whispered.

He closed his eyes to keep a tear from falling, then sniffed. *I'm like Doubting Thomas, Lord, one of Your apostles. Please help my unbelief.* Carlton drifted off to sleep and didn't wake until the car stopped in front of his apartment building.

Chapter Twenty-seven

Sinclaire was in her deep sleep when the annoying ringtone of Carlton's phone stirred her awake. She rolled over and looked at the time. Two-thirty-four in the morning. Sinclaire frowned. Who would be calling her son that late?

The house rule at bedtime was Carlton had to turn over his phone until the morning. Throwing the covers back, Sinclaire slipped out of bed and picked up the phone off her dresser. *Harry.*

"Hello, Harry. What's wrong?"

"My mom…" His voice shook as he began to ramble. "My mom's sick."

Sinclaire paced the floor. "What do you mean sick? What's going on?"

"I think she's dead."

"What?" Sinclaire gasped as she grabbed her clothes to slip over her nightgown. "Are you safe?"

"Yes, ma'am. I want my brother." He started to whine.

If she woke Carlton, which she wouldn't, she would have two hysterical boys on her hands. "I want you to call 9-1-1 and go lock yourself in the bathroom. I'm on my way."

Sinclaire didn't want to sever the connection, so she kept him on the line. Sinclaire needed to start waking people up, so she grabbed her cell phone. Jude was her first call. He answered with sleep deep in his voice.

"Hello."

"Jude," she paused, whimpered, then became hysterical.

"Sinclaire, what's wrong?" The sleep in his voice became a crisp tone.

"Harry called saying Zanetta is dead. I told him to call 9-1-1, and I'm heading over there. Can you come stay at my house until I get back?"

"Absolutely not."

Sinclaire blinked. He had never told her no. What was his problem?

"Give me the address, and I'll meet you there. Call Omega and ask her to come to your place." He ended the call.

That was the second time Jude bossed her around, first with the gun and now. She smiled and did as he said and called Omega. "There's an emergency at Harry's house." She tried to keep her voice low. "I'm heading over there. I called Jude to come, but he wants to meet me at her house, so you're next on my list. The children are sleeping."

She heard Mitchell in the background, yawning. "Hey, sis. Give us ten minutes, and we're out the door."

Lord, I don't know what to do: Stay here and protect my children or leave them here to save someone else. Jesus, I need direction. A tear fell down her cheek as her bedroom door opened, and Carlton stuck his head inside.

"Mom, where are you going? Who were you talking to? Why are you crying?"

"Carlton, I'm sorry to wake you. There is an emergency, so I have to leave. Auntie Omega and Brother Mitchell will stay here until I get back."

Her son didn't move as she slipped on a light jacket and picked up her keys. "Is something wrong with Harry?"

She frowned. "Why?"

"Because you have my phone and yours in your hands." Carlton pointed. "Mom, is he okay?" His lips quivered as his eyes glossed over.

"Harry is okay. His mother isn't. That's why I'm going now." She heard Harry's whimpers. Otherwise, Sinclaire would have him reassure Carlton.

"I want to go too." His son raced back into his bedroom.

"You can't. Someone has to stay with Sissy and TJ. I will leave your phone here," against her better judgment as Sinclaire discontinued the call, "but do not call or text Harry. Wait for him to text you. Do you understand me?"

Carlton nodded.

"I need a verbal answer. If you disobey me, then..." She didn't have time to devise a punishment for a minor infraction. "Do not disobey me."

Sinclaire tapped her shoe. "Come on, Omega," she mumbled and peeped out the window. "Come on, come, come on." After the incident with Nikki, there was no way she was going to leave her children alone again, even though there weren't guns in the house.

Her phone rang again. Omega. "Where are you?"

"Sis, we're turning into your apartment complex now."

Grabbing her keys, Sinclaire opened her door while Carlton watched from the sofa.

Omega and Mitchell jogged up the stairs to her landing, out of breath. "Go. We'll be praying." They hurried into her apartment, and Sinclaire took off for her car.

University City, right outside the St. Louis city limits, was a thirty-minute drive without traffic. She programmed Zanetta's address into her GPS and drove away. "Lord, post an angel at my door tonight and be with Harry too."

So many questions raced through her mind as she tried not to speed to get to the highway. If Zanetta was dead, who killed her? An intruder, ex-lover, or was Harry defending himself?

Jude's call came through her car speakers ten minutes from her destination. "Sinclaire, I'm here. So are the police and ambulance. They won't let me enter the house, so I don't know what happened."

"Have you seen Harry?"

"No."

"Lord Jesus, please let him be okay." Sinclaire took a deep breath and exited the highway. She glanced at her navigation map. Two minutes away.

Omega texted her. **Please let us know ASAP what is going on. Carlton is beside himself, worried about his brother.**

Will do.

She arrived on the block and saw Jude waving her down. After she parked, he opened her door. He wrapped his arms around her in a comforting hug.

Sinclaire exhaled and stepped back. "I didn't know I needed that." She swallowed. "Now, let's find out what's going on." She walked ahead until it became a jog.

"Hi. I'm Sinclaire Oliver," she said to the first officer she approached. My son and Zanetta's son are brothers. Harry called me, and I told him to lock himself in the bathroom, not knowing what was happening. Have you found him?"

"Yes, and he's in shock," Officer Branson said.

Her heart ached for him.

He needed nurturing.

He needed a hug.

He needed his mother.

"Can I see him?"

"We just put him in the ambulance to calm him down. He said he was waiting for you and his brother. Follow me." Sinclaire linked her fingers through Jude's for strength, and he walked beside her.

Harry looked up. He leaped out of the ambulance and ran toward her.

"Miss Sinclaire." The force of Harry's speed would have body-slammed her if Jude hadn't blocked.

Sinclaire leaned down and hugged him. She kissed his forehead as if she would Carlton. She examined him—no injuries—then hugged him. "Sweetie, are you okay?"

He nodded.

"What happened to your mother?"

A paramedic approached and saved Harry from answering. "She fainted."

Sinclaire felt faint after releasing the heavy anxiety of not knowing that it wasn't something more serious. "But she is alive?"

"Yes, and alert," he answered, "but we're taking her to the hospital so a doctor can run tests to determine a cause."

"Well, Harry can't stay here alone." She stepped into the role of an advocate.

Officer Branson returned. "Are you his next of kin?"

Sinclaire opened her mouth to say no, but Harry blurted out. "She's my brother's mother, so she's my next of kin to me."

"Where's your father, son?"

"Dead." Harry dropped his head to his chest in shame.

"Sorry to hear that. What about aunts, uncles, grandparents?" the officer pressed.

"I want to go with Miss Sinclaire and Minister Jude. She will take care of me until my mother is better."

"Determined little boy, aren't you?" Officer Branson looked back at another ambulance. "Wait here." He spoke to a paramedic, then waved them over.

That's when Sinclaire saw Zanetta. Her eyes were open, but she looked dazed. "How are you?"

"I'm better, I guess." Her voice was weak. "Must have really scared Harry to call you. Sorry."

Sinclaire took her hand. "You have nothing to be sorry for. Is it okay for me to take Harry home overnight and bring him back tomorrow?"

Zanetta looked at her with worry in her eyes. "Are you sure? I know you don't allow sleepovers."

"This is an emergency. Things change." She patted Zanetta's shoulder.

"Thank you." Zanetta sniffed, then opened her arms for her son. "Harry, you be good for Sinclaire, okay?"

He nodded.

"And don't forget to pray for me."

"We will," Sinclaire, Jude, and Harry said in chorus.

Never say never, Sinclaire scolded herself when she thought back to telling Zanetta she didn't do sleepovers. And that's precisely what was about to happen. *Lord, I repent for my attitude.*

"Miss Sinclaire, I couldn't sleep. It seemed like someone was shaking my bed. I opened my eyes, and I think an angel told me to pray, so I did. Mama heard me and came into my room. She fainted, so I thought I had killed her."

Sinclaire could see how a child could think that. She wrapped her arm around him. "Everything is going to be okay." As she followed Harry into the small, neat bungalow, Sinclaire was relieved that this wasn't anything more serious. She couldn't take another parent attempting to murder their child.

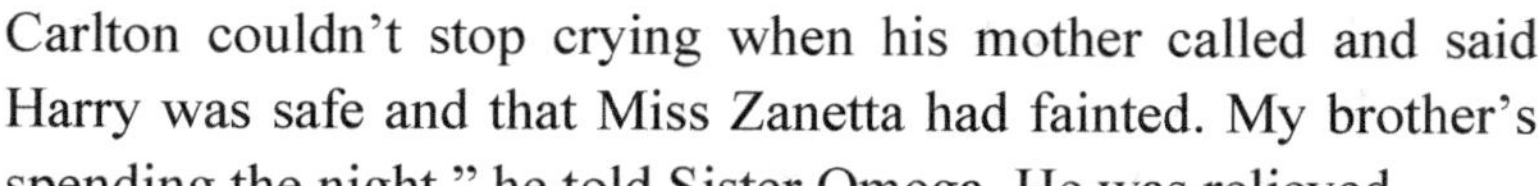

Carlton couldn't stop crying when his mother called and said Harry was safe and that Miss Zanetta had fainted. My brother's spending the night," he told Sister Omega. He was relieved.

It took forever for them to come, and Carlton was getting tired. When the front door opened, Harry walked in with his mother and Minister Jude.

The brothers hugged as his mother told them to share his room and get some sleep.

Sinclaire told his babysitters what happened as they got ready to leave.

"I'll let human resources know you'll take off tomorrow," Omega said.

Carlton closed his bedroom door so Harry could change. "I have a pull-out bed. You can sleep on the bottom."

"Okay."

Minutes later, they kneeled together, and Carlton prayed. "Lord, thank You for protecting my brother, in Jesus' name. Amen."

After they climbed into their beds, Harry said, "Now I know how scared you were with Dad. Mama didn't like me praying too loud, but I couldn't help it. God gets loud when I pray to Him."

His mom didn't wake them early for school and let all of them sleep late.

When Carlton sniffed bacon, he sat up and looked down. It wasn't a dream. His brother was there with him and safe. Carlton used the bathroom before going into the kitchen. "Good morning, Mom."

"Morning, baby. You be quiet so your brother can sleep. He had a rough night. After he eats, I'll take him to the hospital to see his mother. He'll probably go back home with her if she's discharged—and she should be."

"I wish he could stay longer." Carlton frowned his displeasure.

"Maybe one day." She tweaked his nose. "But not today. His mom needs him right now, and we keep praying for her. Okay?"

"Yes, ma'am."

While Sinclaire finished cooking breakfast, she wondered what would it take for Zanetta to surrender her soul to Christ? If this health scare didn't make her run to Jesus for salvation, then what would?

Chapter Twenty-eight

And we know that all things work together for good to them that love
God, to them who are called according to his purpose. —Romans 8:28

"Why didn't you wake me?" Jude scolded Sinclaire when he called her mid-morning.

"Because I had already woke you once this morning, and that was enough. Harry's packing the few things he brought so we can go to the hospital."

"Oh, is he old enough to visit?"

"Twelve and under need an adult, so I will stay with him."

"Do you want me to go with you?" Jude asked.

"I don't…but Harry could use some fatherly comfort right now."

Jude chuckled, and that made Sinclaire smile. "Let me know when you head out, and I'll meet you at the hospital." He paused. "What about the other children?"

"Business as usual for Carlton and Sissy. They will get to school late, but I hope it will be a distraction. I'm dropping off TJ at Mother Kincaid's place."

Sinclaire ended the call to check whether the children were dressed. Walking closer to Carlton's room, she heard an explosion of heavenly tongues as the brothers worshipped God uninhibited.

She opened the door. Carlton had his hands on Harry's shoulders, praying for him.

Harry's arms were stretched toward heaven. Sinclaire could feel the heaviness of God's anointing and the Holy Ghost's power. She closed the door, then went to check on Sissy and TJ, who were half dressed—shoes, but no socks and tops, but no bottoms.

Sinclaire hurried them. At least the older boys looked ready to go. If it were Sinclaire in the hospital, she would want to see all her babies as soon as possible. Zanetta probably felt the same way, but she hadn't called.

Once Harry had all his belongings, Sinclaire did the drop-offs at each destination until it was only her and Harry. She texted Jude.

We're on our way.

I'll pack up my work and meet you in the hospital lobby, he texted back.

Harry was quiet as he looked out the window.

She couldn't imagine how he felt without siblings and a grandmother who seemed detached from his life. "Are you ready to see your mother?"

"If she's not dead," Harry said sorrowfully.

Of course, she's not dead, Sinclaire wanted to say. Only seeing her would make Harry believe. "She isn't sweetie. Zanetta just fainted. I know you were scared when you called me early this morning, and I'm glad you did. All of us are here for you, including Minister Jude. He's coming to the hospital to make sure you're alright."

"I hope he will help me pray for my mama so she will be okay."

"I heard you and Carlton praying. Don't underestimate the power of the Holy Ghost the Lord gifted you. The Lord saved you for His purpose. You keep praying for your mom."

"Yes, ma'am." Harry nodded.

Soon, they arrived at the hospital, and Sinclaire parked.

"Do you think my mama will come home today?"

"I hope so." Sinclaire took his hand like she would Carlton's. If he was uncomfortable with her gesture, he didn't voice it.

They entered the lobby, and Sinclaire asked the information clerk for Zanetta Erving's room number. As she turned around, Jude strolled in, wearing a crisp blue shirt, printed tie, dark dress slacks, and a crossbody leather bag. He removed his sunglasses and smiled. Why he was still a single man at the church was a mystery.

Jude walked up to them and hugged Harry like he did Carlton. "Hey, buddy. You ready to check on your mom?"

The boy nodded, then Jude greeted Sinclaire.

She squinted. "How come you look like you got eight hours of sleep and then some, and I feel and look like I've worked a twenty-four-hour shift?"

"Number one, you always look pretty," he said, and she blushed. "Plus, I'm accustomed to getting up in the middle of the night to pray, and when I fall back to sleep, all I can do is ask God to multiply my hours of rest."

Good strategy. Sinclaire led the way to the set of elevators and stepped inside the first open doors. Jude and Harry trailed her and rode silently to the sixth floor. They stepped out, read the signs, then veered to the right for Room 626.

"Wait." Jude stopped a few doors from Zanetta's room, "Shouldn't we have balloons, flowers, or something for her?"

"Yeah." Harry got excited.

"Tell you what, Harry and I will go to the gift shop and get his mother something while you see her first."

Sinclaire nodded, continued on her way, then knocked on the door.

"Come in." Zanetta's voice feigned cheerfulness to Sinclaire.

She walked in. Zanetta didn't look ready to be discharged, not with an IV in her hand. "Hey. You gave us a scare last night—or rather early this morning."

Zanetta angled her body to look around Sinclaire. "Where's Harry?"

"He went downstairs with Jude to get you something from the gift shop."

"Oh. That's nice." She nodded and motioned for Sinclaire to close the door, then waved her closer to the bed. "The doctors ran tests. My blood sugar is down, and I'm borderline diabetic…" She paused and didn't meet Sinclaire's eyes.

That was manageable. She sensed there was more. Sinclaire's heart rate accelerated. "Is there something else?"

"My bloodwork also indicates I have abnormal cells. The doctors asked me some questions, and I was checking all their boxes. The big thing is my unexplained fatigue. Sometimes, a room of twenty-three seven-year-olds can wipe you out, depending on the day." She smiled, but Sinclaire wasn't buying it. "Doctors want to run more tests to rule out cancer, but I'm thinking positive."

Zanetta was not coming home today and was not okay.

The moment was surreal as Sinclaire thought about Zanetta and her son. "Regardless of what the doctor says—"

"I plan to think positive and not speak that terrible disease into my life." Zanetta lifted her chin but didn't look convinced she believed what she uttered.

"Jesus is the Great Physician. Whatever the doctors on earth decide, we can take it to the Lord in prayer at His altar and ask for healing." Sinclaire paused. "It's going to take prayer to get you through this, Zanetta, not positive energy to keep misfortune at bay."

They stared at each other as Harry and Jude's voices grew louder.

"*Knock, knock*," Jude announced as he tapped the door. Harry burst through with a force that seemed to shake the room.

"Mama!" Harry leaped on her bed and rested his head on her chest.

"We'll wait outside, and oh," Sinclaire said. "if you want, you can add me to your emergency contact at the school in case I need to pick up Harry."

"I will." Zanetta's eyes watered as Harry hugged her. "Thank you for being there for us." She sniffed, then closed her eyes.

"Here's the goodies Harry got for you." Jude grinned and handed Zanetta a bag. "Take as much time as you and Harry need. We won't be far."

When Sinclaire and Jude were alone in the hall, he asked, "Well, is she okay?" The concern was etched on his brows.

"The doctors suspect more than exhaustion is going on with her that caused her to faint." Sinclaire didn't want to say more without Zanetta's permission.

"Understood. Pastor Rodney agreed to call for an additional shut-in service for this Friday. Looks like we have even more to pray for."

Sinclaire's list was ever-growing. She peeked inside the room. Harry had his hand on Zanetta's shoulder, and his lips moved in whispered prayers.

They walked the short distance to the family lounge. She took a seat. Jude sat at a nearby table and pulled a small computer from his crossbody bag.

"You don't have to stay," Sinclaire told him. "I could be here a long time."

Jude shrugged. "Don't forget Harry lost a father, and he may feel like he's going to lose his mother. He needs us."

"You're a compassionate man and minister." She admired his wisdom and love of others, then called Omega with an update and a favor to pick up the children. Once confirmed, Sinclaire closed her eyes and prayed. "Lord, if this is Your will, please soften Zanetta's heart toward You."

"Amen, Sister Oliver. Love to hear you pray." That stare Jude gave her was filled with adoration.

Since they were on a first-name basis outside of church, it was more of an endearment and a reminder that she was a saint of God. "The same could be said about you. However, I don't know how effective my petitions are."

"When your faith behind your prayers grows, you'll see God move."

"Amen," she said as Zanetta's door opened and Harry called for her.

"Miss Sinclaire, my mom wants to speak with you."

"Coming." Sinclaire stood and left Jude working. She followed Harry back inside Zanetta's room. "Do you mind if Harry stays another night with you?"

Sinclaire lowered her head in shame, then looked up at Zanetta with tears in her eyes. The two had become unexpected friends. "That will never be an issue again—ever. I'm sorry, and I repented for my attitude. Harry is welcome at any time. If he spends Friday night, we will attend our church's shut-in service from 10 p.m. to 7 a.m. If you don't want him to go—"

"Can I, Mama?" Harry jumped from his chair. His eyes were bright.

"Prayer changes things," Sinclaire said.

"Yes." Zanetta didn't put up a fight.

Friday morning, Zanetta called Sinclaire with the bad news. "The doctors say I have an aggressive type of cancer." She was calm, but her voice was shaky.

Sinclaire's stomach dropped. "What's the name of the cancer?"

When Zanetta told her, Sinclaire couldn't pronounce it, much less spell it correctly. "I'm glad you consented for Harry to attend church for all-night prayer. We're taking this condition before the Lord."

Zanetta was quiet. "I know our children haven't been friends long, but I get good vibes from you that Harry would be safe and thrive with his brother more than with Harrison's mother or aunt. Since they wanted me to split Harrison's life insurance, I put money in a trust fund for Harry. They can't touch it. I also have a life insurance policy with the school district. I'm telling you all this because if something happened to me, I'd be at peace knowing you had custody of Harry."

"I would." Sinclaire choked, then walked into her bedroom and slid to her knees. She cried out, *Lord, please don't let Zanetta Irving die from this condition....*

"Are we going to pray all night?" Harry asked from the backseat as Sinclaire drove them to church for the shut-in service. She brought pillows and blankets for TJ and Sissy.

"Yep." Carlton enjoyed the shut-in service, which only happened two to three times a year. "It's so cool. I've seen angels walk up and down ladders as if they're carrying our prayers up to God."

"Really? I hope they take my prayers about my mama up to Jesus. I'm also glad Mama said it was okay for me to get baptized in water, in Jesus' name. I love Jesus!"

"She did?" Carlton didn't know.

"Yes, Miss Zanetta did, son," Sinclaire said. It had been a surprise to Sinclaire, too, but God was changing Zanetta's heart.

When Sinclaire called Harry "son," the brothers couldn't stop grinning. Was that by accident? Carlton didn't care. They were like twins since they were the same age.

Once they arrived at Christ For All Church, Carlton sought out Minister Jude as soon as they were in the foyer. When he spotted him, Carlton waved, calling his name. Harry did the same as they ran to him.

"Boys, stop running before you knock someone down," Sinclaire said.

Minister Jude grinned and shook both their hands before hugging them.

"Mama said I can get baptized." Harry was almost out of breath.

"Yeah." Carlton couldn't contain his excitement.

"She did? Well, this is a good night for it. Let me verify that with your mom, then find our pastor and see if I can baptize you in Jesus' name before we begin all-night prayer."

The pair raced back to Sinclaire, and Carlton said, "Mom, Minister Jude is going to baptize my brother!"

"I'm sure the angels are already dancing." Sinclaire was as happy as they were.

"For real?" Harry's eyes widened in disbelief.

"Yes. The Bible says in Luke, I think it's the fifteenth chapter, that there is joy in the presence of God's angels over one sinner who repents."

"I already repented and—"

Minister Jude approached. TJ and Sissy hugged his legs, then he lifted them in each arm. "Pastor Rodney okayed it. But she doesn't want to witness this magnificent event?" He frowned and looked to Sinclaire for answers.

"No, but she gave her consent for some reason, so we should take the win," Sinclaire said.

"What's all this excitement?" Brother Mitchell teased as he walked into the building, holding hands with Sister Omega.

"I'm about to get baptized, in Jesus' name!" Harry answered.

"And we get to witness it," Omega said, dancing from side to side.

Brother Randall walked in with Tally at his side. "What's going on?"

Carlton told him, and Randall clapped.

Everyone gathered in the sanctuary as Pastor Rodney made the announcement. "Praise the Lord, saints. Tonight, we come before God with some good news! Our dear Carlton's brother is about to finish his salvation requirement with the water baptism in Jesus' name. He already has received the Holy Spirit's baptism. That means he'll be caught in the air to meet Jesus when He returns."

"Amen!" several shouted, including Mother Kincaid, who began to sing, *"Take me to the water, take me to the water to be baptized..."*

"In the name of Jesus," the rest of the congregation joined in as the light illuminated the baptismal pool, and Minister Jude stepped down into the water and stretched his hand for Harry to come.

Carlton jumped up and down, and Sissy and TJ mimicked him.

Dressed in a white T-shirt, pants, and socks, Harry entered the pool and followed Minister Jude's instructions to cross his arms over his chest.

With a grip on the back of Carlton's shirt, Minister Jude lifted one arm and, with a loud voice that echoed and caused a hush throughout the sanctuary, said, "My dear brother Harry, upon the confession of your faith and repentance in the blessed Word of God, concerning His death, burial, and grand resurrection, I now indeed baptize you in the name—the only name under heaven given by which we must be saved. That is the Lord Jesus Christ for the remission of your sins. Amen."

The sanctuary roared with applause and praise as Harry was submerged, then he seemed to float to the top as if his arms pushed through the water. Carlton and his siblings tried to clap the loudest.

"Amen!" Pastor Rodney rejoiced. "Since the presence of the Lord is here, let's make our requests—whatever they are—before the Lord. Please remember we are still under God's judgment with the children, so we are happy that Harry was spared. But there are other children out there who need to be rescued. Pray for their salvation."

Chapter Twenty-nine

Therefore, if anyone is in Christ, he is a new creation.
The old has passed away. Behold, all things have become new!
—2 Corinthians 5:17

Saturday morning, after the prayer shut-in, Sinclaire ushered her family inside her apartment. She was dragging. Jude trailed behind her, carrying TJ and Sissy.

All the children headed to bed, except for Harry. Despite the exhaustion from praying overnight, the child seemed to glow with energy.

"Get some rest. See you tomorrow," Jude said and left.

"Thank you." Sinclaire nodded and turned to Harry. "Aren't you tired?" She stifled a yawn.

"No. I want to go see my mom, please."

"Sure. We'll go later after we all take naps and refresh ourselves."

"No. It has to be now," Harry demanded.

Sinclaire was seconds away from reminding him she was in control of the Oliver house, when God spoke to her.

My timing is everything. I have given Harry an assignment. Go, God whispered.

"Lord, renew my strength," Sinclaire said before she called Mother Kincaid to come and stay with the children while they slept. Although the elderly woman was at the shut-in service, midnight was the last chance for people to leave, and she always did.

The woman had gotten her rest. Sinclaire explained Harry's request.

"Then you have to go. I'm dressed and had my morning coffee. I'll be there in half an hour."

Sinclaire sat on the sofa to wait and dozed off. A knock on her door stirred her awake.

"Miss Sinclaire, that's probably Mother Kincaid." Harry shook her until she stood, then opened the door.

Mother Kincaid walked in, hugged her, then nudged Sinclaire and Harry out the door.

In the car, she faced Harry. "I'm going to need you to pray that I stay awake while driving."

"Yes, ma'am."

They arrived safely in no time and rode the elevator to the sixth floor. Harry walked ahead of Sinclaire on a mission to Zanetta's room. A nurse was prepping Zanetta for something.

"Stop right there, please," Harry said respectfully as Sinclaire closed the door and stood silently.

Zanetta looked up, and happiness filled her face. "Harry, what are you doing here? Shouldn't you be asleep after staying up late last night with the Olivers?"

"I came to pray."

"Well, can you make it quick? I have my orders," the nurse said. Ruby was written on the erase board.

He walked to the bed, touched his mother's stomach, and lifted his hand. "Father, in the name of Jesus, You told me to prophesy over my mother's health that she would live and not die from the cancer in her body…"

Sinclaire frowned. How did Harry know that? She didn't tell him, and Sinclaire doubted his mother had mentioned it.

"In Jesus' name, remove the tumors the doctors see and can't see. I command sickness to leave." He pushed on Zanetta's stomach, and she yelped. Sinclaire felt the presence of God in the room.

It was powerful. Even Nurse Ruby was on her knees, shaking.

Zanetta, who appeared weak in bed when they came in, was sitting up. She grabbed the plastic pan by her bedside and vomited blood until nothing else came, then stared at her son. "I believe. I believe."

The door opened, and another nurse stood in the doorway. "What's going on in here? Voices could be heard at the end of the hall."

A doctor strolled into the room bewildered and repeated the question.

"I'm going home." Zanetta grinned.

"Miss Irving," he said, pausing and looking at the nurse still on her knees. Her hands were lifted, and she was crying, bowing. "Nurse Ruby, compose yourself and prepare the patient for the procedure."

"Mom won't need it. She's healed," Harry said.

The physician chuckled. "I'm the doctor, and her tests say otherwise." He challenged with a scowl.

"I'm her son, and I say run the tests again." Harry didn't back down, sat on Zanetta's bed, and then folded her hands.

"Miss Irving, I don't have time for this. Please silence your child." The doctor didn't hide his irritation.

"You're bringing bad energy into this room. I'm going home so you can halt everything."

Shaking her head, Sinclaire knew Zanetta would soon learn that all good things come from above, and anything contrary that she called bad energy was the demon's presence.

"Then you will be discharging yourself against doctor's orders." The doctor huffed and walked out.

While he was gone, the nurse's hands shook as she seemed to operate in a daze. Harry told Nurse Ruby about being baptized and praying all night at the church. "God told me you have cancer, and the doctors wouldn't be able to get it all, but He knew the hidden places." Harry took a breath. "He said I have to push. The blood you spit up were the tumors, Mom."

Sinclaire took a seat. She was wide awake as Zanetta got her clothes and shoes, headed to the bathroom, and paused. "Nurse Ruby, you heard what my son said. I think someone should take my blood and compare it with the blood I vomited."

"If that is true," the nurse said, "I will believe. Let me talk to my supervisor to see if another doctor will order tests."

Zanetta folded her arms. "Okay. I can stick around for that."

For the next hour, Sinclaire sat in a chair, fully alert, watching the nurses and a new doctor enter the room.

The new doctor agreed to order another blood test and compare it with what she regurgitated. "I'll put a rush on it. Maybe we can get the results back within the hour."

"Thank you, but I am checking myself out so I can go home and rest. Will you call me with the results?"

The doctor smiled. "I could use a miracle after the night I've had. I hope you're right."

As Sinclaire took Zanetta and Harry home, she smiled to herself. Without realizing it, she felt she had gained a sister, not just a friend.

En route to Zanetta's home, Harry talked nonstop about all the things Jesus had spoken to him in prayer, and his mother listened without interrupting.

Sinclaire parked in front of Zanetta's place. "Please call me as soon as you hear." Then she headed home. Despite her exhaustion, how was she supposed to go to sleep now?

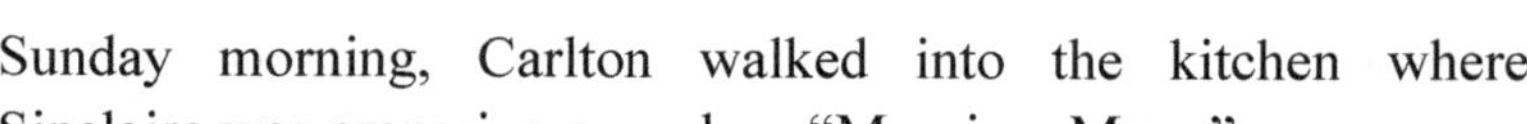

Sunday morning, Carlton walked into the kitchen where Sinclaire was preparing pancakes. "Morning, Mom."

She looked over her shoulder and smiled. "Hey, son."

"Can I ask you a question?"

"Sure. First, wash your hands, then you can help me butter the pancakes."

Carlton did, then made himself comfortable. "Mom, can I change my name from Oliver to Wakefield so Harry and I can have the same last name?"

Sinclaire was quiet. Harrison hadn't wanted their son to have any part of Harrison's name. His reasoning was he could do that when they married. He was a liar from the beginning, knowing there would be no marriage, and he already had a son who bore his first and last name.

"Harrison told me to wait. By blood, you are a Wakefield. I hoped that if I ever got married, your new dad would adopt you so we all could have the same name."

"I'd like that too." Carlton tilted his head, gave it some thought, then shrugged. "I guess it depends on who you'll marry and who will be my new dad. He may be mean and not nice like Minister Jude. That's who you should marry, Mom."

Carlton walked into his siblings' room to wake them up.

Is my son trying to get me a husband, she thought as Jude called and asked about Zanetta.

"She *had* cancer."

"Oh, I'm sorry to hear that. Harry needs his mother…"

"Jude, I said 'had.' After the prayer shut-in service, Harry went to the hospital and prayed for her. She threw up the cancerous blood. By the time I got home after dropping her off, the nurse called with the results, confirming Harry's testimony. No cancer was found. Zanetta is healed."

"Hallelujah!" Jude shouted at the top of his lungs. "Won't He do it?"

"Yes, Jesus will."

"I called her this morning, and she said Carlton witnessed to the nurse over the phone, so I wouldn't be surprised if Nurse Ruby shows up for church, and Zanetta said she would be there."

"Looks like this is one service neither of us should miss. See you at church." Jude ended the call.

Sinclaire rejoiced for Zanetta's testimony but searched her heart for the answer to allow Carlton to change his last name. Wasn't Harrison's name listed on his birth certificate good enough?

Chapter Thirty

What shall I render unto the LORD for all his benefits toward me? I will take the cup of salvation and call upon the name of the LORD. I will pay my vows unto the LORD now in the presence of all His people.
—Psalm 116:12–14

It was a good day, Sinclaire thought as she walked into the church foyer and looked around for Zanetta and Harry.

"You see them, Mom?" Carlton asked, cranking his neck in both directions.

"Not yet." Sinclaire sighed. She refused to let doubt set in after witnessing Zanetta's miracle.

"I'm going to take Sissy and TJ to their classrooms and come right back, so Harry and I can sit with you and Miss Zanetta, okay?"

"That's fine." She rubbed the waves in his hair before he hurried to youth church.

Moments later, Harry opened the door for Zanetta. He escorted his mother inside with pride and confidence in his steps.

"Zanetta, you look well. How do you feel?" Sinclaire hugged her and Harry.

"Amazing," she said with such awe. "The fact that God revealed my illness to my son, who then turned around and healed me with God's help..." Zanetta shook her head as if in disbelief. "I give God all the props." Her face glowed with happiness.

"I'm so glad you're here." Sinclaire smiled. "Carlton took his siblings to youth church." She blinked. In record time, her son returned.

"Yes!" Harry pumped his fist in the air. "There he is. Hey, brother."

Sinclaire and Zanetta laughed as the two boys performed a handshake routine.

"Let's go into the sanctuary. I hear the praise team has started," Sinclaire said as their sons rested their arms around each other's shoulders and entered the sanctuary. Anyone could see how much the newfound brothers loved each other. Because of their bond, Sinclaire thought it would be unfair not to consider Carlton's request to change his surname.

Surprisingly, Zanetta looped her arm through Sinclaire's. Both grinned and followed their sons.

The singers ushered in the spirit of praise with William McDowell's old hit, "Here I Am to Worship."

Sinclaire hugged Omega and Tally, and their husbands. Zanetta gave them a friendly nod. She didn't stand with others in her pew to participate in praise and worship, but she did sway to the beat of the music.

When the praise-and-worship segment quieted, Pastor Rodney walked to the podium.

Pastor Rodney, please bring the right message for Zanetta and others today, Sinclaire silently prayed as she closed her eyes and her mind to any distractions.

"Welcome, saints and friends and our guests," the pastor said. "Before I get to this morning's sermon, I want to say that although judgment is reigning in this world, God is still blessing, protecting, healing, and delivering His own, which is why belonging to God is important. After Friday's shut-in service, I received so many testimonies. Brother Harry Wakefield, congratulations on your baptism and God healing your mother."

A hearty applause roared throughout the sanctuary.

Zanetta closed her eyes and smiled. Sinclaire squeezed her shoulder, happy for her.

Pastor Rodney nodded, then continued. "I'm encouraged today because people are beginning to cry out to God on all social media platforms for their sick children or loved ones. People are not ashamed to ask for prayer for celebrities in trouble with life-threatening conditions. My message today is a common scripture from Second Chronicles, seven and fourteen: *'If my people, which are called by my name, shall humble themselves, and pray, and seek my face, and turn from their wicked ways; then will I hear from heaven, and will forgive their sin, and will heal their land.'* This is a simple formula, saints! Sin got us in this mess. Repentance, which is humility, gets us out."

Zanetta exhaled. "Finally, a little inspiration."

Pastor Rodney was silent. "But humility is not in our DNA. Sin is in the bloodline, and the water baptism washes that away. As the devil continues to wage spiritual war against us, let us arm ourselves with the Word of God so we won't get caught up in Satan's snare."

"Amens" were shouted around them.

"So finally, friends, let me invite you to come and suit up for battle. The Lord has all the equipment we need. If I'm talking to you today, come. Repent. Be genuinely sorry for the sins you've committed against yourself and others. Come on, let Jesus wash those hidden sins away, and God will fill you with His Holy Ghost."

To the surprise of Sinclaire and everybody sitting on their pew, Zanetta didn't budge.

Why? Sinclaire and Omega exchanged sly glances.

After the benediction, Sinclaire didn't press Zanetta with questions. What more would God have to do for Harry's mom to relinquish her will? They chatted for a few minutes, and then Zanetta said goodbye.

"Harry and I will definitely be back." Zanetta watched the brothers hug, and they left.

Sinclaire turned to her friends and shrugged. "I don't get it."

Tally's husband, Randall, rubbed the back of his head. "Some people need more convincing than others. I was literally a dead man. When God restored me, I was ready for salvation."

"When Mitchell and I saw those angels protecting us during that gas station robbery," his sister, Omega, said, "we became believers."

"Whew!" Mitchell slipped his hands into his pants pockets. "I was too scared not to have Jesus."

Tally squeezed Sinclaire's hands. "Let God's loving kindness draw her, and we continue to show God's love until she's ready."

The group nodded as Carlton spoke up. Sinclaire had forgotten her son was present when she expressed concern to the adults.

"Mom, aunties, and uncles don't worry. God's not done with her yet," Carlton said with confidence, grinned, and left to get his siblings from youth church.

"We need to have a child's blind faith," Omega said.

Carlton had high hopes for his last counseling session with Dr. Abbott. While his mother worked to show Christ's love to Miss Zanetta, Carlton's other mission would be his counselor. He didn't think she knew who Jesus was, and it was up to Carlton to testify to her about God.

Dr. Abbott smiled at him and his mother. "Carlton, it's been a pleasure seeing you, and I'm impressed by your resilience."

"Thank you," Carlton said.

"So… have you had any more bad dreams or scary situations?" She looked at Carlton and then his mother.

Sinclaire cleared her throat. "Dr. Abbott, this is a bad world because we live in an evil time, but during the last months, whatever the devil meant for bad to destroy my son, God meant it for good and strengthened his faith."

"Uh-huh. Well, yes."

Carlton wiggled in his seat. "Dr. Abbott, I've learned a lot from you." He grinned. "Have you learned anything from me?" He held his breath, hopeful she would want to know more about Jesus.

His counselor nodded. "Why, yes. God has helped you out of dangerous situations that were not of your doing, and…" She paused. "I downloaded a Bible app on my phone and read the scripture I received daily."

Sinclair chuckled. "Then it looks like our jobs are done."

I always have a plan, God whispered.

Carlton couldn't sit still as he danced in his seat as the meeting concluded. "Yay."

Harry's counseling session ended the following week, but he was sad when Carlton spoke to him. "I don't understand why my mom won't come back because she said she liked the service."

They had been on the phone after school for an hour, trying to find Scriptures that might help convince Miss Zanetta that God could save her soul as well as heal her body. "All of us are praying, Harry. At least she lets us take you to church."

"Yeah." Harry became quiet, then suddenly said, "Hey, I almost forgot, I've been talking to the kids at my school about Jesus. Some are mean, but I hear God tell me who to pray for."

Getting excited, Carlton bounced on his bed. "One time, angels followed me into the building and protected me from a bully. Everyone in class saw them. That was cool. A lot of people wanted to be my friend after that."

"That hasn't happened to me yet, but I like to pray for them because I don't know if the devil wants to hurt them, but something is going to happen. God whispered in my ear and told me to read Psalm 91:7."

"I know that verse! My teacher taught us that in youth church. *'A thousand may fall at your side, And ten thousand at your right hand. But it shall not come near you. '*"

"Carlton," his mother yelled, "dinner."

"Okay, Mom," he shouted back. "I've got to go."

"Thanks, brother. I'm glad we get to talk every day."

"Me too." Carlton ended the call as God whispered, *I'm coming for the children.*

Now what? he wondered.

Chapter Thirty-one

*For when they shall say, Peace and safety, then sudden destruction
comes upon them as travail upon a woman with child,
and they shall not escape.* —1 Thessalonians 5:3

For weeks, God seemed to give the world a reprieve from His judgments, but Jude could sense a storm was brewing in the atmosphere, and he had prayed for discernment.

But God was silent.

Then the breaking news flashed on his phone: *Five students at Scully Elementary School in University City make a suicide pact. Three are dead, and two are in critical condition.*

"What?" That was Harry's school. Jude's heart pounded with fear as his coworkers' heads popped from their workstations to give Jude odd expressions.

He closed his eyes to pray for the surviving students. What was the world coming to was on the tip of his tongue. Jude already knew the answer outlined in the passage in Matthew 24, beginning in verse four: *wars and rumors of wars, famines, pestilences, and earthquakes. Disasters everywhere…*

All these are the beginning of sorrows, God whispered.

Jude caught a tear. Take him to heaven now because this world was going nowhere fast. He called Sinclaire, and it went to voicemail, so he texted her. **Call me when you get a chance.**

Two minutes ticked by. Jude couldn't work. He sent Sinclaire another text. **Call me as soon as you can.** If that didn't sound the alarm, Jude was about to take an early lunch break and show up at Harry's school because he didn't have Zanetta's number.

Sinclaire couldn't believe what Zanetta was telling her.

The woman was frantic when she called Sinclaire at work. Sniffing, she barely got the words out, "I walked into my classroom…and the children…they were hanging from the hooks in the back of the room." She sobbed, sniffed, and sobbed again. "Five of them! I can't get those images out of my head."

Sinclaire couldn't imagine the horror. "What about Harry? I hope he didn't see any of that."

"Yes…yes, he did. I told him to get the principal and have her call 9-1-1 as I tried to untie them. They were so tight. They must have helped each other until the last one. Who would have thought these bullies would hang themselves? I guess karma does work."

Bullies were created, not born. These were babies as far as Sinclaire was concerned. An incoming call from Jude made her pause, but she allowed it to default to voicemail. Although she wanted to talk to him, Zanetta sounded like she needed her more.

"The paramedics were able to find a pulse on two of them. I'm hoping they pull through. One little boy was in my class last year but had to repeat the curriculum. I knew he was having problems at home, but I kept sending positive energy his way."

"Zanetta, positive energy doesn't affect God's will. We need to send prayers to the living God who gives life and grants permission to the Death Angel to take us from this world. Jesus is also a healer. Please come to church and trust God to finish His work in you."

"Harry has been trying to teach me to pray like him, but I don't feel connected."

Sinclaire rubbed her forehead. Her stomach was turning from the lunch she just had with Omega. "You need to receive God's gift of the Holy Ghost for the connection." Sinclaire closed her eyes to pray. "Lord, in the name of Jesus, You have warned us of the sabotage of the devil, but we need You to deliver us. Comfort the students at the school and their parents. And Lord, revive those children the devil tried to destroy, in Jesus' name. Amen."

"Amen," Zanetta whispered as someone came into the room. "I've got to go. Thanks for taking my call."

"Any time, day or night. We are connected, sis. Please keep me posted. I'll come by with the children after I get off work. Sounds like you'll both need a hug."

Sinclaire ended the call and immediately walked down the short hall to Omega's office, but someone was in there. She returned to her office and held her head in her hands. "A week before Thanksgiving. Those poor families. Sinclaire blinked away tears as she sent a group text to Jude, Mother Kincaid, Omega, and Tally.

Code pray: Suicides. Children. Then she saw Jude's texts and called him.

He answered immediately. "Sinclaire, isn't that Harry's school where there are reports of suicides? Is he okay?"

"Harry is safe, but Zanetta found the students. She's not okay. Zanetta and that school needs our prayers."

"I hate the devil," Jude said with venom. "I can't wait for the Lord to return, and we're caught up with Him, and then Satan is going down."

The Sunday before Thanksgiving, Zanetta called Sinclaire with the news that she was ready to surrender. "I can't take any more negative vibes from this world, or I'll crack."

Sinclaire did a praise dance in her kitchen and shouted, "Hallelujah!"

The children joined in on the dance without knowing what she was thanking God for.

"Mom, is that Miss Zanetta?" Carlton asked, but Sinclaire couldn't answer, so she handed Carlton the phone.

"Hi, Miss Zanetta. I'm so glad today is your day of salvation. We'll see you at church." He ended the call and returned to his room to get ready for service.

Sinclaire didn't know how her son knew that—whether God had revealed it to him or Harry had told him.

Zanetta had put up a long, hard fight. Sinclaire was glad today was her day.

She ain't made it to church yet. A demon had the nerve to try and shake her faith.

"Oh, the devil is a lie! You cannot pluck her out of God's hands." Sinclaire scrunched her nose for emphasis as she called the children for breakfast, then she hurried to dress so she could greet Zanetta and Harry when they walked through the church doors.

Pastor Rodney's sermon was short and direct before he made the invitation to come to Christ, and Sinclaire prayed throughout his altar call. "You are here today because you are hungry." He smiled. "The table is set—and I'm not talking about Thanksgiving dinner. The feast of the Lord is going on. Christ For All Church members believe the Bible when the Lord tells us to live holy, for He is holy. Some television preachers give you a little of Jesus in their sermons and a whole lot of lies. The Spirit of the Anti-Christ is working overtime to keep you deceived. A little lie is not the truth…."

Zanetta leaned forward and listened attentively. Sinclaire exchanged sly glances with Omega, then Tally. All of them were praying for the same outcome—surrender.

"Now, who wants to be saved by repenting of your sins?"

It was an open invitation to the church, but Zanetta jumped up and waved her hands. "Me!"

Chapter Thirty-two

In early December, Jude was at his desk, staring out the window at the sunshine God had given St. Louis, when his phone alerted him of breaking news.

He didn't want to look. What judgment was coming next on a world that refused to follow Jesus? Jude reflected on the Book of Revelation, where seven angels would release the wrath of God on the earth. What was happening now was a precursor.

Thank God the saints wouldn't be around to suffer through those. However, Jude wished the Lord had given the Christians choices on this.

Grabbing his phone, Jude prepared for the worst. He blinked at the news alert: *After six months, All Missing Children Worldwide Have Re-Appeared.*

Thank You, Jesus. Jude's eyes watered, and he swallowed the fear he was bracing for. Exhaling, his spirit rejoiced. God had come for the children.

Some had perished.

Others He preserved for His reasons.

Jude clicked on the video. "Sources say the children were seen outside random churches, begging strangers to come inside and see the salvation of God. They didn't appear drugged or coerced but nonchalant about their whereabouts."

One reporter on the local news interviewed one little girl, Sarah Humphries, who might have been seven or eight.

"I've been with Jesus, and we've been watching all the horrible things mommies and daddies are doing on earth." She scrunched her nose. "They aren't nice people, and adults aren't teaching us about Jesus. That made me and all the other kids, as well as Jesus, sad. We wanted to stay with God, but He said we had to go back and remind people that Jesus loves them."

Sara looked point-blank at the reporter. "Do you love Jesus?"

Viewers never heard the woman's answer.

Next, a foreign correspondent interviewed a little boy in Japan whose response was translated to English in closed caption. "God showed us children doing bad things because they don't know who Jesus is. That made us sad." The child looked hopeless and stomped his foot. "I want to go back to Jesus because people in this world hate God and don't like each other."

"Where did you go?" The male reporter was unfazed. "Was it heaven?"

The boy laughed at him. "Don't you know anything? We can't go to heaven until Jesus returns for people who love Him and do His will, even if they're young or old. They have to get their sins washed away first. Have you?"

The reporter, who seemed skeptical, didn't answer but pressed the child for more information.

The girl became annoyed. "Aren't you listening to anything I'm telling you? We didn't have these bodies you see here. It was just our spirits…"

Jude picked up his office phone and called Sinclaire. "Have you been checking out the news on the missing children?"

"Yep. Omega and I are sitting in my office with the door closed, rejoicing." Sinclaire's smile came through the phone. "What do you think this means regarding God's judgment?"

"I'm clueless." Jude exhaled. "God hasn't shown Omega any visions, has He?" He listened as she asked Omega.

"Nope. I feel like we're in a holding pattern or something." Sinclaire didn't hide her anxiety.

"Maybe the world has learned its lessons, and God has given us a reprieve from his judgment. I don't know," Jude said as a fellow engineer approached his desk. "Talk to you both later."

Chapter Thirty-three

For just as rain and snow fall from heaven and do not return without watering the earth, making it bud and sprout, and providing seed to sow and food to eat, so My word that proceeds from My mouth will not return to Me empty, but it will accomplish what I please, and it will prosper where I send it. —Isaiah 55:10–11

It was the week before Christmas, and Jude prayed for the void in families this time of year. Although the world had a reason to celebrate, like the reappearance of the missing children, many others weren't fortunate.

Thousands of children had committed suicides, were murdered, or were killed in car crashes, earthquakes, fires, and countless other horrors that Jude lost track of. The good news was that two of the five students who attempted suicide recovered, suffering minimal brain damage.

Jude switched his mind to more pleasant thoughts. Sinclaire's children would be out of school tomorrow for the Christmas holiday. Still calling him Dad, Carlton asked Jude to take them shopping so they could buy something for their mother.

"Of course." Jude was honored to be asked, and Sinclaire was clueless about their conspiracy.

While they were out, Jude could get a hint of what they liked. Carlton understood that it was Jesus' birthday and to give Him their best in offering over whatever presents were purchased for others.

Jude's mother had already shopped for Sinclaire and her children.

While in the department store, TJ picked out cartoon house slippers for Sinclaire and wanted a smaller pair for himself.

"No, TJ. This is for Mommy." Carlton put the item back.

Carlton's younger brother didn't seem happy about relinquishing his gift idea, and Jude took notes. Sissy liked a blue sweater with pearls. It was soft to the touch, and it cost thirty-two dollars. She looked to Carlton. "Do I have enough money, Carlton?" Her eyes filled with hope.

Jude watched as Carlton counted twenty-seven dollars. He wondered how she had earned that much money. Smiling at Sinclaire's only daughter's dilemma, he was ready to step in, but Carlton took the lead. "I have money." He counted out his fives, tens, and singles. The church paid the boys in the mentor program a stipend for working around the church and assisting seniors.

"But I've got to get Mom something." Carlton frowned in deep thought. "She likes to paint her nails. I should have enough to buy her polish that matches the sweater." He looked at Jude. "What do you think, Dad?"

Finally, Jude was asked for his input. "I think you have enough for polish and maybe earrings. I'm sure whatever you give her, she will love because she loves you."

Jude could think of many possibilities for a gift, but they weren't in a relationship, so he didn't want to offend her. He would give her a gift card for whatever she wanted to match with it.

"Since we don't have any more money, will you treat us to a hamburger and fries, Dad?" Sissy asked. Since Carlton called him Dad, his younger siblings mimicked him, although they knew their father, Tyler, was alive but had little involvement in their lives.

"Yes, ma'am." Jude loved the innocence of a child. He could understand the Lord's anger toward the world for not instructing them in God's way.

When they returned hours later, Sinclaire's face glowed from the excitement and happiness on her children's faces. After they hugged him goodbye, they raced to their rooms to wrap their gifts.

"Thank you for taking me and spoiling their appetite for dinner, Minister Jude Morgan."

"Guilty." Jude feigned remorse. "But the hamburger and fries were good." He handed her the carryout box.

"Bribing the mother, huh?" They laughed together. "So, while they're wrapping their gifts, how about a slice of my sweet potato pie?"

"No way am I saying no to sweet potato anything." He washed his hands and sat at the counter as Sinclaire's phone rang.

"What?" Sinclaire's scream alarmed Jude.

When tears began to fall, Jude's heart sank. *Lord…* He couldn't find words to petition God.

"Congratulations. I'm so happy for you." She grinned.

Jude exhaled. Good news. *Whew. Thank You, Jesus, for whatever it is.*

"Yes. Jude is here. I'll tell him." She lifted her hand to praise the Lord.

"What?" He waited before he sampled a slice of the pie.

"Hold on." She answered another call. "Tally! I just spoke with Omega, and… What? You too?" Her giggles turned to laughter. "Yes! Congratulations, and Merry Christmas."

Pushing his dessert aside, Jude folded his arms, tired of being in the dark. He slipped the phone from her hands. "Can you share the news—please?"

"God's judgment is complete! Hallelujah. Thank You, Jesus." She began to praise God until heavenly tongues filled her mouth, and she worshipped God in the spirit.

Jude suspected he knew but didn't want to speculate. Then, his phone alerted him to breaking news. He couldn't believe what he was reading: *An all-time low earlier this year, birth rates are exploding, and gynecologists can't handle the load and are pleading for labor and delivery nurses and doctors to come out of retirement....*

He shouted, "Hallelujah," loud enough that the younger children came to investigate.

Carlton followed, saying, "Yes, Lord. Yes, Lord," between speaking in heavenly tongues.

The seven-month judgment had ended. The atmosphere shifted as the Lord's presence filled the apartment, and they praised God for everything.

Carlton wiped his eyes and grinned. He hugged Jude with all the strength Jude didn't know the boy had. "I love you, Dad." His siblings did the same.

"Love you, too, buddy." He kissed him on his head and repeated the same sentiments with Sissy and TJ, then all three ran to Carlton's bedroom.

Sinclaire sniffed and wiped her eyes as she walked toward him, shaking her head. "I tried to tell you our friends were pregnant, but God took control and made me praise Him before I could tell a soul."

"I caught on." Jude chuckled as he studied her flushed face.

Sinclaire squinted, folded her arms, then leaned against the wall. "Question."

Jude wasn't sure he had an answer, but he nodded. "Go ahead."

"How come you've never asked me out, like to dinner or a movie? Is it because of my single-mom status?"

Was she holding her breath, thinking he would hurt her? Was this a trick question where there was no correct answer?

The truth works.

"I adore your children." He stepped closer and inhaled a hint of her perfume. "Sinclaire, you rebelled against the Lord after you had experienced what you called church hurt from men who lied about caring for you. That was a mess God wasn't in. It was people hurt. I didn't want you to think I was another man in the church who would subject you to people hurt."

"Well," she jutted her chin, "I challenge anyone who has experienced church hurt like I called it to change church memberships. I would have missed out on everything God had for me if not for Tally, then meeting true believers who love God's people at Christ For All Church." She started to count her benefits. "I got my current job because Tally introduced me to Omega. Mother Kincaid has not turned me down once for babysitting. The brothers at Christ For All Church have mentored Carlton…"

"What about me?" Jude towered over her. Height usually intimidated people, but this woman was making him weak. "Not that I'm looking for accolades, but do I get credit for anything—like sometimes brunch on Saturdays?"

"You," she said, smiling and wagging her finger, "you have been like a plastic surgeon to my heart. There is no evidence of my scars."

"I praise God for His healing power—spiritually and physically—but I was hoping for a special place in your life. If you permit me, I would like to take you out. Mother Kincaid has already offered her babysitting services as a gift because she says I finally found my perfect match with you." He grunted. "Trust me, that's a compliment because she and others have tried to set me up."

"Good answer." Sinclaire lowered her lashes, then closed her eyes. "You have permission."

Jude tugged her closer, wrapped his arms around her small waist, and kissed her for all the times he wished he had.

Epilogue

*And we know that all things work together for good to them
who love God, to them who are the called according
to His purpose.* —Romans 8:28

Three months later.

Sinclaire admired the brilliant diamond on her ring finger. In sixty days, she would become Mrs. Jude Morgan. She couldn't stop blushing whenever Sinclaire thought about Jude's romantic side.

Serious as a minister of God.

Committed as a mentor.

And attentive as a boyfriend. Jude never missed a beat separating "their time" from time spent with her children.

Omega often caught her daydreaming at work, like today when she knocked before entering Sinclaire's workspace. She glowed in her pregnancy as she rubbed her baby bump, making herself comfortable on the cushioned chair.

"Are you sure you want two pregnant women in your wedding?" Omega laughed.

"Of course. I'd have it no other way." Sinclaire finger-combed her fresh salon curls and leaned back in her chair. "You, Tally, Mother Kincaid, and all of Christ For All Christ has been a part of my spiritual growth. Your pregnancies are a testament to God's promise after His judgment, and my wedding photos will remind us of God's mercies with those baby bumps."

"Zanetta may be jealous," Omega teased. "I'm glad you two have become friends."

"We're like sisters, just like you and Tally." Then, her mind drifted as she spied the fresh bouquet of flowers on her desk.

Jude said he couldn't wait for Valentine's Day to propose, so he took her to a restaurant with fireside dining on a cold January evening.

He held her hand at every opportunity. His embraces were warm, reassuring, and full of love, and the brushes of his lips on her cheeks made her shiver with bliss.

After so many relationship heartaches, Sinclaire found love, or rather, love found her wrapped in a handsome package.

Once they ordered their appetizers, Jude looked at her with such intensity that she blushed.

"Sinclaire Oliver, your children have claimed me as their daddy. Now, I want to claim their mother as my wife. I love you and have for a long time. I waited patiently for you to see me more than as your son's mentor. Marry me, and make me an honest husband." He chuckled.

Sinclaire laughed, then giggled. Jude nor anyone at church made her feel ashamed of her past decisions.

"And before you say yes—"

Humph. She jutted her chin in a tease. "What if I say no?"

Jude squinted. "I wouldn't if I were you." He smiled. "It would be four against one. Carlton, Sissy, and TJ have my back."

Since she had yet to answer him, Sinclaire thought about Carlton's request to change his last name.

"I'm not liking your hesitation. Don't break my heart, Sinclaire, because you have it."

Covering his hands, she brought them to her lips. "I would never say no to you, but…it's Carlton. He wants his last name changed to Wakefield like Harry's."

Jude had been quiet. He seemed thoughtful, then nodded. "As his dad over the last couple of months, I know how much he loves Harry. I think that's a good idea."

"You do?" Sinclaire blinked. "Are you sure? I mean, I had hoped that if I ever married, my family would have the same last name."

"Sweetheart, this is bigger than a name. This is about a connection that never would have happened if Harrison had lived. So," he said, tilting his head, then pushing back his chair and kneeling, "Will you be my Valentine—forever—as my wife?"

"Yes!"

Book Club Discussion

1. What came to your mind when God told Jude that He was "coming for the children?"

2. What are your thoughts about Carlton attending his father's funeral after the incident?

3. Discuss Sinclaire's resolve about not allowing sleepovers until Harry needed to stay over. How many times have you eaten your words about something?

4. Name a couple of incidents in the story that you see happening today.

5. Discuss Sinclaire's focus on evangelizing to Nikki while making a judgment call on Zanetta, which was God's focus.

About the Author

Pat Simmons is a multi-published Christian romance author of forty-plus titles. She is a self-proclaimed genealogy sleuth passionate about researching her ancestors and casting them in starring roles in her novels. She is a five-time recipient of the RSJ Emma Rodgers Award for Best Inspirational Romance: *Still Guilty, Crowning Glory, The Confession, Christmas Dinner*, and *Queen's Surrender (To A Higher Calling)*. Pat's first inspirational women's fiction, *Lean On Me*, with Sourcebooks, was the national library system's February/March Together We Read Digital Book Club pick. *Here for You* and *Stand by Me* are also part of the Family is Forever series. Her holiday indie release, *Christmas Dinner*, and traditionally published, *Here for You*, were featured in *Woman's World*, a national magazine. *Here for You* was also listed in the "7 Great Reads That Help to Keep the Faith" by Sisters From AARP. She contributed an article, "I'm Listening," in the *Chicken Soup for the Soul: I'm Speaking Now* (2021). Pat is the recipient of the 2022 Leslie Esdaile "Trailblazer" Award given by Building Relationships Around Books Readers' Choice for her work in the Christian fiction genre.

As a Christian, Pat describes the evidence of the gift of the Holy Ghost as a life-altering experience. She has been a featured speaker and workshop presenter at various venues nationwide. Pat has converted her sofa-strapped sports fanatical husband into an amateur travel agent, untrained bodyguard, GPS-guided chauffeur, and administrative assistant who is constantly on probation. They have a son and a daughter. Pat holds a B.S. in mass communications from Emerson College in Boston, Massachusetts, and has worked in radio, television, and print media for over twenty years. She oversaw the media publicity for the annual RT Booklovers Conventions for fourteen years. Visit her at www.patsimmons.net.

Other Christian Titles

The Jamieson Legacy
Book 1: Guilty of Love
Book 2: Not Guilty of Love
Book 3: Still Guilty
Book 4: The Acquittal
Book 5: Guilty by Association
Book 6: The Guilt Trip
Book 7: Free from Guilt
Book 8: Sandra Nicholson's Backstory
Book 9: The Confession
Book 10: The Guilty Generation
Book 11: Queen's Surrender (To a Higher Calling)
Book 12: Contempt: Grandma BB's Shenanigans
Book 13: Christmas Takeover (The Next Generation)
Book 14: Accomplices in Love (The Next Generation)

The Intercessors
Book 1: Day Not Promised
Book 2: Day She Prayed
Book 3: Days Are Coming
Book 4: Day of Hope

The Carmen Sisters
Book 1: No Easy Catch
Book 2: In Defense of Love
Book 3: Driven to Be Loved
Book 4: Redeeming Heart
Love at the Crossroads
Book 1: Stopping Traffic

Book 2: A Baby for Christmas
Book 3: The Keepsake
Book 4: What God Has for Me
Book 5: Every Woman Needs a Praying Man

Restore My Soul
Book 1: Crowning Glory
Book 2: Jet: The Back Story
Book 3: Love Led by the Spirit

Family is Forever
Book 1: Lean on Me
Book 2: Here For You
Book 3: Stand by Me

Making Love Work Anthology
Book 1: Love at Work
Book 2: Words of Love
Book 3: A Mother's Love

God's Gifts
Book 1: Couple by Christmas
Book 2: Prayers Answered by Christmas

Perfect Chance at Love series
Book 1: Love by Delivery
Book 2: Late Summer Love

Single titles
Talk to Me
Her Dress
House Calls for the Holidays (short story)
Christmas Dinner

Christmas Greetings
Taye's Gift
Waiting for Christmas
House Calls for the Holidays

Anderson Brothers
Book 1: Love for the Holidays (Three novellas):
A Christian Christmas
A Christian Easter
A Christian Father's Day
Book 2: A Woman After David's Heart (A Valentine's Day Story)
Book 3: A Noelle for Nathan

In *Crowning Glory*, Cinderella had a prince; Karyn Wallace has a King. While Karyn served four years in prison for an unthinkable crime, she embraced salvation through Crowns for Christ outreach ministry. After her release, Karyn stays strong and confident, despite the stigma society places on ex-offenders. Since Christ strengthens the underdog, Karyn refuses to sway away from the scripture, "He who the Son has set free is free indeed." Levi Tolliver, for the most part, is a practicing Christian. One contradiction is he doesn't believe in turning the other cheek. He's steadfast there is a price to pay for every sin committed, especially after the untimely death of his wife during a robbery. Then Karyn enters Levi's life. He is enthralled not only with her beauty, but her sweet spirit until he learns about her incarceration. If Levi can accept that Christ paid Karyn's debt in full, then a treasure awaits him. This is a powerful tale and reminds readers of the permanency of redemption.

Jet: The Back Story to Love Led By the Spirit, to say Jesetta "Jet" Hutchens has issues is an understatement. In Crowning Glory, Book 1 of the Restoring My Soul series, she releases a firestorm of anger with an unforgiving heart. But every hurting soul has a history. In Jet: The Back Story to Love Led by the Spirit, Jet doesn't know how to cope with the loss of her younger sister, Diane. But God sets her on the road to a spiritual recovery. To make sure she doesn't get lost, Jesus sends the handsome and single Minister Rossi Tolliver to be her guide. Psalm 147:3 says

Jesus can heal the brokenhearted and bind up their wounds. That sets the stage for Love Led by the Spirit.

In Love Led By the Spirit, Minister Rossi Tolliver is ready to settle down. Besides the outwardly attraction, he desires a woman who is sweet, humble, and loves church folks. Sounds simple enough on paper, but when he gets off his knees, praying for that special someone to come into his life, God opens his eyes to the woman who has been there all along. There is only a slight problem. Love is the farthest thing from Jesetta "Jet" Hutchens' mind. But Rossi, the man and the minister, is hard to resist. Is Jet ready to allow the Holy Spirit to lead her to love?

In *Stopping Traffic*, Book 1, Candace Clark has a phobia about crossing the street, and for a good reason. As fate would have it, her daughter's principal assigns her to crossing guard duties as part of the school's Parent Participation program. With no choice in the matter, Candace begrudgingly accepts her stop sign and safety vest, then reports to her designated crosswalk. Once Candace is determined to overcome her fears, God opens the door for a blessing, and Royce Kavanaugh enters her life, a firefighter built to rescue any damsel in distress. When a spark of attraction ignites, Candace and Royce soon discover more than one way to stop traffic.

In *A Baby For Christmas*, Book 2, yes, diamonds are a girl's best friend, but in Solae Wyatt-Palmer's case, she desires something more valuable. Captain Hershel Kavanaugh is a divorcee and the father of two adorable little boys. Solae has never been married and longs to be a mother. Although Hershel showers her with expensive gifts, his hesitation about proposing causes Solae to walk and never look back. As the holidays approach, Hershel must convince Solae she has everything he could ever want for Christmas.

In *The Keepsake*, Book 3, Until death us do part…or until Desiree walks away. Desiree "Desi" Bishop is devastated when she finds evidence of her husband's affair. God knew she didn't get married only to one day have to stand before a judge and file for a divorce. But Desi wants out no matter how much her heart says to forgive Michael. That isn't easier said than done. She sees God's one acceptable reason for a divorce as the only opt-out clause in her marriage. Michael Bishop is a repenting man who loves his wife of three years. If only…he had paid attention to the red flags God sent to keep him from falling into the devil's snares. But Michael didn't and fell. Although God forgives him instantly when he repents, Desi's forgiveness is moving as a snail's pace. In the end, after all the tears have been shed and forgiveness granted and received, the couple learns that some marriages are worth keeping.

In *What God Has For Me*, Book 4, pregnant or not, Halcyon Holland is leaving her boyfriend. When her ex makes no attempts to reconcile their relationship, Halcyon begins to second-guess whether or not she compromised her chance for a happily ever after. But Zachary Bishop has had his eye on Halcyon since he first saw her. What one man doesn't cherish, Zach is ready to treasure. He's on a mission to offer her a second chance at love that she can't refuse: unconditional love for a ready-made family. Halcyon will soon learn that her past circumstances won't hinder the Lord's blessings for them.

In *Every Woman Needs A Praying Man*, Book 5, first impressions can make or break a business deal, and they definitely could be a relationship buster, but an ill-timed panic attack draws two strangers together. Unlike firefighters who run into danger, instincts tell businessman Tyson Graham to be weary of a certain damsel in distress and run. Days later, the same woman struts through his door for a job interview. Monica Wyatt might possess the outward beauty and the brains on paper, but Tyson doesn't trust her to work for his firm, or maybe he doesn't trust his heart around her.

In *Guilty of Love*, when do you know the most important decision of your life is the right one? Reaping the seeds from what she's sown; Cheney Reynolds moves into a historic neighborhood in Ferguson, Missouri, and becomes a reclusive. Her first neighbor, the incomparable Mrs. Beatrice Tilley Beacon aka Grandma BB, is an opinionated childless widow. Grandma BB is a self-proclaimed expert on topics Cheney isn't seeking advice—everything from landscaping to hip-hop dancing to romance. Then there is Parke Kokumuo Jamison VI, a direct descendant of a royal African tribe. He learned his family ancestry, African history, and lineage preservation before he could count. Unwittingly, they are drawn to each other, but it takes Christ to weave their lives into a spiritual bliss while He exonerates their past indiscretions.

In *Not Guilty*, one man, one woman, one God, and one big problem. Malcolm Jamieson wasn't the man who got away, but the man God instructed Hallison Dinkins to set free. Instead of their explosive love affair leading them to the wedding altar, God diverted Hallison to the prayer altar during her first visit back to church in years. Malcolm was convinced that his woman had loss her mind to break off their engagement. Didn't Hallison know that Malcolm, a tenth-generation descendant of a royal African tribe, couldn't be replaced? Once Malcolm concedes that their relationship can't be savaged, he issues Hallison his own edict, "If we're meant to be with each other, we'll find our way back. If not, that means there's a love stronger than we had." His words begin to haunt Hallison until she begins to regret their break up, and that's where their story begins. Someone has to retreat, and God never loses a battle.

In *Still Guilty*, Cheney Reynolds Jamieson made a choice years ago that is now shaping her future and the future of the men she loves. A botched abortion prevented her from carrying a baby to term, and her husband, Parke K. Jamison VI, is expected to produce heirs. With a wife who cannot give him a child, Parke vows to find and get custody of his illegitimate son by any means necessary. Meanwhile, Cheney's twin brother, Rainey, struggles with his anger over his ex-girlfriend's actions that haunt him, and their father, Dr. Roland Reynolds, fights to keep an old secret in the past.

In *The Acquittal*, two worlds apart, but their hearts dance to the same African drum beat. On a professional level, Dr. Rainey Reynolds is a competent, highly sought-after orthodontist. Inwardly, he needs to be set free from the chaos of revelations that make him question if happiness is obtainable. To get away from the drama, Rainey is willing to leave the country under the guise of a mission trip with Dentist Without Borders. Will changing his surroundings really change him? If one woman can heal his wounds, then he will believe that there is really peace after the storm.

Ghanaian beauty Josephine Abena Yaa Amoah returns to Africa after completing her studies as an exchange student in St. Louis, Missouri. Although her heart bleeds for his peace, she knows she must step back and pray for Rainey's surrender to Christ so God can acquit him of his self-inflicted mental torture. In the Motherland of Ghana, Africa, Rainey not only visits the places of his ancestors, will he embrace the liberty that Christ's Blood does set every man free.

In *Guilty By Association*, how important is a name? To the St. Louis Jamiesons, tenth-generation descendants of a royal African tribe—everything. To the Boston Jamiesons whose father never married their mother—there is no loyalty or legacy. Kidd Jamieson suffers from the "angry" male syndrome because his father was absent in the home, but insisted his two sons carry his last name. It takes an old woman who mingles genealogy truths and Bible verses together for Kidd to realize his worth as a strong black man. He learns it's not his association with the name that identifies him, but the man he becomes that defines him.

In *The Guilt Trip*, Aaron "Ace" Jamieson lives carefree. He's good-looking, and respectable when he's in the mood, but his weakness is women. If a woman tries to ambush him with a pregnancy, he takes off in the other direction. It's a lesson learned from his absentee father that responsibility is optional. Talise Rogers has a bright future ahead of her. She's pretty and has no problem catching a man's eye, which is exactly what she does with Ace. Trapping Ace Jamieson is the furthest thing from Talise's mind when she learns she is pregnant and Ace rejects her. "I want nothing from you Ace, not even your name." And Talise meant it.

In *Free From Guilt*, it's salvation round-up time and Cameron Jamieson's name is on God's hit list. Although his brothers and cousins embraced God—thanks to the women in their lives—the two-degreed MIT graduate isn't going to let any woman take him down that path without a fight. He's satisfied with his career, social calendar, and good genes. But God uses a beautiful messenger, Gabrielle Dupree, to show him that he's in a spiritual deficit. Cameron learns the hard way that man's wisdom is like foolishness to God. For every philosophical argument he throws her way, Gabrielle exposes him to scriptures that makes him question his worldly knowledge.

In *Sandra Nicholson's Backstory*, Sandra has made good and bad choices throughout the years, but the best one was to give her life to Christ when her sons were small and to rear them up in the best Christian way she knew how. That was thirty-something years ago and Sandra has evolved from a young single mother of two rambunctious boys: Kidd and Ace Jamieson, to a godly woman seasoned with wisdom. Despite the challenges and trials of rearing two strong-willed personalities, Sandra maintained her sanity through the grace of God, which kept gray strands at bay. But there is something to be said about a woman's first love. Kidd and Ace Jamieson's father, Samuel Jamieson broke their mother's heart. Can Sandra recover? Her sons don't believe any man is good enough for her, especially their absent father. Kidd doesn't deny his mother should find love again since she never married Samuel. But will she fall for a carbon copy of his father? God's love gives second chances.

In *The Confession*, Sandra Nicholson had made good and bad choices throughout the years, but the best one was to give her life to Christ when her sons were small and to rear them up in the best Christian way she knew how. That was thirty-something years ago and Sandra has evolved from a young single mother of two rambunctious boys, Kidd and Ace Jamieson to a godly woman seasoned with wisdom. Despite the challenges and trials of rearing two strong-willed personalities, Sandra maintained her sanity through the grace of God, which kept gray strands at bay.

Now, Sandra Nicholson is on the threshold of happiness, but Kidd believes no man is good enough for his mother, especially if her love interest could be a man just like his absentee father.

In *The Guilty Generation*, seventeen-year-old Kami Jamieson is so over being daddy's little girl. Now that she has captured the attention of Tango, the bad boy from her school, Kami's love for her family and God have taken a backseat to her teen crush.

Although the Jamiesons have instilled godly principles in Kami since she was young, they will stop at nothing, including prayer and fasting, to protect her from falling prey to society's peer pressure. Can Kami survive her teen rebellion, or will she be guilty of dividing the next generation?

In *Queen's Surrender (To a Higher Calling)*, Opposites attract...or clash. The Jamieson saga continues with the Queen of the family in this inspirational romance. She's the mistress of flirtation but Philip is unaffected by her charm. The two enjoy a harmless banter about God's will versus Queen's, who prefers her own free-will lifestyle. Philip doesn't judge her choices—most of the time—and Queen respects his opinions—most of the time. It's perfect harmony sometimes. Queen, the youngest sister of the Jamieson clan, wears her name as if it's a crown. She's single, sassy, and most of the time, loving her status, but she's about to strut down an unexpected spiritual path. Evangelist Philip Dupree is on the hot seat as the trial pastor at Total Surrender Church. The stalemate: They want a family man to lead their flock. The board's ultimatum is enough to make him quit the ministry. But can a man of God walk away from his calling? Can two people with different lifestyles and priorities cross paths and continue the journey as one? Who is going to be the first to surrender?

In *Contempt (Grandma BB's Shenanigans)*, Grandma BB, the unofficial matriarch of the Jamieson clan, is getting her house in order for the perfect homegoing celebration. After all, she's eighty-something. She summons Parke Jamieson VI, his brothers, cousins, and their families to play a part in the practice funeral program—only if they follow her instructions to the letter. Since the Jamiesons are at her house with bodyguards Chip and Dale, they might have an impromptu family game night. The evening is full of surprises, especially when an unexpected visitor shows up to steal the show. With more work that needs to be done, Grandma BB plans to put her funeral on hold and stick around for a couple more generations.

In *Fun and Games with the Jamieson Men*, The Jamieson Legacy series inspired this game book of fun activities:• Brain Teasers• Crossword Puzzles• Word Searches •Sudoku •Mazes •Coloring Pages. The Jamiesons are fictional characters that put emphasis on Black Heritage, which includes Black American History tidbits, African American genealogy, and strong Black families. Relax, grab a pencil and play along.

THE CARMEN SISTERS SERIES

In *No Easy Catch*, Book 1, Shae Carmen hasn't lost her faith in God, only the men she's come across. Shae's recent heartbreak was discovering that her boyfriend was not only married, but on the verge of reconciling with his estranged wife. Humiliated, Shae begins to second guess herself as why she didn't see the signs that he was nothing more than a devil's decoy masquerading as a devout Christian man. St. Louis Outfielder Rahn Maxwell finds himself a victim of an attempted carjacking. The Lord guides him out of harms' way by opening the gunmen's eyes to Rahn's identity. The crook instead becomes infatuated fan and asks for Rahn's autograph, and as a good will gesture, directs Rahn out of the ambush! When the news media gets wind of what happened with the baseball player, Shae's television station lands an exclusive interview. Shae and Rahn's chance meeting sets in motion a relationship where Rahn not only surrenders to Christ, but pursues Shae with a purpose to prove that good men are still out there. After letting her guard down, Shae is faced with another scandal that rocks her world. This time the stakes are higher. Not only is her heart on the line, so is her professional credibility. She and Rahn are at odds as how to handle it and friction erupts between them. Will she strike out at love again? The Lord shows Rahn that nothing happens by chance, and everything is done for Him to get the glory.

In *Defense of Love*, Book 2, lately, nothing in Garrett Nash's life has made sense. When two people close to the U.S. Marshal wrong him deeply, Garrett expects God to remove them from his life. Instead, the Lord relocates Garrett to another city to start over, as if he were the offender instead of the victim. Criminal attorney Shari Carmen is comfortable in her own skin—most of the time. Being a "dark and lovely" African-American sister has its challenges, especially when it comes to relationships. Although she's a fireball in the courtroom, she knows how to fade into the background and keep the proverbial spotlight off her personal life. But literal spotlights are a different matter altogether. While playing tenor saxophone at an anniversary party, she grabs the attention of Garrett Nash. And as God draws them closer together, He makes another request of Garrett, one to which it will prove far more difficult to say "Yes, Lord."

In *Redeeming Heart*, Book 3, Landon Thomas (In Defense of Love) brings a new definition to the word "prodigal," as in prodigal son, brother or anything else imaginable. It's a good thing that God's love covers a multitude of sins, but He isn't letting Landon off easy. His journey from riches to rags proves to be humbling and a lesson well learned. Real Estate Agent Octavia Winston is a woman on a mission, whether it's God's or hers professionally. One thing is for certain, she's not about to compromise when it comes to a Christian mate, so why did God send a homeless man to steal her heart? Minister Rossi Tolliver (Crowning Glory) knows how to minister to God's lost sheep and through God's redemption, the game changes for Landon and Octavia.

In *Driven to Be Loved*, Book 4, on the surface, Brecee Carmen has nothing in common with Adrian Cole. She is a pediatrician certified in trauma care; he is a transportation problem solver for a luxury car dealership (a.k.a., a car salesman). Despite their slow but steady attraction to each other, neither one of them are sure that they're compatible. To complicate matters, Brecee is the sole unattached Carmen when it seems as though everyone else around her—family and friends—are finding love, except her. Through a series of discoveries, Adrian and Brecee learn that things don't happen by coincidence. Generational forces are at work, keeping promises, protecting family members, and perhaps even drawing Adrian back to the church. For Brecee and Adrian, God has been hard at work, playing matchmaker all along the way for their paths cross at the right time and the right place.

Lean on Me, Book 1. No one should have to go it alone... Caregivers sometimes need a little TLC too.

Tabitha Knicely believes in family before everything. She may be overwhelmed caring for her beloved great-aunt, but she would never turn her back on the woman who raised her, even if Aunt Tweet's dementia is getting worse. Tabitha is sure she can do this on her own. But when Aunt Tweet ends up on her neighbor's front porch, and the man has the audacity to accuse Tabitha of elder abuse, things go from bad to awful. Marcus Whittington feels a mountain of regret at causing problems for Tabitha and her great-aunt. How was he to know the frail older woman's niece was doing the best she could? As Marcus gets to know Aunt Tweet and sees how hard Tabitha is fighting to keep everything together, he can't walk away from the pair. Particularly when helping Tabitha care for her great-aunt leads the two of them on a spiritual journey of faith and surrender.

Here For You, Book 2. Rachel Knicely's life has been on hold for six months while she takes care of her great aunt, who has Alzheimer's. Putting her aunt first was an easy decision—accepting that Aunt Tweet is nearing the end of her battle is far more difficult. Nicholas Adams's ministry is bringing comfort to those who are sick and homebound. He responds to a request for help for an ailing woman but when he meets the Knicelys, he realizes Rachel is the one who needs support the most. Nicholas is charmed by and attracted to Rachel, but then devastating news brings both a crisis of faith and roadblocks to their budding relationship that neither could have anticipated. This beautifully emotional and clean story contains a hero and heroine who are better at taking care of other people than themselves, a dark moment that shakes their faith, and a well-earned happily ever after.

Stand by Me, Book 3. An uplifting story about embracing love and giving others—and yourself—one more chance. When it comes to being a caregiver, Kym Knicely has been there and done that. Then she meets Charles "Chaz" Banks and soon learns that every caregiving situation is different. Chaz takes care of his seven-year-old autistic granddaughter, Chauncy. Although Kym's attraction to Chaz is strong, she has to decide whether a romantic relationship can survive and thrive between two people at different stages in life. It's a journey with a different set of rules that Kym has to play by if she and Chaz are to have their happily ever after and the faith and family they envision.

About *Waiting for Christmas*,

A chance meeting. An undeniable attraction.

And a first date that starts with a stakeout that leads to a winner takes all shopping spree. It's the making of a holiday romance. While philanthropist Sterling Price believes in charitable causes, he and licensed social worker Ciara Summers have a difference of opinion on how to bless others. Ciara is a rebel with a cause and a hundred reasons why helping those less fortunate is important. Sterling is a man of means who believes there is a financial responsibility that comes with giving.

The Lord will make sure everyone's needs are met, and He has something extra for Sterling and Ciara that can't wait until Christmas.

About *Christmas Dinner*,

How do you celebrate the holidays after losing a loved one? Take the journey, beginning with Christmas Dinner. For months, Darcelle Price has suffered depression in silence. But things are about to change as she plans to celebrate Christmas Eve with family and share her journey. Darcelle invites them via group text, not knowing she had included her ex. Evanston Giles is surprised to hear from the woman he loved after months following their breakup. Seeking closure, he shows up on her doorstep for answers. A lot can happen on Christmas Eve. Restoring family ties, building her faith in God, and falling in love again is just the beginning of the night of miracles.

About *Taye's Gift*,
Welcome to Snowflake, Colorado—a small town where wishes come true! When six old high school friends receive a letter that their fellow friend, Charity Hart, wrote before she passed away, their lives take an unexpected turn. She leaves them each a check for $1,500 and asks them to grant a wish—a secret wish—for someone else by Christmas. Who lays off someone before the holidays? Taye Thomas' employer did, so instead of Christmas shopping, she's job hunting. More devastating news comes when an old high school friend passed away. Could God be answering her prayers for help when she learns that Charity Hart left a $1500 check? No, the caveat is it's more blessed to give than receive. Taye has 30 days to find someone else in need to bless. To complicate matters, she's lives in Kansas City, which is more than eight hours away from Snowflake and she can't do it alone. Keeping a secret has never been so much work.

About *Couple by Christmas*,
Holidays haven't been the same for Derek Washington since his divorce. He and his ex-wife, Robyn, go out of their way to avoid each other. This Christmas may be different when he decides to give his son, Tyler, the family he once had before they split. Derek's going to need the Lord's intervention to soften her heart to agree to some outings. God's help doesn't come in the way he expected, but it's all good because everything falls in place for them to be a couple by Christmas.

About *Prayers Answered By Christmas*,
Christmas is coming. While other children are compiling their lists for a fictional Santa, eight-year-old Mikaela Washington is on her knees, making her requests known to the Lord: One mommy for Christmas please. Portia Hunter refuses to let her ex-husband cheat her out of the family she wants. Her prayer is for God to send the right man into her life. Marlon Washington will do anything for his two little girls, but can he find a mommy for

them and a love for himself? Since Christmas is the time of year to remember the many gifts God has given men, maybe these three souls will get their heart s desire.

About *A Noelle for Nathan*,
A Noelle for Nathan is a story of kindness, selflessness, and falling in love during the Christmas season. Andersen Investors & Consultants, LLC, CFO Nathan Andersen (A Christian Christmas) isn't looking for attention when he buys a homeless man a meal, but grade school teacher Noelle Foster is watching his every move with admiration. His generosity makes him a man after her own heart. While donors give more to children and families in need around the holiday season, Noelle Foster believes in giving year-round after seeing many of her students struggle with hunger and finding a warm bed at night. At a second-chance meeting, sparks fly when Noelle and Nathan share a kindred spirit with their passion to help those less fortunate. Whether they're doing charity work or attending Christmas parties, the couple becomes inseparable. Although Noelle and Nathan exchange gifts, the biggest present is the one from Christ.

One reader says, "A Noelle for Nathan makes you fall in love with love…the love of mankind and the love of God. You cannot read this without having a desire to give and do more, all while being appreciative of what you have."

About *Christmas Greetings*,
Saige Carter loves everything about Christmas: the shopping, the food, the lights, and of course, Christmas wouldn't be complete without family and friends to share in the traditions they've created together. Plus, Saige is extra excited about her line of Christmas greeting cards hitting store shelves, but when she gets devastating news around the holidays, she wonders if she'll ever look at Christmas the same again. Daniel Washington is no Scrooge, but he'd rather skip the holidays altogether than spend

them with his estranged family. After one too many arguments around the dinner table one year, Daniel had enough and walked away from the drama. As one year has turned into many, no one seems willing to take the first step toward reconciliation. When Daniel reads one of Saige's greeting cards, he's unsure if the words inside are enough to erase the pain and bring about forgiveness. Once God reveals His purpose for their lives to them, they will have a reason to rejoice. *Come unto me, all ye that labor and are heavily laden, and I will give you rest. Take my yoke upon you, and learn of me; for I am meek and lowly in heart: and ye shall find rest unto your souls.* Matthew 11:28-29

About *A Baby for Christmas,*
Yes, diamonds are a girl's best friend, but unless the jewel is going on Solae Wyatt-Palmer's ring finger, they hold little value to her. When she meets Fire Captain Hershel Kavanaugh, their magnetism is undeniable and there's no doubt that it's love at first sight. Since Solae adores Hershel's two boys from his failed marriage, she wouldn't blink at the chance to become a mother to them. But when it seems as if Hershel doesn't have a proposal on his agenda, she has no choice but to cut her losses and move on. But Christmas is coming. And in order to win Solae back, Hershel must resolve some past issues before convincing her that she possesses everything he wants.

About *A Christian Christmas,*
Christmas will never be the same for Joy Knight if Christian Andersen has his way. Not to be confused with a secret Santa, Christian and his family are busier than Santa's elves making sure the Lord's blessings are distributed to those less fortunate by Christmas day. Joy is playing the hand that life dealt her, rearing four children in a home that is on the brink of foreclosure. She's not looking for a handout, but when Christian rescues her in the checkout line; her niece thinks Christian is an angel. Joy thinks he's just another man who will eventually

leave, disappointing her and the children. Although Christian is a servant of the Lord, he is a flesh and blood man and all he wants for Christmas is Joy Knight. Can time spent with Christian turn Joy's attention from her financial woes to the real meaning of Christmas—and true love? A Christian Christmas is a holiday novella to be enjoyed any time of the year.

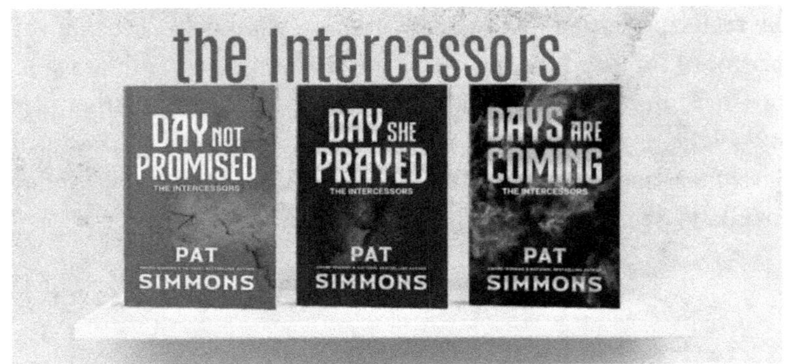

Pat Simmons introduces a new Christian fiction series that reminds readers that the bad guys don't always win, especially when the Lord fights our battles.

In *Day Not Promised*, Omega Addams thought it was a typical workday until a detour on the way home changes everything. She's almost killed, but an innocent bystander, Mitchell Franklin, takes a bullet for Omega during a gas station robbery. In the aftermath, Omega has no idea that God expects her to "pray it forward" until a spiritual battle unfolds before her eyes. Another innocent bystander is in trouble; unless Omega gets her prayer life together, others will die without Christ. It's a chain reaction that highlights the responsibility of a Christian--hot, cold, or lukewarm. It's time to get our acts together. We are our brother's keeper.

In *Day She Prayed*, New Christian convert Tally Gilbert knows the power of prayer and the pain of walking away. She's witnessed family and friends' healing, salvation, and deliverance. There's one holdout, and he's at the top of her prayer list. The love of her life, Randall Addams, won't surrender to the Lord, so Tally ends the relationship. What will it take for Randall to turn to God? Will Tally's prayers be answered, or will Randall—and their love—be lost forever?

Don't underestimate a woman who knows how to pray, has backup, and believes "The Word of God is quick, and powerful, and sharper than any two-edged sword, piercing even to the dividing the soul from the spirit, and of the joints and marrow, and is a discerner of the thoughts and intents of the heart." Hebrews 4:12.

If the devil wants a battle, he picks the wrong woman to fight.

In *Days Are Coming*, the spiritual battle is heating up in the lives of Omega and her friends. God is about to proclaim a punishment on the world because of their sins. Can prayer change things?